INHERITORS

INHERITORS

Asako Serizawa

RANDOM HOUSE
LARGE PRINT

Published in the United States of America by Random House Large Print in association with Doubleday, a division of Penguin Random House LLC, New York, and distributed in Canada by Penguin Random House Canada Limited, Toronto.

Several pieces first appeared, in different form, in the following publications: "Flight" in **The Southern Review** (Spring 2005); "Luna" in **Prairie Schooner** (Summer 2008); "Allegiance" (Spring 2012) and "Train to Harbin" (Autumn 2014) in **The Hudson Review**; and "Echolocation" in **Copper Nickel** (Spring 2019).

Cover composite images: Hiroshima after the atomic bomb (detail). Roger Viollet / Getty Images; (paper cutout) Merkushev Vasily / Shutterstock
Cover design by Michael J. Windsor

The Library of Congress has established a Cataloging-in-Publication record for this title.

ISBN: 978-0-593-21482-4

www.penguinrandomhouse.com/large-print-format-books

FIRST LARGE PRINT EDITION

Printed in the United States of America

10 9 8 7 6 5 4 3 2 1

This Large Print edition published in accord with the standards of the N.A.V.H.

Yet the fully enlightened earth radiates disaster triumphant.

—Theodor W. Adorno and Max Horkheimer, **Dialectic of Enlightenment**

CONTENTS

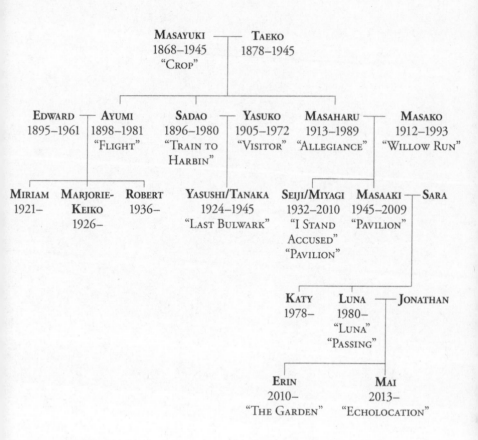

MASAYUKI 1868–1945 "CROP" — TAEKO 1878–1945

EDWARD 1895–1961 — AYUMI 1898–1981 "FLIGHT"

SADAO 1896–1980 "TRAIN TO HARBIN" — YASUKO 1905–1972 "VISITOR"

MASAHARU 1913–1989 "ALLEGIANCE"

MASAKO 1912–1993 "WILLOW RUN"

MIRIAM 1921–

MARJORIE-KEIKO 1926–

ROBERT 1936–

YASUSHI/TANAKA 1924–1945 "LAST BULWARK"

SEIJI/MIYAGI 1932–2010 "I STAND ACCUSED" "PAVILION"

MASAAKI 1945–2009 "PAVILION" — SARA

KATY 1978–

LUNA 1980– "LUNA" "PASSING" — JONATHAN

ERIN 2010– "THE GARDEN"

MAI 2013– "ECHOLOCATION"

ONE

FLIGHT

First it was the names that went. Names of her neighbors, names of her grandchildren. Sometimes the names of her two daughters, her only son.

She knew their faces, of course. The daughter with the sharp eyes, always inspecting her, pressing her onward—always onward!—to the bathroom, the kitchen, anywhere that was away from the door, where she'd hesitated, no longer certain of her direction, or why.

The other daughter was pale-faced and forgiving. When she wandered lost among the tomato vines in her yard, it was this daughter who clasped her hands firmly in hers.

The son did not visit often. He called once a month. Who could blame him? His mother, who couldn't be trusted with the baby. Who couldn't be trusted with herself. Even as a boy he'd been prudent. Preserving himself against the world's imperfections.

Then, one day, the streets began to go. The stark, narrow one, shortcut to the schoolyard where her children used to wait, fidgeting and hungry, racing at the sight of her. Then the route to the drugstore; the turn to the post office; the short leafy distance to the bakery with shelves of cinnamon bread she liked, lightly buttered, on rainy afternoons.

Her neighbors began finding her. Strolling up and down the road, peering into windows she recognized but could no longer place. Sometimes they found her at the bus stop considering the direction of her home, which was not on any bus route. Each time, the neighbors took her elbow— the younger ones kindly, the older ones angrily—all of them threatening to tell on her.

But how could she stay home? The sky shimmering outside her window, the trees like shadow puppets dancing on the lawn, the promise of her tomatoes plumping in the yard Edward had cleared for her, years ago, when they were both still young and had half the mortgage to pay. She couldn't help it, her body yearning for the weight of the globes, warm under cool running water. There was no room for her daughters' warnings or her neighbors' pity. Her feet simply took her there, down the steps into her bright garden.

HER FIRST tomato came to her in 1911, the year she turned thirteen, the year she first visited America. Small, yellow, pear-shaped: it was a gift from her father, plucked from the land that was to be her new summer home in California. The seeds were slimy, and the first time she bit the fruit, they splattered the soil, a dark phlegmy embarrassment. She hastily toed the spot, but her father, catching her, laughed. **Watch out, everything root here.**

She ended up potting that patch of soil and placing the terra-cotta by her bedroom window in the farmhouse that now held her summer things. Like her new frock, uncomfortably buxom beside her yukata, which waved like a happy kite when the breeze

blew in from the rice paddy that belonged
to her father's cousin Bob. Bob, like her
father, was an agronomist. Once known as
Mitsuru, he was a reckless fox of a man, his
many pockets jingling with ideas too modern for their hometown in Niigata, a rice
farming region on the west coast of Japan.
Her father, though, could never resist their
allure, and Mitsuru, knowing this, often en-
tangled him in regrettable schemes.

Bob left for California in 1906, and for
over two years no one heard from him. But
of course it was her father to whom Bob
eventually wrote, telling him about the new
strain of rice he was cultivating, sweet like
home but suited to the California soil and
climate. Her father leapt at the prospect.
And though it would take a few seasons,
the strain, a robust hybrid, would prove
successful, surviving all the Land Acts and
even the arsonists sent by the Asiatic Exclusion League, until Executive Order 9066
rounded up all the Bobs and transplanted
them to Manzanar.

Yellow Pear, her father said, testing the
shape of the language that would one day
replace her own. **That's name.**

The plant grew, despite the confines of the pot and window, and produced a single cluster of tomatoes that collected like dewdrops. It sat there enjoying the sun that dazzled the room every summer for three years until one afternoon an avalanche of books, loosed by an earthquake, battered its limbs and broke its spine.

Oh well, her father had laughed, squeezing his shoulders to his ears like his Americanized cousin. **That's life, huh!**

SOMETIME IN the fall the kind-faced daughter began staying with her. At first she stayed only on weekends, then during the week as well. This daughter was quiet. She did not disturb the house even when she washed dishes or folded laundry. While this daughter was around, TV was forbidden, so they sat in the kitchen with a pot of tea and talked about the new hiring the daughter was in charge of: gentle prattle that soon gave way to a gentle prodding of memory.

Remember when we went apple-picking and you got caught with your mouth full of Gala—or was it McIntosh?

Remember the time at the movies when you got up to use the bathroom and ended up in the exact seat you'd left, but in a different theater, next to a different family, without realizing it?

Of course she did not remember these stories, which nudged a darkness but did not illuminate it. What flared in her were childhood images. Like the time her father took her ice-skating on the lake behind the house in Niigata. She was six then, enamored of her skates, which smelled of new leather and not the usual musk of her brother's feet.

Hot sun on her shivery back. She remembered the glint of the ice, her slashing blades, her fear of sliced fingers. Her skates skipped: the surprise of hard ice on her back and her father's swishing blades crisscrossing so close to her face she could taste the metal slicing her breath.

Two years later she did rip open her face. A deep curve from her left ear to her chin. An unbelievably clean wound for such a messy incident. Grabbing the leg of a sleeping dog! But how could she have known? The dog was a friend. So fortunate the scar had followed her jawline. So fortunate she had a pretty face, astonishingly hard to ruin. Naughty girl.

Only one girl ever asked about her scar. This girl was fair-haired and fair-skinned and spoke with a foreign accent. New to Niigata, she was prickly, her turbulent face flashing at the sound of her name, which no one could pronounce. **Mar. Joh. Ree!** One day Marjorie sat next to her. Parting her hair, she inspected her face and, just like that, asked about it. What could she say to enchant this girl? She leaned into her ear—so pale she could see the blue and red lattice as delicate as the crazing in her family's finest Imari china—and whispered that it was her father who'd done it. Flayed open her face with ice skates.

She never forgot Marjorie, or the lie, and became ill when her cherished friend transferred to another school in another part of the country, where her diplomatic father was reassigned.

Years later she believed she saw her, though who could be sure? It was 1919, and they were women now, on an entirely different continent, in an entirely different hemisphere, far from the classroom in

Niigata. It was a glorious day, the California sun invigorating the streets, and as she lifted her face in spontaneous praise of its vitality, she caught another face doing the same. **Marjorie!** Her mouth shaped the name no longer so difficult to pronounce. But the woman only lowered her gaze and hurried off, the fair crowd swallowing her up.

THE FIRST time she was hospitalized was three years ago, in 1978, the year Robert announced his engagement. Robert, her son. She was admitted for pneumonia but diagnosed with cirrhosis on top of a bad case of the flu. The cirrhosis was a shock; she was a proper woman. When the doctors asked after her medications, she produced her modest list. Nobody could have suspected that the prescription she'd dutifully filled had been treating a healthy heart but destroying her liver.

Six months later she was admitted again. Fainting on the way to the market. She was treated for a concussion but diagnosed with malnutrition; she was prescribed a four-day stay that dribbled into two weeks.

At first her children worried. Then they

were angry. They blamed each other, then blamed her. When, finally, they realized she hadn't uttered a word for days, they called in more doctors, more men who touched and probed her, first with words, then with beeping objects, finally turning to her children to inquire after her daily functioning, her history of diagnosed depression, neither of which they knew anything about.

The test results came back inconclusive, but one thing was certain: her brain had changed; age had worn holes in it, siphoning her ability to cope with a world that had become complicated with a tangle of things she couldn't or shouldn't do. For months, perhaps years, she'd been losing herself, her body and thoughts, even her feelings, no longer hers to command or own.

But of course her children were a worry. Like the sharp-eyed one, still unmarried at fifty-two. Some days, when she thought about this daughter, she was glad of the house Edward had left them. Other days she couldn't place this face, this sharp pair of eyes, which she mistook as belonging to the nurse who asked brisk, disgraceful questions to expose her. One day, quite without warning, she sharpened her own eyes and said, **Marjorie, Marjorie-Keiko, you'll never bring home a husband, will you?**

SHE RECEIVED her second tomato in 1920. Six weeks pregnant and wild with fever, she'd even frightened Edward, who'd cursed the June heat, unaware that it was an entirely different fire that was stoking her furnace. As always, the Exclusion League was fanning the national passions, igniting the resentment of even their own neighbors—Edward's family friends!—who spat in her direction behind his back and hurled rocks at their windows when he was out. She almost cost herself and Edward his heir, flying out to confront the vandal who, luckily, turned out to be a lone, unarmed boy of barely fifteen. Then it was over: a new Alien Land Law passed, shuttering all the remaining Japanese-run farms in the region.

Cherokee Purple: the fruits were large, the color of bruises. When she tried one, she was surprised to find it sweet, nothing at all like blood.

Four years later America closed its ports to all Asian immigrants, special cases pending. When Edward brought the news, she expected his usual tirade, but all that came was the angry thwack of the newspaper striking his open palm. The sound itself was startling, but it was the snap in it that flipped her heart, uncovering a coil of fear that had been fattening there. After all, with the borders officially closed, she'd ceased to be Edward's romantic commitment and become instead his permanent liability. For the first time she found herself cursing her father, his optimism that had let him leave her, his then fifteen-year-old daughter, here. Of course, it was still 1913 then; they'd assumed he'd return as usual, if not the following summer then the one after.

But the world turned out to be tired of the usual, and in retrospect it was only hopeful ignorance that had allowed them to stand on the pier that final morning, her father becoming in his gray suit, she unbecoming in her frock, cut and sewn to complement Edward's cream jacket. The ship, **Hikari,** sleek and modern, was admitting passengers, and her father, a lover of technology, paused to admire it.

The sea was calm, polished to a high gleam, and so was her father when he turned to offer his hand, first to Bob, then to Edward, then finally to her, pulling her in at the last moment to squeeze her shoulders, once, twice, before scissoring his legs and severing himself from them. Was she disappointed? Of course she was. But what words, what gestures, could they have exchanged? The horn bellowed; the passengers waved and shouted. Like her father, she corralled her face. The horn bellowed again, and soon the ramps lifted; water began rippling along the ship's keel, and a sick feeling pushed into her chest, propelling her arms into a wave. She waved and waved, two frantic flags. But his face, a rapidly diminishing button, never changed, his eyes transmitting nothing, not to her, not to Edward, who had kept his hand firmly around her waist.

IN THE winter the sharp-eyed daughter began staying with her. This daughter stayed in the living room even when the wind howled and the cold drifted in through the picture window.

Sometimes the daughters' visits overlapped, and their voices rose to bitter, ac-
cusatory shouts before dropping again to
apologetic whispers, the faithful picture
window reflecting the shoulders of the two
women resigned to an unpleasant but necessary collaboration. Once in a while, one
or the other stormed out, slamming the
door and paralyzing the house. On these
nights she prayed for deliverance, summoning her father, mother, and brothers—and
even Edward, who was annoyingly swift to
respond. One by one, they gathered atop
a mountain whose gentle peak, neon with
green grass, beckoned to her, and in time
she understood that this was her destination
too. This landscape, canopied by a giant
mushroom cloud, binding them together.

ONLY ONCE did Edward turn his back on
her. Edward the chivalrous. He was halfway
up the drive with the morning papers when
he froze, a slightly paunchy statue who
pivoted the next moment to the compost
pile, unaware of her shape in the picture
window.

Minutes later, they met in the house, and before she could utter a greeting he pivoted for a second time, unhooking his coat and leaving without breakfast. Of course she went to investigate. Sprinkled with yesterday's scraps, the newspaper was wet but whole, and it still took her some time to find the article so tiny she might've missed it anyway in her afternoon skim between housekeeping and dinner. HIROSHIMA MAIDENS ARRIVE FOR FREE TREATMENT. The story, seven lines total, praised the spirit of American charity, magnanimous enough to welcome the "grateful girls, survivors of the world's first atomic blast."

She broke five plates that afternoon, her furious hands dropping his heirloom china in purposeful succession: two for the silenced girls; two for the phrasing (**grateful!**); and one for her outrage at Edward, who hadn't bothered to shred the shameful report.

Over the weeks, more newspapers turned up in that corner of the yard as the maidens were treated and displayed. Then, four years later, she found a page carefully splayed on the dining table. JAPAN'S FIRST

MISS UNIVERSE. She read the feature, the headline large enough that she would never have missed it, and fed strips of it to the rotting pile.

Mother!

To her surprise, it was the kind-faced daughter—but when had she gotten so old?—tearing through the door, her hands separating the plastic brush from the dustpan to sweep the breakfast bowl mysteriously shattered like ice floes across the blue and green linoleum.

THEY FORMALIZED their engagement in 1914. She was sixteen, Edward nineteen; they were together for forty-seven years. Forty-seven that would've been sixty-seven had he not fallen from the chair while changing the lightbulb above the foyer cabinet. The cabinet, teak with grooved beveling, stood on six legs and held all of their shoes. If only the lightbulb hadn't died. If only the cabinet had stopped his fall. She no longer remembered what she was doing—drying her hands on her daisy dishcloth? All that survived was a series of tumbling sounds:

wood chair against the wood door that had come unlatched, and the astonished look on Edward's face, staring up at the May sky.

Edward died the following afternoon, surrounded by friends and flowers that spilled from the nightstand beside the hospital bed. She remembered thinking **1961** and catching her own aging reflection in the bathroom mirror. She was in black, her pale face like an old scuttling nun's, and somehow this struck her as perverse, as though she'd glimpsed something she had no business witnessing. Like the time she caught her visiting neighbor, Elizabeth—Elizabeth Derby!—stroking the tie that was draped on the armchair, which Edward was fond of and wore often.

The voice in her head, which was not her own, said: **Everything turns out as it must.**

SOLACE CAME intermittently, like the bumpy signal of the radio she used to listen to in the few stolen minutes before dinnertime, alone in the shed behind the house in Niigata.

One morning, in a moment of such

absolute peace, she looked out the window to discover snow had fallen. When had it fallen? Time had become glassy. She stared at the cup in her hand. How long had she been holding it? When she realized she'd been observing a robin twittering on the birdbath in January, she was surprised to find that she'd been resentful of Edward all these years for leaving her so abruptly.

SHE WAS hospitalized for the final time in the spring. She was coming down the stairs from her bedroom; the pain dazzled her. When she came to, she was in darkness, a faint sizzle still beneath her. When she moved, it flashed from her legs into her eye sockets, clarifying her body's borders.

The injury was to her left tibia. It required a cast and did not set right. The doctor, a prim fellow less than half her age, clucked his tongue with all the reprimand of a wagging finger, as though she'd fiddled with the cast and displaced the bone.

Her daughters did not blame the doctor but did not blame her either. You know how she is, this small child who cannot be blamed for her mistakes. She looked at her new, bow-shaped leg and thought: at least she'd been faithful to Edward.

SUMMER SAW her get temporarily better. She remembered the names of her daughters, the name of her son. She even recognized their faces, knew their exact relationship to her, and asked about the people in the pictures they brought, nodding when she was spoken to. Her daughters were elated. They pushed her to widen her world, one inch at a time, always one more inch.

Soon her son's children came to visit. They were bigger than in the pictures, and knobbier. She stared at them, her foreign grandchildren (but how familiar their chins!), until they hid behind their mother, whom she recognized from the pictures, but of whom she did not have a single memory.

Her eldest, Miriam, said, "Tell us everything about Japan."

Her son, Robert, said, "Where did she put those Super Eights?"

Her other daughter, Marjorie-Keiko, said, "Mother, you do exactly what you want."

The voice in her head, which was very much her own, said: **When will they stop demanding?**

EDWARD DID marry her, but not until 1948, when California repealed its antimiscegenation law. They could have married as early as 1942, when the first Civilian Exclusion Order nudged them to the liberal East, to the house Edward had bought, sight unseen, with his late mother's money. But at that time world freedom was under attack, democracy at risk, and afterward, after the war, they were too tired to bother with what was a formality, until the repeal made the headlines and reminded them of not only the principle but the practicality of it. They, after all, had had three children technically outside of wedlock.

The house was a two-story Cape Cod. It had three bedrooms and a kitchen that opened into a living room overlooking a lawn divided by a pebble walkway, also visible from the attic with its lone cataract window that appealed to no one.

She spent three years confined to this house, to this view of the lawn and the backyard where she hung the laundry with her teenage girls and homeschooled her son, who looked so much like Edward but also enough like her to be bullied. **Ching chang chong!** It was the longest three years of her life, its taut monotony stretched by a shifting fear that made her rage at her children who couldn't help testing the lockdown, lured by the voices of other children, other teenagers. For the first time, three decades since she'd last been in Niigata, she allowed herself to admit she was homesick, her heart squeezing with irrational longing, especially for her brother, who, as rough as boys were, had taken her gently by the hand to feed the ducks in the lake.

One night, unable to settle, she composed a letter to her family, but Edward—Edward!—had forbidden her to mail it, telling her they shouldn't risk it, not even in liberal Massachusetts. **Damn war.**

She ended up complying—he was right: who knew when this country would come for them?—but she never forgave him this restriction. But maybe it wasn't this or that confinement; what she resented was her own dependence, his complete authority over her. After all, these were prohibited days she'd been granted; unlike Bob, she'd escaped uninterned. What right had she to raise her voice? She pictured their house back west, the letters from Niigata, fed through the mail slot, piling by the door. She watched her children and reminded herself to be grateful for all that she'd kept, which did not include her yukata, just in case.

She did send that letter in 1961. It required additional postage, and she mailed it in a new envelope with a second letter, praying for her family's safety and health.

A reply arrived weeks later in a large envelope containing both her letters, plus another in handwriting she didn't recognize. For the rest of her life, she'd wonder how it might have turned out had Edward mailed her letter all those years ago.

According to the house's current owner, her family home had been officially declared abandoned in 1951; he regretted knowing nothing further.

HER FINAL tomato came to her by chance. She didn't discover it until it blossomed and

ripened at the edge of the yard where the
weeds gripped the ground and did not per-
mit much growth.

The stalks were feeble and the fruits
sparse, but so was she by this time, alive
closer to the end of the century than she'd
ever imagined possible. She never learned
the name of the tomato, which yielded only
once, exhibiting their spectacular rainbow
colors before they were plundered by crows
and other small animals that lived in the
woods behind the yard.

IN THE fall, her very last, her daughters
rented a minivan to take her west to tour
the place she had once lived. The drive was
long, spread over seven days and six nights,
and her daughters took turns fussing over
her comfort and pointing out signs—
MOOSE CROSSING, CAMPGROUND—in loud
cheery voices meant to snap her attention.
"It'll be worth it," they kept reassuring her.
Certainly, it was worth it to **them.**

Haight-Ashbury. Chinatown. Golden
Gate Bridge. The daughters moved her closer
to the car window where sunlight, crosshatched with wind, clawed at her face and

stung her eyes. When her daughters noticed her tears, they stopped the car and watched her look. She gazed at the water, shimmering with boats. She gazed at the sky, twiddling the sun. After a moment, sharp-eyed Marjorie said, "No, Mother. Angel Island is over **there.**"

She remembered the overcrowded immigration building, the gloved fingers prying her eyelids, the cheap falling sleeves of the kimonoed picture brides. She remembered the miracle of her walk across the Golden Gate Bridge on Pedestrian Day. Then she remembered Dr. Kerr, a small man with slim fingers, who had talked Edward into a **pessaire** (as he said, delicately, in French). How they'd fought, she and Edward! Not that she wanted another child—Miriam, at three, was a horror, with her doughy obedience and costly appetite—but it was **her** body they were conspiring to plug.

In the end she submitted to the trespass, opening her legs for Dr. Kerr's fingers, which probed and groped for an eternity, intent on finding the "slant" he wished to detail in his new book. When at last he conceded that she was no different from any normal woman, he jammed the pessary (as she insisted on calling it, in English), locking her in.

But her body refused to be sealed, and she gave birth to their second daughter a year later. **Marjorie-Keiko.** She announced the name and refused to retract it. Not for another dead ancestor who had helped spread Edward's family line.

She did not fight the device after that and appreciated its practicality during the Depression. It would be ten years before she'd be pregnant again, and after that—the Caesarean, infection, and fever—it would strike her that she hadn't wanted any of these children—not Miriam or Robert, or even Marjorie-Keiko, her sole successful act of mutiny.

NO! THAT wasn't true! **She** had **coached** Edward to make the argument—better education, more opportunities—to persuade her idealistic father to leave her behind.

SHE LAY in the bed she'd slept in every night since Edward's death. At the foot of her bed was her trunk. The trunk was packed. In the morning her daughters were taking her to a new home. She stood by her window. Something had woken her, compelling her to draw back the curtains.

Not much had changed over the years: the square yard barren in the wintertime, the bare flowerbeds empty of the colors that spilled from them in the summertime. She touched the windowpane; she knew by the feel there was frost in the beds. High in the sky, the moon radiated luminous rings of yellow and pink.

At this hour between night and morning, her fingers were stiff, but she swept them through her empty drawers. Where were her letters? Her thoughts drifted with the clouds that passed over the moon. When was the last time she'd left the house?

A few flakes squeezed themselves from the sky, and she felt weightless, illuminated by moonlight. In this luminescence she was light.

She had taken these stairs many times before; as usual they were cold, but today there were no specific memories attached to them, and her feet were fluent over their surfaces.

Outside, the air was clear, and it gave incredible range to her eyesight. Here was the pebble walkway, here the low wooden gate with the rusted latch. The gate creaked when she opened it.

No lights were on at her neighbors', and the street was latticed with shadows. When she peered down, she saw the road zooming into the sky. The openness delighted her. She was delighted by the dark and the quiet that had conspired to make it so.

A breeze fluttered her nightgown. She had not dressed properly. In this light, her nightgown was translucent, the naughty hem uncovering her knees. But what did she care? This morning, she was utterly careless, her thoughts and feelings flapping as though teased by a miraculous gale. Later, they may settle into their hard, familiar forms. But for now there were only sensations skimming her skin and scattering her memories. Today, her heart was flying, and so were her feet. She ran into the crisp horizon just beginning to break.

TWO

LUNA

Luna hadn't slept all night. She hadn't slept because she couldn't get the feeling of water out of her ear, the left one, which felt numb, rubbery and dense, as if it no longer belonged to her.

All night she conjured birds and fields, then roads to bisect the fields, then cars to put on the roads, cars with rolled-down windows, and, in one, pigtails that belonged to her sister Katy. Then there was the ticking car; the rustling shade; a pair of hands setting out all her favorite things—chicken, gravy, mashed potatoes. She saw her own fingers elongate across the picnic blanket, then the sudden flash—her sister covered her mouth—and Luna heard it again. That plugged sound. Like the sound of water underwater. It flung open her eyes.

Then it was morning. The room was milky with sunlight, and her father, who had come to wake her, was disappearing into the seam of the half-open door. She pulled on her clothes and was sitting at the dining table staring at a plate of scrambled eggs, two sausages grinning like a clown. Her mother said, "Your shirt's backwards."

Katy laughed. But when Luna opened her mouth, her sister's laugh muted on one side, and she remembered her ear; her protest shriveled back down her throat.

THE PROBLEM with her ear had been coming and going all week—Luna knew exactly where it started. **Shōnan-kaigan.** Her father had pointed out the beach on the map. **See, here?** A nick on the belly of the seahorse: the eastern shore of Japan. Katy, as she was prone to these days, rolled her eyes, but Luna liked this about her father, the way he spoke to her as though to his university students. That morning, when he looked up from the map, he'd said, **It's important to remember where you've been.**

But Luna, at six, never remembered.

This was their third consecutive summer in Japan, but it might as well have
been her first, except that she was familiar with her grandparents' house, where
they'd stayed their first two visits. She
liked it there, despite her grandfather's
room, always closed, the white door emanating an incubated silence, like an eye
turned inward. On his good days, her
ojīsan used to slip out of his room to tend
to his shapely plants in the foyer, and Luna
remembered how, the first time she and
Katy happened upon him, he'd surprised
them by inquiring in gentlemanly English
whether they were enjoying their day. Later,
her father explained that both her ojīsan
and obāsan knew some English from the
American Occupation days, but unlike
Ojīsan, Obāsan never gave herself away,
prattling on in Japanese, content to transmit only her feelings: an open warmth, like
the house itself.

Now Ojīsan was confined to a room at
the hospital, but Luna never forgot how,
on that first foyer encounter, he'd pressed a
finger to his lips and, eyes glinting, shuffled

into his sandals to show them the white peaks of Mount Fuji protruding like a giant tooth above the telephone wires.

Fujisan. It was the first word he'd taught them, telling them about their ancestors who congregated on the mountain to watch over the house. By the end of that first visit, even Luna, still three then, could follow his ritual, clapping her hands three times and pressing her palms together, eyes closed, a prayer for Fuji-**san**, his mountain god. Keeper of health.

Ojīsan recovered that time, but her parents had already decided to spend a few weeks every summer in Japan. This summer, their third, they were staying two months in a rented apartment midway between the hospital and her grandparents' house.

MODEST ON the map, Shōnan-kaigan was a surfer's hub teeming with colors: blue tubes, green boogie boards, towels like puddles of paint, the occasional rainbow parasol adrift in smoke billowing from the beachside cuttlefish stands.

All summer they'd gone to beaches along this coast, but none had been like this, with pink-lipped women, hair the color of hay, their men equally bleached and beaked with visors. At first their mother sat in the car, observing, and Luna worried that another afternoon might be ruined. But then her mother opened the door, plunging her hand into her bag—Luna knew exactly what she was looking for, what she was always looking for in Japan: sunglasses. Her father, who had also been watching, placed his hand on her head and said, **Go help your sister.**

Up ahead, Katy was inflating a beach ball. She'd already inflated their tubes, which were looped around her shoulders. The ball was enormous, and as Katy tried to inflate it further it kicked off her face. Luna laughed, but when she turned to see if her father had witnessed it too, she heard her mother say, **I'm sick of being stared at. I feel so goddamn white.**

But nobody noticed her mother here, and soon everybody nestled into their patches of sand as the sun drifted and the clouds flickered, brightening, then graying, stirring up a breeze that roughened the waves and lifted the tide, reminding the sisters of their afternoon's last task: to choose their seashells,

pearly pink ones today, pierced like ear-
lobes. Luna wanted the whole pile to add to
her collection. Katy planned to string hers
together, like the necklaces she'd seen at a
shop near the giant statue of the goddess
their father had called the Kannon. Behind
them, their mother was powering through
her paperback, her brown sunglasses occasionally rising like a camel's back to check
on them. Down by the shoreline, their father was combing through bands of seaweed
for the larger shells that washed up there.

"Hey," Katy said, nudging her sister.

Ankle-deep in seaweed, their father was
holding up a palm-sized shell. They raced
to inspect it: a peach-colored dome shaped
like a snail. No holes in this one, and too
big for a necklace: Katy discarded it into
Luna's hand.

The shell was light, warm like an egg.
When she turned it over, it looked like an
ear. Her father said if she listened, she could
hear the entire ocean inside.

Luna matched the shell to her ear. She
heard the roar of the surf, the trill of the
wind, and then: absence; the deafening
slap. Her father spun around. **Say,** he said.

Her mother, horrified, retracted her hand. **Masa.** She pointed at the gray spider retreating across the sand. **It could've bit her.**

"LUNA?" HER mother was staring at her. "Aren't you going to eat?"

Luna blinked at the egg-sausage-milk combo. The eggs looked spongy. She rolled the sausages from side to side. "I'm not hungry."

Katy, quicker than a cat, speared the sausages.

"Katy." Her father lowered the newspaper. "Let Luna decide if she's finished."

"She said she doesn't want them."

Everyone looked at Luna, who covered her ear. "I'm not hungry."

Her father gently pried her hand. "What's wrong?"

"I'm not hungry," she repeated.

Her mother folded her napkin. "She's fine. She can eat later."

Her father's mouth tightened, but he closed his paper and scraped back his chair. "All right, I'm off. I'll make sure I'm back around lunch," he said. These days, he'd taken to visiting the hospital alone, his promise to return in thirty stretching into four, five hours. "I'll give your bracelet to your ojīsan. He'll love it," he told the girls, who'd used their shells to make him a charm. "Don't forget dinner's at six," he told their mother. "Let's hope they'll let my father out for a few hours."

"But I thought we were having lunch at your parents'," her mother said.

"My mother wants us all to have a nice dinner."

"Masa, didn't we agree—"

Her father scooped up the keys. "It could be his last time—can't you see that?"

Her mother stared at him, face set.

Luna peeked at her sister, who was fighting to chew the egg and sausage she'd sulkily crammed into her mouth. Every summer, on their last day, Obāsan made **osekihan** and **yakitori** for Luna and Katy. Luna loved her grandmother's **osekihan,** sticky rice plumped with red beans, a pinch of salt and black sesame sprinkled on top. She'd been anticipating it all week. She pushed her plate away. Her mother's gaze fell on her.

"At least finish your milk."

The milk was sweaty and as white as

Elmer's. When Luna brought it to her face, a sweet gamy smell wafted up her nose. She glanced at her mother, but she was looking out the window, watching her father traverse the little parking lot to their rented car. Luna shut her eyes and, in one queasy chug, drank the entire glass and carried it, sick and wobbly, to the kitchen.

HER FATHER did return just after lunch, in time to take them to the neighborhood shrine he'd been talking up, someplace he and Ojīsan used to stop at on their walks to the vegetable stands along the back roads where the farmers lived. The stands were still there, rickety and weather-beaten, piled with seconds, a slotted box nailed to the wooden pillar to collect the proceeds. Luna loved feeding the box, the sound of the coins working their way down the obstacle course of paper bills, but she'd never noticed a shrine. Her father explained that this was because it was on a different road, a footpath, and unlike the popular shrines in the region, this one was local, shabby and small, dating back a thousand years or more, which might sound old but was in fact nothing compared to the sacred tree that stood beside it, its trunk so wide it took at least five adults to encircle it. The tree was the reason the shrine was there; its majesty had caught the eye of a traveling priest.

"Is it open to the public? Is it safe?" her mother asked.

Even a month ago, her father would've laughed—**the conscientious tourist**—but now he replied that all shrines were open to the public, and if it was safe for their neighbors it was safe for them.

"Do spirits live there?" Luna asked. Her father had told them many stories about the mountain fox and raccoon spirits who liked to venture into town to prank people.

Her father nodded gravely. "There's a rumor that an actual god lives there. Jurōjin." He stretched out the syllable for Luna and Katy. "Jurōjin is one of the Shichifukujin, the seven gods of fortune. Remember?"

They nodded dubiously.

"Jurōjin's superpower is longevity," he went on. "We're lucky he's the one who lives here."

"He can cure Ojīsan?" Luna asked, eyes shining.

"We'll see." He smiled. Then he told them a secret: Jurōjin was actually **not** Japanese but Chinese, and long ago, before he became a proper god, he'd been a gambling pirate who lost all his treasures to Sinbad. Luna was astounded. "He knew Sinbad?" Katy was convinced their father was making it up, but Luna could tell she was excited. They jumped into action, Katy dashing for the sunscreen, Luna for their fugitive hats.

THEY PARKED in the carport attached to Ojīsan's house. Usually when Obāsan heard the car she came to the door to invite them for snacks, but today they were greeted with sweet and savory aromas, the door closed to company. In the heat it was impossible not to feel cheated, and Luna's ear itched, the lobe oversoft like microwaved gummy bears. She plodded on, lagging behind Katy and her parents, and followed the wrong turn at the split, veering onto a dirt path that vanished into the backwoods. She was halfway down the path, kicking up dust, when her father called to her. She trudged back, and though it was muggy he squeezed her close, leaning her this way and that as the road narrowed, ambushed by a bamboo grove. When Luna asked how much longer, he told her that if they were home in Urbana, it would be like going from their house to the playground.

They emerged onto a proper road, regulated by traffic lights and flanked by small businesses, one jammed with stationery, another displaying mannequins and posters of makeup and beauty creams. There was a pharmacy, a salon, then a shelter of rice vending machines. Katy ran to investigate them. "What do they say?" she demanded, pressing all the buttons. Their father read her the options, from the type (short, long, sticky) to the quality (premium to regular) to the level of processing (whole to brown to polished). "Some people take the husks, too," he said. Luna pictured bowls of husks appearing in the morning. Katy wondered if she could make a mattress out of them. Their father laughed. "At this rate, we'll need an extra suitcase to bring the husks home." Their mother, quiet since the morning, turned away.

They passed a boutique, a noodle shop,

then a field, metal baseball bats clanging in the distance, the sky winking with summer kites. Their mother dabbed their faces and passed around the water bottle.

"Are we there yet?" Katy asked, but her father, lost in thought, kept marching, his neck darkening in the sun.

At last the blinding road began to dapple again, the mown field bursting into tall weeds, which thickened into brush, interspersed with spindly trees that soon broadened into real trees that sifted the sun. Their father finally stopped and pointed at a hill, a dark mouth gaping at the base.

"I thought we were going to the shrine," Katy said.

"We are. We're just taking a detour—a special one," he said.

The heat rose, the cicadas buzzed; no one said anything.

THE TUNNEL was old, with a scraggly beard and a mossy forehead that sprouted a forest before vanishing up the hill. From above—a plane, say, or a parachute—the tunnel was invisible. Their father told them that for centuries it had been a vital pass linking the surrounding villages. During the war, though, it took on a different function. "Do you know what it was?"

The girls frowned, wary of the chilly mouth, the dot of light on the other end forbiddingly far. Their mother said, "Masa, it's hot."

"Well, you'll just have to see for yourself, then," he said.

"Luna loves seeing for herself," Katy said.

This was true, but Luna was apprehensive of this tunnel, the seeping darkness that swallowed the sunlight and returned nothing. "I want to go back," she said.

Her father wiped her hair off her face. "Let's give things a chance."

But the tunnel was dark, the ground wet, its mineral breath furring the wall. Luna clutched her sister's arm, and Katy let her, the two of them stepping cautiously, the wet crunch of their footsteps echoing like a cacophony of bats. Luna wiggled her ear; the tunnel's clammy pressure had a plugging effect, darkening the dark on that side of her head, throwing off her balance. Katy pulled her closer and whispered, "It's a dungeon."

Sure enough, Luna could see the outlines

along the wall, the row of roughly filled pas-
sages, some streaked with slivers of what
looked like metal. Then, astonishingly, an
open mouth, fanged with bars.

"Is it really a dungeon?" Luna asked, feeling the suck of air, the eternal inhalation.

Her father palmed her head. "Good
guess, but no. It's a decommissioned bomb
shelter. Bōkūgo. They're filled now"—he
reached to trace a seam—"but they used to
extend pretty far into these hills."

"What are the bars for, then?" Katy asked.

Luna edged behind her sister and felt
the press of her mother's hand on her back.
"Masa, you're scaring them."

Her father curled a hand around a bar
and reassured them that they weren't bars
so much as gates people could close when
parachutes dropped from the sky. "It was
the safest place. Like wearing a magic cloak
and armor."

But it wasn't remotely like that; Luna
could see the ghostly knuckles powdering
the bars. In a dark this dark, someone could
still be huddled there, unseen, waiting for
bombs and parachutes to fall from the sky.
"What if we get trapped?" she asked.

Her mother squeezed her shoulder. "No one will get trapped. The war was a long time ago. Air raids don't happen like that anymore."

"Actually," her father said, inspecting a remnant of a latch, "wars are happening all the time. In some places, children like you and Katy make themselves into bombs."

"Bombs?" Katy said. "Like how?"

Luna glanced back at the daylight shimmering behind them; diminished to a patch, it was now equal in size to the one ahead of them. "I won't be a bomb. I **refuse,**" she said.

"Sometimes we don't have that choice," her father said.

"And other times we do," her mother said. "Come on, that's enough." She grabbed their arms and pulled them toward the light.

Her father trailed along, running his hand over the wall's depressions. "You know your ojīsan and obāsan lived through it. They survived, but it was a scary time. All the lives lost. Soldiers and civilians. To say nothing of the colonial conscripts." His voice vanished in the cackle of the tunnel.

Her mother swiveled. "Really? This is why you dragged them here?"

Her father's shoes scraped to a stop. "This is important. It's their history."

"For god sake."

"Everyone should know their roots, Say."

"Come on," their mother said, prodding them forward.

"They're half mine too."

His words bounced off the wall and chased each other through the tunnel of Luna's own ears. She'd never considered herself this way before—half—like something mashed together and pulling apart, like the dogs she'd once seen, joined by their bums and scrabbling in opposite directions. There had been a blind woman on the sidewalk too; disturbed by the mewling scuffle, she'd cried out. Luna's mother had tried to explain, but the dogs, ever more panicked, yipped and tumbled, knocking the woman's cane. Her mother rushed to help, and in that moment the woman, lost in the sudden vastness of space, had looked straight at Luna, her milky-white eyes darting behind her skewed sunglasses.

"Mom?" Katy said. "Luna's going to cry."

Her mother drew her in. "It's okay," she said, but Luna twisted away and ran, her plugged ear echoing like the tunnel, her whole being yearning for the sunlight, where she'd be able to see their faces and feel her father's fingers work their way through her hair. And when she thought about that, she couldn't control her tears.

DINNER WAS quiet that evening. Despite Obāsan's hopes, Ojīsan couldn't be discharged, and an eerie absence emanated from the spot Obāsan had set for him. Katy couldn't understand why anyone would set the table for an absent person. "It's creepy," she said, watching her grandmother arrange a small plate for Ojīsan.

"Your obāsan misses him. This way, it's like he's here with us," her mother said.

Her father ladled soup into their bowls, a consommé Obāsan thought their mother would like. "It's a gesture of respect, Katy. Your grandmother wants you to know how much your ojīsan wanted to come."

"It's still creepy." Katy took the piece of

sweet **tamagoyaki** Obāsan was holding out to her.

Luna sat on her hands, eyeing the crock of **osekihan.** "Katy didn't say **arigatō,**" she said.

"Loser," Katy said.

"Well?" her mother said.

Katy mumbled her **arigatō.**

Obāsan nodded, folding back the sleeves of her perfectly pressed blouse. Even alone in her own home she dressed this way—a generational propriety, her mother had explained; a side effect of the Depression and the war, her father had explained. Obāsan held out a heaping plate. "Yakitori?"

"Thank you, **arigatō,**" their mother said, accepting the skewers and distributing them among their plates. "Girls?"

They said their **arigatō**s.

Obāsan's eyes lit with pity. "Kawaisō ne."

Luna looked at her father, who, for once, was uneager to translate. "What do you say before you eat?" he asked.

"Itadakimasu," the sisters chimed in unison.

Their father reached for the dish of pickled cucumbers, his favorite. After a moment, he said, "Guess what I learned the other day."

Luna dipped her chopsticks into her soup, chasing elusive slivers of carrots and onions.

"I found out I was adopted."

"You were an orphan?" Katy said.

"What's an orphan?" Luna said.

"It's when you have no mom or dad," Katy said.

Luna frowned at her father and her grandmother.

Her father brushed a dot of rice from her chin. "Katy's right. But, luckily, your obāsan and ojīsan adopted me right away, after my mother died, just after the war. She was very sick, isn't that right?" He spoke to his mother in Japanese.

Obāsan nodded wearily. She explained through him that food and access to medicine were limited. She said something else with "America" in it, but he chose not to translate it.

"Did she live in the tunnel?" Luna asked.

"Honey, no one lived in the tunnel," her mother said.

"Actually, she **did,**" her father said. "Not

the tunnel we went to, but a bigger one in a town called Matsushiro. The tunnels there were built to form a huge underground maze, designed to hide the Emperor. Many people died during the construction. Most were Korean, forced to work there by the Japanese."

Her mother scooped a mound of sesame spinach. "How about we talk about this later? Your mother is already sad." She smiled at Obāsan.

Luna peered at her grandmother, who did seem sad.

Her father lowered his chopsticks. "One day it'll matter to them. They deserve to know."

"So we'll talk about it later," she repeated.

Her father lifted his bowl. "All I want to say is that it was strange to find out my parents were Korean. I've been Japanese for forty-one years—my own parents' **colonizer.**"

"What's a colonizer?" Katy asked.

Her mother, still a mask of pleasantness, said, "My mother's parents came from Germany. But so what? It's wild to find out you were adopted, but it's not as if you've suddenly become a different person. You're no more Korean than I'm German."

Katy's eyes widened. "We're Korean?"

"Like Jurōjin?" Luna asked.

"Jurōjin's Chinese, stupid," Katy said.

Her father shook his head. "You make it sound like nothing has changed. As though identity is a choice. It's not a choice."

"But what has changed? You're claiming something that played no part in your life."

Luna watched her parents, the rising pitch not yet touching their faces. She saw that Obāsan was watching them too.

Her father sighed. "We're not separate from our histories, Say; I can't separate myself from my roots. To sever that connection would be calamitous. Why can't you understand that?"

Her mother, catching Obāsan's eyes, shook her head apologetically. "Sometimes I think you forget what's real in your life, what's important in the here and now. Maybe you're right. Maybe I don't understand. But you're making a choice—you realize that, right?"

"And you're not?"

They regarded each other, their faces

neutral but joined by an invisible bridge, words Luna couldn't hear passing between them. Their mother finally said, "You keep saying they deserve to know. Well, you're right." She turned to them. "Girls—"

"Don't—"

"Your father's not coming back with us tomorrow."

Luna stared at her father, his face still with disbelief.

"Why?" Katy asked.

"Are you going to stay until The Fall?" Luna asked. Fall was a big deal in their house, marking and regulating their life, which revolved around the school calendar.

He rubbed his forehead. "Your grandfather is very sick. I'm going to stay for a while to help your obāsan."

Her mother made a snorting sort of noise. "Oh, that's rich. Don't lie to them."

"It's not a lie."

"Is it because you're Korean now?" Luna asked.

Her father blinked. Then he brushed her cheek. "It's just for a time, until I sort things out. Anyway, you'll be so busy," he said, reminding her that school would soon be starting, and she'd have swim practice and sleepovers and Oatmeal Cream Pies and Suzy-U's—

"Suzy-**Q**'s," Katy corrected.

"Suzy-Q's," he said.

Obāsan gripped the collar of her blouse and began coughing.

Their mother jumped up. "Are you okay?"

Obāsan pointed at the water glass.

"She's crying," Katy observed.

"She just swallowed the wrong way," their mother said, gently thumping Obāsan's back.

Their father rose to refill her glass. At the sink, with his head bent, he looked worn, his back like someone else's old coat.

Luna clutched her ear. "Are you divorcing us?"

Her father turned. "Of course not," he said, but his face flushed a shade of red she only saw when he drank with his colleagues. Katy knocked back her chair and burst out of the room. "Liar," she screamed. Luna covered her ears as the front door slammed.

Obāsan, coughing, got up. Tucking her chair neatly under the table, she quietly

followed Katy outside. Through the sliding glass doors, still pale with summer
light, they watched her approach the curled
shape on the bench in Ojīsan's garden. Luna
slipped out of her own chair to join them,
and nobody stopped her.

Outside, the cicadas were loud, the air a
filtered gray, almost dizzying. When Luna
reached them, Obāsan nudged Katy and
made room for her. Luna sat against her
grandmother, her steady warmth radiant,
like the walls of their house in Urbana at
midday but softer. It was a pleasant evening,
the breeze dispersing her grandmother's
patter, pollinating the air with her twin-
kling words. Above, the clouds pinked, then
blued. Obāsan patted their knees. "Hotaru,"
she said, pronouncing the word she knew
they knew because she'd taught it to them.
And it was true: a whole galaxy of fireflies
were flashing in the grass.

IN THE morning, they drove to the airport in the cloying rental car. Usually, they
arrived early to shop for snacks and last-
minute gifts, but today they didn't even eat
at the restaurant overlooking the runway.

They headed straight to check-in and pretended not to see their father extracting his passport from their bundle. At the security gate, he took out the camera: two solemn children and a grim mother. Katy gasped. "We forgot the mikans!"

Luna pictured the mikans, plump and soft to peel; they always got a pack, bunched in a net, at the kiosk. "Can we get them?"

Her father glanced at the clock. "Maybe they'll have them at Duty Free?"

Her mother, checking the zippers on the bags, didn't reply.

"I'm sure they'll have them at Duty Free," he said.

Luna, though, was sure they didn't. "They only have them **there.**" She pointed at the glittery shops down the concourse.

"Listen." He knelt. "You'll miss your flight. You can forgo them this once."

Luna stared past him. "I want them."

"All right," he said. "We'll make a deal. I'll bring you a whole crate when I fly home."

Luna studied her father, the glowing crate the size of a small mountain materializing between them. "Really?"

He nodded.

"Do you promise?"

Her father closed his eyes. When he opened them again, they were shiny with pain, his lips twitching as he worked to control them. Then his face tightened, and Luna knew he was shaping his words, words like "love" and "miss" and "soon," which he would say because they were true—Luna knew they were true but not the entire truth, only what he wished most to be true. So she waited for it, that moment she knew would come, the moment when his tongue hefted his words for the last time. And when it came, the telltale pinch of his lips, just before he did it—opened his mouth and lied to her—she turned her head, the good side, away from him. But Luna didn't need to hear his words or his exact tone—apologetic and full of promise—she could simply feel it, his breath like a small devastation inside her ear. And because she didn't want him to suspect, or see him cry again, when he moved back to look at her, she gave him a full smile, as if she'd been listening and believed what he said.

Later, Luna will learn words like "biculturalism" and "fracture" to explain the pain that will skim her heart whenever someone mentions something that reminds her of summer in Japan. Like her father, she will learn to find solace in the rigor of academic practice, and in this way she'll compensate for the loss, which she will not confront until she is in her late twenties, pregnant with her first child, her home a happiness that will blemish her, the way it will touch and terrify her deeper than any hurt. Then she'll discover that, despite the anguish and disappointment, she'd loved her father, loved him irreplaceably.

But for now Luna has no words to describe this feeling, this weight, which has traveled from her ear to her chest, constricting the tears that are refusing to come, even here, at the boarding gate, where they can see him waving behind the glass panel that now separates them. For now, Luna is focused on the plane, where she will sit between her sister and mother, enjoying her orange juice and peanuts, not knowing that it will be years before she'll see him again, older and unable to look directly at her.

THREE

ALLEGIANCE

He was a man of principle, Masaharu told himself. After all, he'd kept his head, even in the midst of that nonsense war, which had gone much too far—anyone could've told anyone that by the dismal end of it. Even the Emperor, the coward, sacrificing more lives just to save a good patch of his own skin. And now in this burnt-out clutter of defeat, his head was still screwed on tightly, despite the rationed-out years no one could justify now. Only when the Americans made their appearance, dotting the wasteland with their trucks and jeeps, did he become aware of a coldness at the center of his being, a coldness that nipped the belly of his heart before sliding away like a silver fish, back into the black depths of his soul. Then again, maybe this had always been his flaw: his vulnerability to feelings that jeopardized his principles. Masaharu had to allow that.

That morning, they'd had breakfast as usual, he and his wife: thin barley gruel and half a sweet potato. And, as usual, he'd raised his chopsticks, imagining a magnificent breakfast he'd once considered plain: white rice, salted sanma fish, miso soup. He slurped the gruel, snatching hints of the sweetness of white rice, the bitterness of the sanma, relishing them. But the potato was an emaciated stump, unsalvageable even by imagination. He ate it in one bite.

"Would you like mine too?" his wife asked, finishing her smaller bowl of gruel.

Last night he'd watched her from the window of their rented room, carefully roasting the potato, its purple skin blistering in a nest of flames—just like a boy's leg. He speared her untouched potato and swallowed it whole, choking on it.

"Do you want anything else before I go?" she asked, nesting her bowl in his.

Masaharu grunted and slid his chopsticks toward her. A year older than him, his wife was an elegant woman he'd chosen for himself—and for his parents, who'd been anxious to see him married. Of course, like everybody else, she'd thinned out considerably over these years, but she'd done so evenly, with none of the sinking and hollowing he saw in the flesh of others. Still, she barely filled her clothes now, no matter how often she took them in. Masaharu lay back on the grimy tatami floor, wondering why she still asked after his wants when, clearly, every want had to go unfulfilled. Possibly it was habit, thirteen years of being a wife, although Nishi Masako—as he still thought of her sometimes in her maiden name—had never been the subservient type. She'd always made sure he knew what she minded and what she did not. She was a resolute woman, certainly a match for himself.

Tucking her hair behind her ears, she wiped the counter that contained the sink where they also kept their toiletries. Every Sunday, it was the same: his brain withdrew into its stony vault while his wife prepared for work—a typing job secured by an acquaintance of his. It still got to him that she was the one with a job now—but for her to have picked up an extra day? It was enough to fell any man. But actually, that wasn't true, Masaharu thought; Sunday or not, they'd never been short of talk until, one October evening four weeks earlier, she'd returned from work refusing to speak. Her silence was unprecedented, so when the next morning she still didn't explain herself, he'd decided to respect it.

"Well, if there's nothing else." His wife pulled on her sandals, and this time it was Masaharu who did not look at her, even though he could feel her eyes boring into the side of his face.

She picked up her cloth bundle and closed the door behind her.

LISTENING TO his wife's footsteps clanking down the metal stairs, Masaharu wondered again when the idea had come to him, or rather, when it had taken hold of him, this concrete need to act. It couldn't have been long after that silent October evening. But actually, that wasn't true either, Masaharu thought now. As a journalist, that need had fueled his whole career, though it had never gripped him this way. Except, he thought, one other time. It was March then, eight months ago, the worst night in their thirteen years of marriage.

That night, the sky, for once, had been empty of the planes that had begun to burn the country built mostly of wood and paper. Like many people, they'd been ignorant of the realities of incendiaries, and all they'd done to prepare, he and his wife and their thirteen-year-old son, Seiji, was dig a shelter two meters deep and cover it with corrugated tin. When the sirens went off, his wife had headed to the foyer to gather their evacuation bags while he made his way to Seiji's room. In the time it took to cross the hall, there was a series of whistling sounds, followed by a succession of eerie thuds, then an eruption of footsteps as people flooded the streets. It took a moment for the incendiaries to flare, but when they did there was a new combustion of noise: the crash of splintering wood, the juddering roar of the flames as gales of heat and smoke rushed to engulf them. By the time Masaharu and his wife staggered into a district shelter, the whole neighborhood had been razed, the two safest evacuation sites—the Olympic-sized swimming pool and the concrete high school—gutted. All Masaharu and his wife could say for sure was that Seiji wasn't in the house when the siren went off that March night, and afterward he never turned up, not at any shelter, or at any school, or among the things scraped and salvaged from the gummed-up pool.

A hollow clomp resounded on the concrete landing. In a minute his wife would pass under the window on her way to the train station. Masaharu stood. All month he'd asked himself why—why that silence?—and a nameless dread had coalesced in his chest. For here was his wife, a survivor of one of the worst horrors to befall a mother—what could possibly have unnerved her now? Yet she'd come home silent, unable to seamlessly carry on with their domestic routine—an unsettling anomaly for his wife, who'd been trained by years of war to evade the patriotic police.

At the crosswalk, his wife paused, and Masaharu drew back from the window, knowing she'd sensed his presence. They were synchronized in this way, even more so than he and Seiji, who'd resembled each other, casting the same determined shadow when they walked or showing the same propensity for irritation when efficiency was thwarted. She'd connected to Seiji this way as well, the two of them orbiting each other as if their umbilical cord had never been cut. It was something Masaharu had cherished: his little family cell, his wife at the fulcrum keeping them in balance. He'd vowed to do everything he could to keep them intact, even if it meant a little personal compromise.

Masaharu reached for his jacket and cap. Patting his pockets for his keys, he closed the door and quietly descended the metal steps.

TO ACCOUNT for the unpredictability of the world, his wife had taken to leaving early, and she stood on the platform now, with over a half hour to spare, gazing out at the wooded hill studded with scaffolding twenty-five meters high, the framework for what was to become an enormous bust of the Kannon, the Buddhist goddess of mercy. Sixteen years ago, in 1929, a volunteer group had begun building the structure, only to be interrupted five years later

when conflict with China became imminent. Like everything else, the Kannon,
ally of the common people, was sacrificed
for war. When Seiji was born, they'd taken
the train from their home in Tokyo to visit
Masaharu's brother, an esteemed surgeon in
Shizuoka, and glimpsed the construction
from the train window. It seemed anachronistic to build such a monument at a time of
such modernization and militarization, and
they were moved. It was the reason they'd
decided to come here to Ōfuna, this intact
but unfamiliar city, three months ago, when
they'd fled Tokyo after learning that a second "new type" bomb had razed Nagasaki.
If the Americans were willing to obliterate
a Christian city, Tokyo's fate seemed sealed.

"I didn't notice it before, but the Kannon
was being built with Her back to Tokyo,"
his wife had observed the day they arrived in
Ōfuna, clutching their few belongings scavenged from the bombed-out ruins of Tokyo.
"Pity they stopped Her construction—it's a
shame. I'm not surprised we're being oblit-
erated." She gazed up at the abandoned scaffolding. "Our government certainly deserves

nothing less than this. This defeat," she said, the word popping like a rogue balloon.

Masaharu glanced about them. Defeat was surely imminent, but there was no telling who might be listening, even here in this noisy station crowded mostly with refugees like themselves. He took her arm and steered them toward an exit. "It's not like you to be superstitious. If I didn't know you, I'd think you were saying that if She'd been completed, if She'd been facing the right way, She wouldn't have forsaken us."

A prickly light gathered in her eyes. "The Kannon would never forsake us. She'll never forsake her people. No matter which way Her back is turned."

Her vehemence surprised him, and he quickly agreed. "The important thing is that we're here—and we're better off here," he added, even though he knew Ōfuna was home to one of the country's most brutal POW interrogation centers. Though he was unaware of any American or other white prisoners there, with defeat hanging around their necks, he didn't want to consider the ramifications of living in proximity to such

an institution. "Let's see who we can convince to let us a room," he said. But his wife,
inconsolable, refused to brighten, even after
they secured a room in a boardinghouse and
slumped onto the tatami floor. For there
was now no denying they were here. And as
Masaharu sat with this thought, it dawned
on him that what had upset his wife had
perhaps been his word **forsake.** After all, it
was she, Nishi Masako, who'd made the final
decision to turn their backs on the raining
bombs and pitted streets that had refused to
yield even the bones of their only son.

Now, watching her wait for the train,
Masaharu wondered what she saw in the ugly
scaffolding. Did she see hope, the promise
of redemption? Or only regret, the guilt of
choosing to move on?

But his wife, a mask of serenity, betrayed
only that the shade had begun to chill her.

THE TRAIN rattled to a stop. Masaharu
pushed through the crowd to the car he saw
his wife board. Would she sit or stand? Even
thirteen years of marriage couldn't help him
predict that. He lowered his cap and slid

into line, composing an explanation in case she happened upon him.

He spotted her right away, sitting at the opposite end of the car, her coat folded neatly on her lap, her cloth bundle perched above it like an oversized mikan. Darting behind a spindly but tall man, he took up his position, only to be jostled by a throng of katsugiya smugglers transporting rice on their backs. Cooing and swaying, they eddied around him, their precious bundles, convincingly wrapped in the kind of obuihimo his own mother had once used to carry him, pressing him down the aisle. Two more seats, and sure enough, his wife's eyes fastened onto him.

"Are you on your way to Tomita-san's?" she asked, amused by his contortions.

Masaharu grunted. Tomita Yoshiaki was a fellow journalist, a diehard Communist who'd been released from jail after the Allied Forces abolished the Peace Preservation Law once used by the government to suppress "unpatriotic activity." Tomita, initially censured for questioning the legitimacy of the Japanese presence in Manchuria, had been arrested for criticizing Japan's increasingly aggressive foreign policy. He was detained for ten years, a light sentence compared to the hundreds who'd been incarcerated for upwards of twenty. Masaharu took off his sweaty cap. "I forgot we were meeting today. On a Sunday," he mumbled, grateful for the pretext.

"Tomita-san is a zealot. If you weren't so busy brooding, we could've left together," she said, handing him her handkerchief.

Masaharu wiped his face, ignoring her gentle jab. "Tomita needs to be careful. We don't really know how open American-style democracy is."

"I'm sure Tomita-san isn't keen on re-turning to jail. Besides, he might have some job leads for you," she said, turning to ac-knowledge a young woman who'd bumped against her while attempting to unscrew a canteen. She had a small child and a sizable bundle on her lap, the verdant fragrance of tea perfuming her. She bowed apologeti-cally, including Masaharu in the gesture.

"Can I help you with that?" A woman facing them gestured at the canteen. She was wearing a Western-style dress and a pair of Western-style shoes, and her nails were painted a garish red. Oddly, she'd left her face bare, perhaps in consideration of this train ride, or perhaps simply to minimize hostility. The elderly woman next to her sniffed. She was clutching her own bundle, possibly some kimonos she hoped to barter on the black market. The tea peddler glanced about uncomfortably but handed over the canteen. Masaharu turned back to his wife.

"One thing Tomita needs to realize is that it's not Japan, but us men, who were defeated."

"You men have certainly made a mess," his wife agreed, suppressing a smirk.

"That's right," a woman standing near them piped up. "All men do is make war."

"And lose it too," another chimed in.

"I heard they're opening the government to women. Pretty soon women will be running this country," a man behind Masaharu said.

"Lucky for you; you'll never lose another war 'cause we won't make any," a third woman cracked to the others' approval.

Masaharu wondered what these women

would be saying if Japan had won the war; victors could justify anything, and hadn't they thrown themselves into the war effort just months before? The man behind him clucked but didn't reply.

His wife said, "Didn't we all contribute to this war? I certainly didn't do enough to prevent it."

A silence descended over the car, the train's rhythmic clatter unpleasantly marking their progress. Of course she was right; unlike most, he and his wife had at least done their part, boycotting send-offs, contesting propaganda news, but in the end these were small individual acts with no collective reach. If his wife and son hadn't been a factor, Masaharu would've also kept writing, handcopying his exposés and distributing them himself; once upon a time, not so long ago, his name had carried weight. Ultimately, though, he'd never been convinced jail was a useful option, and now, knowing Tomita's ordeal, he had to admit he didn't regret this concession.

Surprisingly, it was the panpan prostitute in the Western-style dress who broke the silence. "But we were deceived, weren't we? We were tricked by the Emperor."

The elderly woman shrank at the blasphemy, but the others murmured their assent. Even the Occupation authorities pushed this logic: they, the Japanese, were simply misguided children in need of a little reeducation, this time to obey the American Father. A thoroughly colonial attitude, thought Masaharu.

"Well, if we were all deceived, we're one stupid country, aren't we? No wonder we lost the war." This time it was the tea peddler with the small child who spoke, once again attuning them to the train's fitful clatter.

The doors rattled open. Masaharu gripped his wife's seat. A few passengers pushed their way out as more squeezed in, among them two GIs who, despite the Occupation's segregation rules, had apparently decided to experience native life. Unlike those who strutted around like roosters, at least this pair seemed well-meaning, if revved by the thrill of disobedience.

"Kunichiwa," they said, their well-fed faces flushed with optimism. "How are you today? My name is Jim," one said, looking at a group of schoolgirls. "What's your name?"

Several women tittered. The men turned away. A ropy silence hung in the air, low grumbles of displeasure rising. "Name?" The soldiers extended their hands. "Nah-meh?"

The schoolgirls giggled nervously. The man behind Masaharu clucked again. "They occupy our country; do they have to occupy our car too?"

"Maybe their car's full," a woman said.

"Ever see more than five or six in their car?" the man retorted.

"They're just kids," someone else snapped.

And that was true, Masaharu thought, turning to his wife. That was the problem with war. "Kids know nothing about consequences—that's what makes them useful in war. Even Seiji—" He swallowed his words; Seiji wasn't a topic they mentioned freely. The last time he'd slipped up they'd ended up pointing fingers at each other with a viciousness that had alarmed them. He glanced at his wife, expecting the doleful smile he found especially withering.

His wife, though, was gazing out the window, the platform beginning to glide;

wrapped in sunlight, she didn't appear to have heard him. Masaharu wiped his forehead with the back of his hand. Something about the way she was sitting, inert and strangely vacant, she looked exactly the way she'd looked when she returned from work that October evening four weeks ago, like a marionette on idle strings, and the memory of how close he'd come to shaking her flashed through his brain. He'd been careful to remove himself then, gently sliding the paper doors behind him.

"Let me see that handkerchief again," he said.

She handed it to him. Shortage had brought a new edge to her face, the kind of sharpness he might have mistaken for hardness if he didn't see her hands, white with nervous pressure. She'd long since mastered her body, but here it was betraying her. Years ago, when the first kenpeitai underlings raided their home, she'd almost undone the family with her hands. Fortunately the soldiers were too green to notice, but it was the first time Masaharu had understood how much his dissidence was wearing on her. He looked at her hands again. What had they been doing that October night? She'd sat at the table, legs folded on the tattered hassock, her face frozen in a stare. But her hands? He wiped his face with the handkerchief.

At the front of the car, a schoolgirl stepped forward. Fist on her hip, she regarded the soldiers with teacherly impatience. "Nah-mah-eh. Kon-nichi-wa," she said.

The soldiers exchanged a glance. "Nahmeh! Kunichiwa!" they said, grinning.

"Nah. Mah. Eh. Kon. Nichi. Wah," the girl repeated.

"Nahmeh! Kunichiwa!" the soldiers cheered.

A loud bang stilled the air as someone punched the side of the car. "Think this is a game? Think you're welcome here? Go back to where you belong." The words were in Japanese, but the tone was clear, and for a moment the soldiers' faces wavered with teenage panic, but their bodies hardened, their hands gripping their rifles. Masaharu felt his wife tense. She was a small woman, her seat sufficiently hidden in the rear of the car, but he moved to shield her anyway. The soldiers trained their eyes on the crowd. "What'd you say?" the one called

Jim shouted. The tea peddler bounced her stirring child. The car swelled with apprehension as the soldiers spoke to each other, their rapid back-and-forth reminding everyone of how decisions were made these days: from on high and in a language as inaccessible as their own Emperor's had been.

"Hey America!" A man stood up. He had the face of someone who, in his youth, had probably carried a little flesh with charm. "Haro! Monay? Gaaru? Chocoraito? Ingurishu prease!" He cupped his ear in humorous apology.

The soldiers swiveled to look at him.

"Ingurishu?" the man tried again.

The soldiers did not move.

"Oh-rai, oh-kay." The man wiped his upper lip. "USA!" He pumped a thumbs-up.

A few women muffled their laughter; the crowd held its breath, fear slowly loosening into a nervous curiosity. Finally, the soldiers' hands slid from their rifle barrels. "Okay." They smiled warily. **"Tomodachi."** They returned a thumbs-up.

Tomodachi. Friend. What a word to use, Masaharu thought. He turned to his wife. An odd expression was crossing her face, the soft light he knew well skewed by it. He glanced at her hands; they were resting on her bundle as still as polished stones. A chill climbed to the base of his head.

"Will you be late tonight?" she asked, startling him.

"You know Tomita," he grumbled, and pulled on his cap.

THEY PARTED at the gate. Masaharu took a few steps, then slid into the milling crowd, looping his way back. Spotting her familiar shape, he wondered at himself. Should he visit Tomita after all? He picked his way after her, picturing Tomita's room, trapped in the quiet of a house its widowed owner had begrudgingly let him. There was no way he'd be there, cooped up on a clear Sunday. Which meant, given his own luck these days, there was a chance his wife could run into him. Would Tomita know to cover for him? She disappeared into the day. Masaharu quickened his pace.

Outside, business was in full swing, the sundry peddlers vying to entice the GIs in search of cheap souvenirs. Melted green glass, uniforms looted from military stockpiles, pipes assembled from antiair-craft shells: these days everything sold as defeat curios—even missing limbs, thought Masaharu, dodging an ex-soldier display-ing his stump for alms. Beside him, a brassy woman in a Western-style dress lit a ciga-rette no doubt supplied by one of her Amer-ican customers. She languidly appraised him as he passed. The unglamorousness of her life was evident on her skin, rough with makeup that did little to mask her plight, but even for Masaharu, who'd never been one to buy his pleasure, the knowledge that he'd been stripped of that privilege rankled him. He looked away, fixing his gaze on his wife's head swinging this way and that as she peered at every sooty orphan. Masaharu thrust his hands into his pockets.

The fact was, no matter how she might feel, they **had** searched for Seiji, scouring the Tokyo streets strewn with dead wires and glowing cinders, clumps of blackened bodies spoiling in the heat. And at first he'd been hopeful too, angling and digging for information, glad for once to be a journal-ist, which had brought nothing but trouble for his family. But as the days passed, and the damage became clearer, he found himself wavering. True, Seiji's missing body was a hopeful sign in the midst of the dead and dying who continued to fill the school grounds where they'd begun volunteering, stoking the pyres and gathering the bones. But unlike his wife, who seemed bolstered by the task, Masaharu couldn't subsist on hope alone, savoring stories of unlikely reunions, perilously sweetened by the words of Seiji's teacher, who'd once come running, claiming to have spotted him blistered but alive.

Spring turned to summer, and the sun, unimpeded by roofs and trees, began hammering down, chipping away at their collective morale already worn by the maddening buzz of the flies, the ripening stench of the corpses, the dips and flares of hope unbearable in the heat. Even his wife sank into a stupor, a prickle of desperation showing in her new, unfocused irritability. And yet, for her, the future continued to hover like an open road; that Seiji could appear on it haunted her. They stayed on, the unadmitted skipping away like a stone.

Then, one night, as he watched the bon-fire cremate the latest B-29 carnage, his wife appeared beside him, her face lit by the heat of the dead. "Do you believe Mori-sensei really saw him?"

The question startled him; it was the closest she'd come to expressing any doubt. He picked up his rod and poked at a half-charred body still too waterlogged to burn. Like so many others, this corpse too had gorged on a river or pond, disbelieving that it had roasted to death. "I suppose nothing's impossible," he said carefully. "But in terms of Mori . . ." He didn't rehash the teacher's recent disappearance, her madly shorn hair scattered like a parting gift in front of their makeshift tent.

"And you?" his wife asked. "What about you? Do you think Seiji . . ."

Masaharu gazed at the crackling pyres glowing like mystical landing lights. "All I can say for myself is that I'm glad it wasn't you."

Instead of shunning him, she had touched his arm and left to pack their things.

———

DRAWN BACK by the noisy street, Masaharu noted with a start that the distance between them had shrunk. He slowed and wiped his face with the handkerchief he realized he'd taken from his wife. Should he or should he not seek out Tomita? He felt sheepish slinking after her like a mole.

At an intersection, his wife paused. Looking left and right, she turned onto a narrower street flanked by shuttered businesses, where only one store flushed with prewar colors. His wife stopped and joined the gathered crowd. Masaharu eased into the throng.

Lacquered mirrors and combs, elaborate entertainment kimonos—he couldn't remember the last time he'd seen such luxuries openly displayed. No doubt they were props consigned for resale by high-class geishas and actors, but even with the discount, which was probably considerable, he couldn't imagine who could afford them. Perhaps a popular yōpan prostitute catering to foreign servicemen. Why his wife, of all people, had to gawk like every other woman was another matter. Behind him a camera clicked, and a foreign reporter scribbled in a notepad. Masaharu could already picture the headline—WAR-TORN WOMEN SEDUCED BY COSMETICS—his wife's face splashed beside it. He pushed into the crowd, craning to see what she was so captivated by. To his shock, his eyes locked with hers in the window's reflection. He jumped back, lunging into an open doorway behind him.

Had she seen him? The bell above the missing door tinkled as he flattened himself against the inside wall of what had obviously been a confectioner's, its broken counter once full of delicate sweets. He peered around the empty window frame. The crowd was shifting, newcomers replacing the old; his wife was gone. He rushed into the blinding street.

HAD HE known the consequences, would he have pursued her? This was a question Masaharu would find himself asking from time to time until the end of his life. Looking back, he'd retrace these steps, searching for those moments when he might have turned back, behaved differently.

But here was the end of the intact street; beyond it, a vast wasteland, rusty girders grazing in the ruin. Masaharu shook out his wife's handkerchief and wiped the grit that had accumulated around his mouth. Ahead, his wife was negotiating a path someone had cleared in the rubble. She disappeared behind a block of crumbled buildings. He hurried after her.

To his surprise, he found himself emerging onto one of the main thoroughfares bisecting the city's amusement district. Once closed by the government, the district was bustling again, its shuttered storefronts gaudily made over in Western style, the now segregated bars and dancehalls thriving despite postwar shortages. Tawdry gangsters, inebriated GIs, rich businessmen profiteering from the war: the streets were lively, petty spats constantly in the making. Masaharu picked his way through the crowd, avoiding groups of hollering soldiers snatching at passing women. Ahead, his wife picked up her pace. Waving to a pack of street kids clearly familiar to her, she crossed the street and disappeared in front of a rickshaw bearer, deftly avoiding a pair of swaggering soldiers whose height and girth reduced Masaharu, not a small man, to the size of an adolescent. He widened his stride, resisting the urge to run.

At a roadblock—a construction zone?— he thought he'd lost her. Then he spotted her, stopped by two MPs, their skin so dark that for a moment Masaharu froze. He'd never seen a black person before, and in a district he'd assumed off-limits to them, based on what he'd learned of his Occupiers, their presence was startling, drawing the attention of the other soldiers, whose pale skin suddenly looked delicate, pink and peeled, like boiled shrimp. The crowd around him bunched and murmured. The MPs seized her.

What had she done? Even in his panic, he knew the question was unimportant. Whatever she had or hadn't done, there would be no recourse. He squinted at the soldiers. They didn't seem angry, but what did he know about foreigners? He peered at his wife, her small face minuscule now, her tiny expression creased by what he could only guess was fear. The MPs panned the crowd. Taking her arms, they began escorting her down the street. Masaharu plunged into the crowd.

When he saw them again, two white servicemen had staggered into the street. They
were shouting at the MPs, their drunken
taunts clearing a ring around them. The
crowd stiffened. Several weeks ago, a spat
like this had escalated into a riot, killing and
injuring hundreds of people caught in the
melee. The Occupation had since increased
patrols, but nobody was reassured. The MPs
kept walking. The white servicemen closed
in. Masaharu felt his back bloom.

At the first sound of scuffling boots, he
began running. The distance was at most
fifteen meters, yet he struggled to traverse
it; from every doorway, it seemed soldiers
were pouring out. He was less than ten meters away when he heard the first exchange
of fists, the heavy thwack ricocheting in his
chest; the crowd erupted, hooting and jeer-
ing. He clawed on, one human wall after
another, until he broke into a band of space
several meters wide. The MPs were still
fighting, their boots corkscrewing the earth,
but he couldn't see his wife. He bobbed and
wove, searching the spaces that winked between the men, but there was no sign of her.
As he expanded his sightline, he caught a

movement, her familiar shape listing as she slipped down an alley. He started after her, only to be blocked by four huffing soldiers who had momentarily united to halt him.

NEVER HAD Masaharu imagined pacing this alley, slick with vomit and urine, looking for his wife. He exited the alley and rounded the corner for the third time. The same MPs, the same line of jittery GIs, the same closed doors. He glanced up at the grandiose sign. The same cheap brushstrokes coaxed up the same cheap waves, one word ostentatiously scrawled across it: OASIS.

At first he failed to connect the dots, his skittering brain unable to grasp anything. Then he did, and for a moment he stood rooted: the MPs; the line of GIs; the alley into which his wife had disappeared. His body shimmered with a new fear. The front doors swung open. He saw the smiling proprietor; he saw the row of women. Their faces were too far for him to make out, but every one of them had the same short bob he'd enjoyed on his wife. The doors slammed shut. Masaharu rushed forward.

Two pairs of hands clamped down on him: the black MPs. "No Japs." They pointed at the sign. Their faces were neutral, betraying none of the hostilities of a moment ago, but their grip was firm. Masaharu stared at their hands. No doubt the world's advances had produced the miracle of bringing them—men from opposite ends of the map—together; yet it was also the madness of those advances that spared them no time to understand each other. What means did he have to explain? He pictured their hands on his wife moments ago; a dim light expanded in his brain. Did they know her? Could they have been protecting her? He looked up at their faces, his meager collection of English words scattering like beads. Behind him, the doors opened again. He twisted around, the English word for "wife" suddenly coming to his mouth. He repeated it, pointing and struggling. The GIs laughed. The MPs shook their heads. The doors closed. "Dah-meh," they told him, emphasizing each syllable, pushing him away.

Back in the street, Masaharu had no idea

what to do. If he'd been a different man, he might have risked the back door and stormed the facility, stripping the curtains to all the cubicles until he found her, sweat-smeared and humiliated. But Masaharu was not a hysterical man; even now, a part of him expected her to emerge, her face lifting with surprise before curling, guessing at his fears. He couldn't imagine her spread on the bedding, her thin body mounted and speared like a pig.

Circling the streets, Masaharu returned again and again to check the alley and the doors. The shoulder-length bob, the new Sunday hours—why hadn't he seen it? He pictured the requisitioned building, the barbed-wire fence, the armed checkpoint to which he'd accompanied her on the first day of her typing job. It had angered him then that they'd barred his way; now he was sour with the irony. Unlike Tomita, he'd banked on Japan's defeat. Every year another year closer to Seiji's conscription, he'd wished for a different life. When the bombings began, Masaharu, if briefly, felt a fizz of hope. It seemed possible that his son, too old to be evacuated to the countryside, might still escape the draft. He never imagined Seiji, so close to the war's end, disappearing.

Looking about the squalid glitter, Masaharu marveled at the world, its history of sanctioned violence that insisted on dividing the victorious from the defeated. For centuries, men, first in the name of blood, then in the name of national interest, had done this: plunder and rape, decimating whole continents as if it were their noble right. Now there were planes and bombs rumored to vanish entire cities—how could they go on? He pictured the burning streets, the half-charred bodies, all the pyres he'd lit. In every corner of the world, someone was still doing as he'd done—grieving all that the greed of men, his own country's too, had helped lay waste to—and the thought filled him with remorse. He looked at the facility, the ever-growing line, his wife's body opening to take every inch of it. He couldn't imagine how he could ever get past it.

IT WAS almost midnight by the time he got off the train and walked the fifteen minutes to the intersection from which he could see their boardinghouse, a single square of light illuminating it. Framed there was his wife, arms on the windowsill, face upturned, as if scrying the stars that were abundant here, unlike in Tokyo, whose spoilt sky showed nothing but a dim smear. But Masaharu knew his wife was merely waiting for him, their best dinner of the week covered by a cloth: the rewards of her labor. Despite himself, his stomach gurgled, and he marveled bitterly at the body's animal will to survive.

Behind him the Kannon's hill loomed unrealized in a dark that hovered there as if held by a new curfew. It occurred to him that he could run away and vanish as many were doing, but after everything, disappearing, he knew, would be nothing short of an apostasy.

Passing under their window, he looked up and met his wife's eyes. There was nothing in them to betray her feelings, but he could feel her agitation, the ripple of worry and perhaps anger competing with her will to spare him the inquisition. He rounded the corner and climbed the metal stairs, his footsteps loud in the chilly air. In less than a month, winter would once again dust these steps, freezing off thousands of the sick and starving, but they would not need to worry.

Loosing his keys from his pocket, he stepped into the shadowy corridor and was again assailed by images of her—her slick mouth and wet thighs, opening for the pleasure of others. For a moment he stood still. How could he do this? He gripped his keys, struggling to recall the person he knew was on the other side of the door, readying his meal, unbegrudgingly. Of course, this was what she'd tried to spare him—he saw that now. And just as she'd tried, he had to try to spare her the knowledge that he knew—that was only fair. After all, they'd chosen to survive; they had a whole life ahead of them to live now, together, in their own silence, separately.

WILLOW RUN

Do you know "Willow Run"?

Yes, "willow" as in the tree, "run" as in the verb. Of course, I had no idea what it meant then, or what he—the soldier—meant by it. But I liked the sound—**willow run**—like something wispy, something escaping. Looking back, I have to laugh. But at the time? I'd repeat the words, so cumbersome on my tongue. Many women took to reciting the sutras. But in that situation . . . I'm sorry—was there some way you wanted me to begin?

*

I WAS born in the first year of Taishō—That's right, 1912. Of course, as a Japanese, I wonder if nuances aren't lost when accounting in the Western way. For example, unlike Meiji people like our parents, we Taishō people were very open to the Western world. Have you heard of "moga," or "modan gaaru"? As a girl, I thought we were quite modern, quite the sophisticates <laugh>.

I'll be seventy-nine in October.

Yes, my husband passed on last year. Which is why I decided to take this chance.

That's right, my son is the scholar. But please, as I mentioned on the telephone, I don't want him implicated—

Yes, yes, you explained very well your legal ambitions. But are you sure my name won't—

No, no, I'm quite prepared to speak. It's just that . . . Well, if I had half your courage, a young woman like yourself, coming all this way from America. You mentioned your parents are Korean?

Then I can understand your interest. But your cameraman—is he a historian too? Why an American man would be interested in . . . I'm sorry, it must be my nerves, chatting away like this <laugh>. Not that people haven't come forward—they've always come forward, haven't they? And now with the Shōwa Emperor just passed and everybody reflecting on His reign . . . You see, when I saw your call for testimonies . . . Well, it was the first time I saw anybody soliciting **that** story. Oh! I'm sorry. The hand towel!

No, no, it's all right. Is the camera still—

*

AT THE time of surrender, my husband and I were already in [Ō]-city. We'd fled Tokyo after we lost our son—

No, no, we only had one child. After the war we adopted our son—

Yes, the scholar. Of course, we should have told him sooner—about his adoption. But back then . . . Well, everything was in tatters. And afterward, we had no desire to look back. You see, we never found our son's body.

He was thirteen. Why he wasn't in his room that night . . .

Yes, the March air raid. Looking back, I see how unprepared we were. I suppose we'd gotten used to the false alarms— all we'd seen was the glow of distant flashes.

But that night . . . We hardly had a minute before we heard the whistling, like a thousand fireworks. Back then, we slept in our clothes, so all we had to do was grab our emergency bags and put on our silly hoods—

Oh, they were just padded pieces of cloth, another thing our government cooked up. Still, we put them on, you know, half of us running around with our hoods on fire <laugh>. We ran and ran, our houses shooting into flames. Until then, I never knew fire could be so loud, crashing about like drunken demons. And the heat. It was like a rubber mask smothering our faces. We couldn't breathe or see; all we could do was run from street corner to street corner, smoke rolling in from every side, shadows appearing and disappearing, sometimes knocked away like bowling pins. Everywhere families were calling each other, and one mother— I'll never forget her—came barging past with a baby strapped to her back. She was so determined, you know. But that poor baby. Its little head was knocked back and running like an egg. There were so many lost children—we tried to take them with us. But they clung to the spots where they thought their parents would come for them. We eventually found a shelter, but the next morning . . . Everything was in piles—even the air was scorched, embers floating like fireflies. Eventually, we all drifted toward our homes, but the bodies, you know. They were sprawled every which way, clogging the ditches, cluttering the streets, and all I could think was whether Seiji, our son, had taken his emergency bag, or whether I'd seen it at the entrance. Now there's little to remind us of that time, but it's the body that remembers. Some people can't stand the sound of fireworks. For myself, it's the smell of roasting meat . . .

*

AT FIRST I had another job. Thanks to my father, I could type. My mother died when I was a little girl, so he'd taken it upon himself to—

A secretarial job. With the American administration. Their headquarters was still in Yokohama then.

Oh, no, my husband loathed the idea

<laugh>. But there was no work for some-
one like him.

He was a newspaperman. A political
journalist.

No, no, he leaned very much to the left.

No, he wasn't a Party member, but in
those days, any "radical" was a "red," and
that never changed with the Americans, so
even after the war, no one wanted to risk
hiring—

During the war? We were visited all
the time by the Tokkō thought police; our
neighbors wouldn't come within ten meters of us <laugh>. As a woman, all I could
do was serve the best tea we could afford
and clean up the "gifts" they liked to leave
behind.

Oh, broken teapots, upturned furniture,
ripped shōji—they never missed an opportunity. Throwing tantrums the way only
men can. Soon we had a spacious home
with very little to tidy.

Twelve of us. They hired twelve of us, all
women in our twenties and thirties.

No, no, not all of us could type. But
we did everything from filing papers to
sweeping the floor. I was part of a group

assigned to type up memos, transcripts, reports.

Well, we weren't privy to that level of information <laugh>. The only reports we saw were ones touting the success of this or that "democratic"—

That was the thing; none of us knew a drop of English <laugh>. Except our supervisor. She—[A]-san—would translate snippets, mostly to make us laugh.

Yes, she was our go-between. Several Americans spoke Japanese, but we rarely—

We did like her; [A]-san was a helpful woman.

Yes, there were people who disliked her, but there are always people who dislike others, aren't there? And given her proximity to the Americans—

We did. We trusted her. As much as anybody could trust anybody in those days. We were all so needy, you know; it wasn't always easy to discern—

Advantage? What do you mean—

Oh. No. No, no. [A]-san wasn't a **liaison** <laugh>. That office wasn't a back door to—

Well, now that you mention it. About a month after I started, I found a piece of paper. I was, as they say, sleuthing <laugh>, looking for information about the air raids. The paper was peeking from beneath the file cabinets. It had rows of our faces printed on it, our names below each.

It was in rōmaji, in English script.

But we could read our names; we knew the alphabet—

At first I thought it was a roster. Some faces were crossed out, and I thought they were women who had left the job. Then, when I realized that most women were still there . . .

About half. Half the women were crossed out, and at the top someone had scribbled the word "moose."

No, not the dessert; the animal <laugh>. Of course I didn't know that then, and my first thought was to show [A]-san.

No, her face wasn't crossed out.

Yes, she was very distraught, very un-forthcoming. Eventually, she asked me if I'd noticed the American fondness for con-tractions.

<Laugh> I must have looked as baffled as you. Do you know the Japanese word for "girl"?

That's right. Musume. Or musume-san, as the Americans liked to say. "Moose" was short for musume. They had a popular game they called Hunting for Moose.

Yes, Hunting for Moose.

Exactly, the paper was their tally sheet.

I suppose we knew **things** went on; most women were widows with small children and parents to support, and the soldiers . . . It wouldn't be unfair to say they were here to enjoy a little—

There were twenty men in that office. Including the officer.

Yes, I believe they were all in on it.

[A]-san? She made me promise to keep it to myself. Not that there was any recourse, you understand. For some time, all I could think of were those faces, those terrible slash marks . . .

I assumed [A]-san disposed of the paper. Though sometimes . . . Well, it's just that one morning, soon after the incident, I arrived at the security gate, and they wouldn't let me through.

Oh, I don't **know** if [A]-san had anything do with it. What could she gain—

Yes, I went back every day for a week,

returning at various times to catch a familiar face. But no one would speak to me. And in the end, I couldn't risk anybody's job.

No, I never saw [A]-san. But it had always been that way. As though she never went in or out of that building. She was always there when I arrived, there when I left—

Oh, no, I don't think **she** was in on it. Though it's true: we all did what we had to. If one of them had told me they could find Seiji for me . . .

Yes, eventually, I met a recruiter.

He was Japanese. A policeman. Working with the Public Safety Association. He got the job because, as a policeman, he knew all the licensed and unlicensed women in his district.

Oh, yes, our government was eager for women—for a "people's diplomacy," they called it <laugh>. Our role was "to soothe foreign tempers and protect the purity of girls and women." It goes to show, doesn't it? They knew exactly what to expect, didn't they? After all, they'd had plenty of experience, all those years setting up ways to cater to our own soldiers' . . . needs.

The recruiter? He was pleasant enough.

He kept reassuring me of the cleanli-
ness of—

Coerced?

Well, he never physically or verbally—

I suppose, yes, it was, as you say, my decision. But "voluntary" isn't exactly—

Well, many women were, as you say,
coerced. But "coerced" is such a . . . cun-
ning word, isn't it?

No, no, I don't mean to trivialize—

But I never said I was coerced. On the
telephone, I only told you—

But you agreed. You agreed to hear my
story, my side—

*

I was fortunate; my shift was during
normal hours. And my husband wasn't the
suspicious type—

Oh, no, I never told him. He was so
frustrated in those days; he couldn't find
work, he'd already had a few run-ins with
the American authorities. But he did follow me one day. Of course, one might have
expected a journalist to be more discreet
<laugh>. You should have seen the fuss he

made at the doors. I was afraid he'd barge right in—

No, no, it was open only to white foreigners.

Yes, there were designated establishments for black soldiers.

Actually, some women preferred it. They claimed they were treated more . . . sympathetically, perhaps because of the soldiers', you know, own plight—

Yes, two guards. They were there mostly to watch the line.

Oh, yes. From opening to closing. All the way around the building. They were usually keyed up too, drinking from first thing in the morning.

Fourteen of us. Though someone was always out sick.

Yes, we did; we had our own designated clinic.

No, they were Japanese. They were overseen by American doctors.

Oh, yes, every week. Why they didn't insist on examining their own soldiers with equal—

Fifteen minutes or a half hour. Most soldiers chose the fifteen.

Forty yen. Can you imagine? Same as a pack of cigarettes.

On average? Between fifteen and twenty. One woman had more than thirty in a day. She was relieved when she was taken out for a course of penicillin.

Yes, for VD.

Well, of course, they were **required.** But we could hardly force them to put them on—

The first time? I never thought I'd make it home, my legs were so shaky. Every few steps I had to stop. And all the way home I bled and bled. And the pain. It was like giving birth all over again. The next day . . . Everything ached, my hips, my joints, and when I passed water, the sting of it . . . Eventually, we all found ways to . . . accommodate things, but I don't think anyone got used to it. Some days we could hardly wash, we were so swollen, you know. And the feeling of seeping, as though everything were rotting out. I never felt clean, always as though it were infected with some terrible odor or disease. I'd wash and wash . . .

No, my husband never said a word. Then afterward, after he followed me, he stopped trying to . . . you know. Except once. He'd been drinking. But when he saw my . . . you know . . .

Oh, I don't think **they** noticed a thing—they might have enjoyed the swelling. Of course, there were always a few who insisted on inspecting . . . things. One of them even brought gloves. But most were ready before they got in the doors.

But in their eyes they were paying customers, weren't they? The things they would demand for forty yen.

What do you expect? Letting loose a pack of boys in a country where they could do as they pleased. Most were curious, many afraid of losing face, but they all got used to it, didn't they? Demanding our "geisha tricks," as they called it. As though we knew such things. Why did they assume—

Occasionally, there were soldiers like that. One soldier came twice a week, making such a racket, clomping up the stairs, shouting to his friends, but once he was in the room—it was really a partition—he never looked my way. Eventually, everyone did what they paid for, even those who fancied themselves different, you know, talking

and caressing, asking us to open more than
our legs. But that soldier? He never did a
thing. When I finally summoned the courage to ask him whether he might know how
to, you know, look for my son, it took him
a long time to find the words. His Japanese
was only slightly better than my English,
which was awful, you understand <laugh>,
but he was kind enough to tell me the truth.
He chided me for presuming they had all
the answers in the world. How many millions of lost people do you think there are?
he asked me. One more lost Japanese boy
was the least of their problems. And he was
right. That soldier was also the one who
mentioned Willow Run. To learn that it was
a place, a factory, all those years later . . .
Do you know they built those B-24s there?

Yes, the ones that bombed Germany. They
were called Liberators, weren't they? Funny,
isn't it? That's what they called themselves,
too, those soldiers. Years later—I think it
was in the eighties—I saw photographs of
Willow Run on NHK. I was watching a
program about your President Roosevelt.
To learn that it was such an important factory . . . Most photographs were of the

assembly line, but one was of a large room with rows and rows of cots. Do you know what the caption said? "A bomber an hour." A bomber an hour! <laugh> Of course, I don't know if that's why that soldier mentioned the place, but it's how he saw us, isn't it? A bomber an hour. Some days, watching all those boys huffing away over me, I couldn't help but wonder if Seiji could have, would have . . . And then I'd wonder what he would've done if he ever found out his own mother . . . And every time, I was grateful he never got that chance. Awful, isn't it? To be grateful for such a thing. But, please, the camera. It's awfully close—

*

[K]-SAN WAS younger, in her twenties. She had a strong, clear voice and was quite the force, standing up to everybody <laugh>. By the time I arrived, she'd been there a month, and she'd already claimed the respect of our manager—

Our manager was older, in her forties or early fifties.

She was fair enough—we weren't un-
lucky. Women like her can be quite cruel
to other women; as a manager, she had to
answer to not just the Americans but our
government too. I certainly didn't envy her
her position.

Yes, she was hard on [K]-san. But I think
she rather liked her too. She put herself out
quite a bit when . . . I'm sorry . . .

No, no, I'm all right. It's just that . . .
You see, there was one soldier. He was a regular, one of those . . . brutes. He liked the
new ones, you know, and we all did what
we could to protect one another. There was
a woman who started after me. We never
got her full story, but we suspected she was
one of those munitions factory girls—you
know, the ones taken to our officers' parties
to be "broken in"? [N]-san was young—
very young. Of course, in those days, it was
hard to tell, everybody was so skinny. Still,
she couldn't have been more than fifteen or
sixteen. And that man. That murderer. He
forced himself into her through the back—

I'm sorry, yes. The anus. Usually, one
of us would have heard something, but

that poor girl . . . When she didn't appear at reception, our manager went looking for her. She was lying on the floor in her own blood. She had soiled herself too. That monster—he had ripped her right up. Nobody even knew her name . . .

Yes, we had assigned names. Kimiko, Emiko, Maiko—something bright and easy to pronounce. I suppose it also helped us keep things . . . separate . . .

[K]-san? She was beside herself. We were all afraid she'd try to hunt him down.

No, [N]-san never came back to work.

Report the soldier? To whom? Our police? <laugh> As for your government . . . Even now, your soldiers only have to make it back to base to evade—

Oh, yes, all the time. Especially in Okinawa. Your government never cooperates, does it? Instead, you shelter your soldiers. Your criminals.

That monster? He came right back. Acting as though nothing had happened. One day he smuggled in a baton—not to beat anyone, you understand. The poor woman. She made sure she screamed and screamed. How anyone could turn out that way, at that age. I'm sure they came from nice families, like our own boys, who committed such unimaginable . . . brutalities.

I was luckier. I was older; I had learned not to be reactive. With the "wrong" kind of journalist for a husband, I had plenty of training <laugh>. [K]-san counseled everyone to do the same. But we're not always under our own control or jurisdiction, are we? Especially when fear—

[K]-san never got over it. One day, about six weeks later, she pulled me aside and asked if I'd do her a favor. She asked if I'd take her baby if something happened to her. I was surprised; I had no idea she had a baby. But [K]-san had been an invaluable friend, and I had no reason to refuse or suspect her. In retrospect, I realize I'd told her all about Seiji; I suppose I'd exposed my susceptibility. It was three weeks after that. She asked me to watch her son for a night.

Yes, she told me she had an errand. Five days later, she turned up in the Sumida River with three beer bottles broken inside her. She had burn marks all over her body and a rope burn around her neck. After that, many of us started carrying cyanide.

Yes, the ones we were given in case we were invaded.

No, we never found out. We assumed it had something to do with that monster, but there was no way for us to know. We were lucky enough that our manager happened to be acquainted with a policeman who happened to recognize her . . .

Yes, when she didn't return for her son, I went straight to our manager. None of us had any idea where she lived. Our manager asked her policeman to look into it. It turned out [K]-san lived not five minutes away, in a tenement apartment, with two other Korean women—

Yes, I believe [K]-san was Korean.

No, she never said as much, but she told me her parents had been conscripted workers, forced into the mines.

Her Japanese was flawless. But she would've been a little girl when she was forced to learn—

No, the women she lived with spoke with an accent.

Well, we didn't ask their profession. They were terrified when we knocked, and we weren't there to interrogate—

I suppose they could've been former—

[K]-san too could have been, as you say, a "comfort woman." But, frankly, at that moment that wasn't at the forefront of my mind—

No, I hadn't a clue. We'd heard the term, some variation or another, but we assumed it was some sort of nurse corps. Of course, insinuations were made about "nurse corps," but insinuations are always being made, aren't they? It's the sort of talk men enjoy over a cup, isn't it? And even if we expected there to be . . . camp followers, we never imagined a whole system of . . . of . . .

. . . thank you, sexual slavery.

Yes, the Tokyo War Crimes Tribunals were going on then, but what with your Occupation censors, even with my husband's connections, information was always second- or thirdhand. But I heard about a group of white women—Dutch, or half Dutch, I think they were, in Indonesia. That country was under the Dutch, wasn't it? Before it was occupied by our men?

Yes, I believe the case was raised during the Tribunals, though I don't think the case went anywhere. It was a male court—

Oh, I don't know if anyone knew the **extent,** all those tens of thousands of women, but I believe the practice was known. Though with men, white men, in charge . . . Even when it concerned white Dutch—

When I first heard the testimonies? I couldn't stop shivering. Those brave Korean women. To come forward like that. All these years later in front of the whole world. I kept wondering what [K]-san would've thought. Of course, I had to rely on subtitles and voiceovers—

<Laugh> You sound just like my son: "recolonization." He especially abhors voiceovers. But what could I do? I hardly know Korean. To see their faces and hear all the things our soldiers, our **military,** had done . . . Then when I saw that interview . . . It was with a former Imperial Army man. He was recounting his war experiences. When the reporter asked him if he'd visited any of those "comfort stations," you should have seen his face. It lit up like a little boy's. He had nothing but fond memories. Can you imagine? It made me wonder what all your American soldiers—

Oh, yes, our circumstances were very different from the women who worked—

—I'm sorry, were **enslaved** at the comfort stations. Of course, I heard many of them were set up like brothels. Not that the women were paid—or that that should excuse the behaviors—

No, no, I don't mean to suggest any **were** brothels—

But I'm not trying to "conflate" my situation. Though one wonders sometimes whether soldiers from one country are so different from another's. Even now, wherever there are foreign soldiers, even peacekeepers . . . Your own troops in Korea, Philippines—

But, surely, this isn't just a "national" issue or a "historical" one. Just last week there was that woman in Okinawa with an umbrella—

Didn't you see it in your newspaper?

But it's hardly an "isolated incident." Why do you think there are so many protests—

Well, it's not the only reason—there are the drunken hit and runs, the environmental destruction—

No, no, I'm not trying to "shift the

blame." Our government, our media, our own men—

Yes, I understand your specific mission, I understand you're advocating—

Yes, that Okinawan woman was, as you say, a "professional." But an **umbrella.**

No, I wasn't a comfort woman, I know my country was the one that perpetrated—

But what are you doing? Where are you—

No, please don't go.

Please, [K]-san was Korean; she was probably—

No, please. You must tell the world. You must tell our—

No, please. You must stop—

Please. Please, think of what [K]-san went through. Please, I promised her—I promised myself. You see, my son—**her** son—

Please!

I STAND ACCUSED,
I, JESUS OF THE RUINS

. . . am I not on target in calling him "the Jesus of the ruins"?
—ISHIKAWA JUN, "JESUS OF THE RUINS"

Q. Where were you on the afternoon of April 29, 1947?

The body, curled in the corner of the dusky room, was still, and the boy, equally still, stood peering at it as the afternoon light caught the lip of the blackout paper covering the window. Outside, businesses had reopened, and he could hear the tinkle of the shop bells, the chime of the tills, the mundane sounds that used to pepper his world before the bombings and the Surrender and now the Occupation. Somewhere in the building, a press was running, its muffled clicks and clacks stapling the air. Behind him, the doorway stood agape, the dark corridor running past it, and someone stepped into it, trailing the smell of hot ink and paper. The boy turned, a slow tropistic pivot, the hairs on his neck standing on end: Furukawa.

WITNESS #1: SATO TOKYO METROPOLITAN POLICE DEPARTMENT, APRIL 29, 1947, 18:00

I know the kid. Met him downtown by what they call Little America about seven months ago. I was with Kiyama, the one you brought me in with. I had business at the CCD, the Occupation's censorship detachment—I work for a publisher, though nowadays that means paging through what magazines we still put out, excising what's "noncompliant" with the American censors. Which is pretty much anything related to the war and the Occupation, which is the most relevant topic, if you ask me. At least I'm not in film, all those retakes Kiyama's got to do because the Yanks want evidence of their presence expunged. First of all, they're everywhere, and second, we're talking down to the tiniest blip of a plane. Now that's true censorship. Makes you wonder what's changed; we had high hopes for this democracy. And you wonder why everyone's flocking to us Commies? Who else is fighting for **our** rights, **our** freedoms, the direction of **our** future?

So, we were in Little America. Afterward we swung by an izakaya, our old haunt from before this mess. Mama there used to feed us for free around exam times. Best noodles, hands down. Only reason we got into university. That night we'd just left Mama's when we saw two Yanks kicking the shit out of this kid. They were in their browns—probably just got off patrol—but they'd had a few, and, like I said, we'd come from Mama's, we'd had a drop or two ourselves, and you know Occupation life. Kowtowing day in and day out like someone snapped your spine. Now don't get me wrong, we're not violent, just 'cause we're Party members—not all of us Commies are radical, you know that, right? We saw the Yanks, we rushed in, we ended up with the kid, face like a plate of soft vegetables. We dragged him back to the shelter you picked us up at, nursed him for days, and the first thing he says? **I thought heaven would be nicer.** Could've clocked him right back to where he came from. What I'm saying is, he's a **kid.** He doesn't plot and plan. He does things for love. Her name? Why should I tell you that? You brought me in to ask about the kid. I'm telling you: he's no schemer. No murderer. You think that kid can overpower a man? He looks thirteen.

Q: Who did you see on the afternoon of April 29, 1947?

Furukawa looked old. Only thirty-two or thirty-three, he was a slip of a man, his gaunt head drooping over his dusty button-down tucked into worn trousers that gave him the appearance of a wilted bean sprout, world-weary but hiding all the vigor necessary to birth a new era. Or so it seemed to the boy, who'd heard legends about this renegade who'd survived the wartime Communist purges that had disappeared hundreds of his comrades. In the dimness, he

looked as grainy as the magazine mugshot
made famous by the boy's own father, a wartime journalist known for his exposés of the
purges. Of all the Communists his father
had profiled, Furukawa had caught his attention. He'd seemed so ordinary, answering
his father's questions with such plain sincer-
ity it had been inspiring. He'd impressed his
father too. Now, though, Furukawa frightened him. Less than a year into the Occupation, the Americans, increasingly alarmed
by the Communists' popularity, had begun
retracting civil liberties, harassing the same
political prisoners they'd made a show of releasing only months earlier. Word was that
Furukawa was on their watch list, and the
restriction, coming from the very power
that had legalized the Party, had soured his
heart, spinning his compass in a new, potentially violent direction. Furukawa, as he
had during the war, had been keeping out
of sight in this defunct press, printing un-
censored news and tracts, allegedly in preparation for a red insurgency.

The boy glanced at the curled body
in the corner, its small back brushed by a
weak light, and quickly introduced himself,

dropping the names of the two university students he knew Furukawa was acquainted with from Party meetings: Kiyama and Sato. "They would've never told me where to find you if it wasn't urgent. I'm looking for Konomi."

Furukawa showed no recognition, and a splash of heat spasmed the boy's carbuncular face. Despite the armor of skin that covered his burns, a result of his failure to outrun the incendiaries that had razed his neighborhood two years earlier, inadequate treatment and nutrition had left him susceptible to eruptions and abscesses. He knew he reeked; for months after the bombing, he'd kept to unpopulated areas, scrabbling in the ruins, avoiding the organized gangs of scavengers who prowled the alleys behind restaurants as well as the black markets that had sprung up across the city. But the previous winter had left his body a bed of bones, and he couldn't shake the fever that had nestled in; following the pull of his feet, he weaved his way into a throng of people that led him to a patch of shade cast by Konomi's stall. Instead of chasing him away, she'd sat him down and fed him a warm bowl of gruel. It

had been the first time in weeks that anyone had spoken to him. That was the end of
April almost exactly a year ago.

He glanced again at the body. It was definitely small enough to be a woman.

Furukawa, watching him, moved into
the room and crouched to check the body's
pulse. Pushing two fingers into the neck, he
lifted the wrist. The arm was still soft.

The boy licked his lips; the tang of pus
coated his tongue. "Listen, I know this isn't
protocol, I know you have no reason to trust
me, but I've got to find her. I know you were
with her," he said, regretting this last part.
The information had come from an uncon-
ventional source: a rōjin who roamed the
city streets in the garb of an Imperial officer,
reporting on the goings-on around town.
He often showed up at the welfare shelter
where the boy had been living for the past
seven months. The rōjin's stories were ranging, picked up from anywhere and everywhere, drawing an attentive crowd. It was
also the one lead he had; Konomi had been
missing for close to a month.

Furukawa continued to regard him. Then
he dropped the wrist and rose to his feet. "I

don't know who your eyes and ears are, but seems like you're getting outdated information. Your friend Konomi is a traitor."

The word hit the surface of the boy's thoughts and rippled through him. "No," he said finally. "She'd never do that."

"No? Then tell me why she's working for the Americans." Furukawa stepped toward the window and ripped back the blackout papers. The dusty light illuminated the body. It was not Konomi but a compact man in a suit. Furukawa's right-hand man: Ōtsuka.

WITNESS #2: KIYAMA TOKYO METROPOLITAN POLICE DEPARTMENT, APRIL 29, 1947, 18:30

As far as I know, Konomi met the kid in Ueno, at the black market you shut down last summer, starving a nice chunk of the population. She had a stall there. Took one look at the kid and took him in. Before long, he was helping her, guarding her from the cads lurking around. You said Sato wouldn't talk about her? I always thought he had a little something for her. Fact is, we haven't seen her in about a month.

Konomi's a unique one. Outspoken, pretty but not in the conventional way; she's . . . alluring, despite her little limp, souvenir from the war. Kid can't stay away from her. It's refreshing, the honesty of a kid living with his whole self. These days everyone's complaining about the spot we're in, how we were "deceived by the Emperor." But is anyone asking **why**? Think about it. We didn't **like** being deprived of food, thoughts, choices; we didn't **want** to be in the line of fire; we didn't **enjoy** killing our fellow men, starving them, torturing them, denying them their homes, families, their right to exist. So why did we do it? Because we lost touch with our humanity and opened our minds to chatter. Before we knew it the strings of other minds had taken hold of our own, and suddenly we were marching to the drum that was drumming the loudest while our hands waved the flag foisted upon us and our mouths hinged open to swallow whatever we were being fed. Once you start, there's no stopping. We marched faster. We waved bigger flags. We built our empire,

sacrificed our children. We did all this—
and lost everything. So now what? How do
we go on?

The kid, though, never lost his humanity.
Is he frustrated? Hunger's an irritant, and so
is pain. Look at his body. Perfect picture of
this country, if I can get him on film. Is he
resentful? He has reasons to be, his family
gone, and he's what, fourteen? Not that I'd
know—he won't talk about his past, says
he's nobody. How sad is that? Is he venge-
ful? Like I said, the kid's **whole.** His mind
doesn't float like oil on top of his watery
heart. He lives for one thing: love. We all
know what that is, but do we live by it? It
didn't keep my parents from sacrificing my
brother to the war. Not that it matters—
everyone's gone. Naturally, it's hard loving a
woman who thinks of you as a kid brother.
Konomi knew that. So she made herself
scarce, and the kid's been moping since.
Don't believe me? That's your problem.

Today, April 29, we were pretty excited
when he came around asking if he could
help with May Day. We told him to show
up and march. Did he seem agitated? He did
not. Did he mention some murder—some

assassination—plot? He did not. You come to us because we're Party members, and you think we're extremists. But, tell me, what's wrong with food for the masses? Security for the workers? Equality and justice for all? Sure, the Party'll go after the mighty, but are we stupid enough to get violent? That stuff's for film. Not that we love this democracy with its double standards rolling back our freedom until—what? We become docile subjects of the American empire?

Q: You were seen at Occupation Headquarters on the afternoon of April 29, 1947. What were you doing there?

Slipping out of the press, he chased the trolley swaying like an old milk cow down the pitted track. Clasping the railing, he swung onto the metal ledge. Inside, the trolley was packed, the old and the young, the fortunate and the less, compressed into one somnolent mass. Once upon a time, when the country still picnicked in flowering parks, he'd been part of the crush, maneuvering to protect his mother, who had to protect their lunch. Now he clung to the railing, breathing in the bitter dust wafting from the wasteland.

All month, he'd feared finding Konomi's body—or worse, never finding a trace—but to think she'd been working for the Americans. Furukawa had spun some story about an infiltration plan organized by Ōtsuka, his now dead right-hand man, to gather information about the Occupation's movements against the Party. Konomi volunteered, securing a job at Occupation Headquarters. This was a month ago, Furukawa had said, which fit the timeline of her disappearance. Three weeks in, Furukawa "caught wind" that Konomi and Ōtsuka had "turned." He was vague, but his eyes, which he kept fixed on the body, were bitter. Then he'd told the boy where to find her.

The tracks smoothed; buildings began assembling into blocks of shops and offices, and at last he glimpsed the Imperial Palace moat. He jumped off, the momentum tumbling him into a school of jinrikisha pulled by leathery men half the size of their white customers. He crossed the intersection, and there it was: the concrete behemoth that now housed Occupation Headquarters, its stark columns made almost majestic by the wide boulevard and the wider mirror of the Palace moat spread beyond it. Surveying the sweep of steps rising to a row of doors, recessed and heavily guarded, he looked for the JAPANESE ONLY sign Furukawa had mentioned. A flock of glances alighted on him, and he moved on, gaze lowered, as soldiers passed, trading language lessons with spirited women who looked resolutely away from him.

On his third pass, he saw Konomi.

WITNESS #3: KONOMI TOKYO METROPOLITAN POLICE DEPARTMENT, APRIL 29, 1947, 20:00

I don't know what those guys Kiyama and Sato told you, but you should know, they aren't real Communists. They talk the talk, but all they care about is their "revolution of the flesh." A fine idea—stripping off false ideologies to get back to our human values—but inviting people to literally strip? Pretty convenient. Not that they're bad guys—they've help me and the boy—but I'm through with them, trust me.

That boy's different. Half his body burned, covered with boils, and he still cares. I've known him a year now, and he's never said a word about his family. Do you know why? Because he **survived.** The least you can do for a boy like that is give him food, medicine, a job. Instead, all you do is round them up, like our Liberators round us up, any woman, to randomly test us for VD. We had proper lives once, you know. Tell me, how many requisitioned family homes did you renovate this month to accommodate "American living standards"? If they think throwing chocolate and chewing gum from their jeeps is sweetening anyone's life, they're wrong.

Threaten me all you want, but that boy's not a murderer. He looked after my father, changing his clothes, wiping his spit and blood—how many people would do that, risking their own health at a time like this? Maybe he hung around a couple of Communists. So what? He's a decent human being, unlike you lackeys, never lifting a finger for any of us, **your own people,** while you pant and jump for the next new powers that be. How can you live with yourselves?

So here's your chance. Let the boy go. If he was at Occupation Headquarters or the American Embassy, it's because he was looking for me. I disappeared on him. I'm not proud of it, but when my father died, I got to thinking about my future. Now I clean toilets for the Americans—who else has a job to give these days? But that boy didn't need to know. Nobody needs to know. How should I know how he tracked me? I don't see what the murder has to do with this. Did you just say **assassination** plot? That's the most absurd thing I've ever heard.

Q. On April 29, 1947, you were also seen at the American Embassy. What were you doing there?

Konomi was skinnier, all bones beneath a blue dress cinched at the waist in a style he'd never seen on her, her feet, like a film star's, pecking the pavement in Western-style heels instead of clomping along in her trademark geta. He hadn't believed Furukawa, but this was definitely Konomi emerging from

Occupation Headquarters, and the sight clipped his heart. Since they'd met at her stall the previous spring, they'd spent almost every hour together, selling her omusubi and busting anyone who gave her trouble. After the police crackdown and the black market's dissolution, he moved into her shanty to help her look after her father while she trawled her new market to sell the only thing left to her. Not that Konomi advertised herself; in fact, **she** chose her customers, shy white soldiers not much older than himself. It burned him, the crawling hours, the pitching fear, the mess of gratitude snarling into anger every time she returned safely. But he also knew it burned her, this self-flagellation, justified every time she exchanged her grubby notes for the supply of penicillin she needed for her father's tuberculosis.

One evening seven months earlier, they were on their way to collect their share of kitchen scraps from a restaurant owner Konomi knew. Near the service alley, they saw the usual mobile food stall crowded with sundry people, two GIs squeezed in among them, slurping from bowls like the others. As they shimmied by, he saw a wallet neglected on the counter below the GI's busy elbow, the leather supple like the one his father used to carry. He slipped his hand over it—and that was it. He woke days later sore to the bones in what appeared at first to be a tent, Konomi's voice mingling with Kiyama's and Sato's. Instead of shaming him, the students invited him to stay with them at the shelter, and knowing how much this would lighten Konomi's load—she had to bribe her shanty manager, who counted not just her father but the boy among her sick—he did. The arrangement suited them all: he helped the students with Party errands and cared for Konomi's father when she needed him to. He found himself relaxing, his days clarified with purpose—until Konomi disappeared.

WITNESS #4: PROF. ISHIKAWA TOKYO METROPOLITAN POLICE DEPARTMENT, APRIL 29, 1947, 21:30

Really, there's no need for this. I wasn't "sniffing around" your station; I have an interest in the youth, who I first laid eyes on last July at the Ueno market. A dirty slip of a thing, covered in rags and boils, he looked as though he'd risen out of the ruins like a prophet of our new era, teeth bared for survival but with a sneer that promised to make a mockery of even his own defeat, if it came to it. One has to admire the energy, the unbridled animal determination emanating from his pores, petrifying even the blackguards of the blackest market. I didn't suspect then that he and a young woman who tended a stall there were close. Half-starved, I was greedy for a taste of life, and he, the pustular youth, charged into my path as the agent of my punishment.

I assure you, my value to you is indisputable. For example, I can confirm that today, April 29, the youth was not only at the shelter but also at the very site of your investigation: the old printing press. For I am no ordinary witness; I've been following him for months.

I was never a strong man. I'd given up physical pursuits for a life of the mind, sacrificing my muscles and bones to feed what I believed to be the higher calling. Especially after defeat I clung to this belief. For isn't it the mind that endows humankind with the faculty of memory, without which there can be no historical awareness, no account-ability? Yet in mere months, tossed into a dog-eat-dog hell, we the defeated have for-gotten all our values except the needs of our bodies. Indeed, dawn has broken over our ruined country, but far from illuminating a new society repentant of modernity's ex-cesses, it has revealed the modern brutality of our civilization, consumed as ever by how to profit off another human's back.

It is in this context that I became keenly aware of a young woman minding a stall at the Ueno market. She wasn't a classical beauty, a limp in her step and her lips trem-bling ever so slightly, but, supple and alive, she catalyzed my reunion with my body. I began buying her exorbitant pellets of rice, my parched fingers reaching like a tongue to skim her palm opened to take my coins . . .

On the last day of July, circumstances lured me to reach for more . . . Suffice it to say I was thwarted by the youth. Humiliated, I beat my retreat, but the youth was not done. I was halfway up Ueno Hill when I saw him loping toward me with feral speed, and in a flash he was upon me. I fought as never before, his flesh and mine locked in a mortal struggle until I, with my flaccid muscles, pinned him down. I cannot describe my elation! As my fingers pressed into his windpipe, engorging his face, I experienced what can only be called ecstasy. I saw the Truth. In my desperate greed for survival, I was choking none other than the suffering Redeemer incarnate.

Let it be known I released my grip and suffered his fists upon my face. Over the following weeks, unable to forget, I roamed the area for another glimpse of him. I finally found him walking with the market woman, the two bumping along like besotted cousins before disappearing into what appeared to be a block of tents but turned out to be a welfare shelter that even the likes of me, debased as I was, dared not enter.

Luck, however, favored me; I heard the woman's voice, and from the gaps in the flimsy panels I saw the pair enter a tent occupied by two young men—students I recognized from my university. It did not take me long to understand that the youth and the students had made this place their home. Where the woman lived, I never learned, but the four convened daily, and I became attached to their shapes moving like a family behind the tarpaulin. Then, a month ago, the students received a visitor. A small fellow in a stuffy suit. The woman was there too, but not the youth. Two days later, the woman stopped showing up. After that, the youth began coming and going unpredictably. There was no doubt he was looking for her. I never saw the visitor again.

Today, April 29, the youth appeared at the shelter around noon. He was agitated, barging into the students' tent and instigating an excited conversation before dashing back out. I followed him. This is how I ended up at the old press. The youth knocked, then tried the door and disappeared inside. He stayed perhaps a half hour before reemerging and leaping onto a tram. I lost him then, but my attention was riveted to the figure who'd emerged with him. A droopy fellow with a wilted profile who stared after the youth with a hateful yearning I recognized:

it was my own face, the animal face of a broken soul.

Let us remember the Messiah comes in many guises. Whether He'll lead with the steps of a man or the hoofs of a beast, what's certain is that the youth are the inheritors of this earth. Whereas you and I are trapped, you in your uniform, I in mine in a manner of speaking, the youth is of a new species rising from the ashes to lead the world of today into what we, with our lost heads and craven spirits, cannot begin to imagine. You mark my words.

Q. You were seen at Occupation Headquarters. You were seen at the American Embassy. Were you planning to attack General MacArthur?

Pecking down the boulevard with a fluency that impressed and frightened him, Konomi headed, as Furukawa had said she would, toward another Occupation building: the American Embassy. Should he show himself? He panned the busy street full of soldiers and military police. He slunk along, hoping she'd turn onto a side street, but the hulking Embassy soon rose before them, and Konomi stopped. Exchanging words with the guards, she disappeared through the gates.

Was Furukawa right? People came and went from the many offices in Occupation Headquarters, but the Embassy, currently housing the American general, was closed. He rubbed his temple; a dull pulse the size of a barley kernel rolled beneath his finger. He knew that since the Americans began cracking down on Party members, the Party, increasingly unnerved by what it saw as the Occupation's authoritarian slide, had begun to agitate; with the ghost of their ineffectual wartime resistance still heavy on their minds, everyone agreed they had to take measures. Furukawa, who favored an armed revolt, gathered his supporters. Konomi and the students, critical of violence even as a means to a revolutionary end, joined the opposition. It was a heated situation, but it was when Furukawa proposed involving the Party's Soviet comrades that everything shifted.

The pulse in his temple grew to the size of a pebble. What if Furukawa was preparing a full-on, possibly Soviet-backed, military coup? Would Konomi, a diehard pacifist, risk working with the Americans to stop him? This morning when he greeted the rōjin, the old man had told him what he then told Furukawa: that he'd seen Furukawa with Konomi. What the boy didn't tell Furukawa was that the rōjin had heard them arguing. Was Furukawa mobilizing against his opposition? He pictured Ōtsuka's curled body, the shock of his pulped face. Furukawa never admitted to killing him, but his bitterness had been real. The boy stood. A sharp pain crazed his skull. Then he was out, dragged away by someone trailing the smell of hot paper and printing ink.

WITNESS #5: PROPRIETOR, THE HEAVENLY CURTAIN HOTEL'S HOUSE OF HOPE TOKYO METROPOLITAN POLICE DEPARTMENT, APRIL 29, 1947, 22:00

He's a nice kid, that one. Covered in boils, but who can judge people by their faces these days? Take my place: The Heavenly Curtain Hotel's House of Hope, The Fortieth Welfare Hostel in trust to, and under the management of, the Greater Tokyo Federation of Non-Luxury Hotel Associations. On the face of it, you'd think it a respectable establishment, with such a grand name and endorsement. In reality, it's a clapboard bunkhouse extended and divided by oiled curtains, also used as roofing to protect our guests from the heavens above. Hence, Heavenly Curtain Hotel's House of Hope. Not to be mistaken for a shelter, mind you. As classifications go, we're a Welfare Hostel, which might lead you to believe there's a social security program in place to support the residents and their place of shelter, such as it is. But let me assure you: there is not, despite our Compassionate Occupiers, the Mighty Democratic Vanguards of the New World. This is the sort of place I run, just to be clear.

The kid's a regular, as regulars go at Heavenly Curtain. He looks to be thirteen or fourteen, kind to the maimed and touched, unlike certain other guests who stay by the hour, despite the lack of privacy, if you get my meaning. Can't complain, though. They pay my Federation fees.

As for the boys, they're regular boys, twenty-two or twenty-three—students, I hear. The girl too. Talks tough but you can tell she's from a good family. She lives with her dad—**consumptive.** It's nice to see these youngsters taking in a kid like that, putting a shine back in his eyes. Some days you can see the man he'll be.

Kids are a different breed these days. One minute, they mug you at knifepoint; the next, they shatter into the five-, ten-, fifteen-year-olds they were when their world fell apart; a week later, they disappear, sometimes forever. But this kid? He'd never hurt a soul, I don't care what evidence you think you have. He's honest, quick to help. I keep telling him that one day when I have a real hostel for people getting back on their feet, he can work for me. If I were you, I'd haul in the man who came poking around this evening, asking about the students. A slinky sort. Smelled like a stack of newspapers . . .

Q. You were at Occupation Headquarters. Thwarted, you headed to the American Embassy. You were planning to assassinate General MacArthur. Are you trying to jeopardize our country? Answer me!

If asked, the boy would've told them he was fifteen, the son of dissident parents, not especially determined himself, not during the war, which meant: he'd had friends; his grades were good but not outstanding; he'd had a crush on his pretty teacher with a face like a powdered confection. He would've said he was happy, despite his journalist father who drew the eyes of the Tokkō thought police, who regularly came to the house to slurp his mother's tea before breaking the warm skulls of her porcelain cups. He would've said it was the most brutally simple time of his life, everything beyond the hour irrelevant, poised to be dashed by bombs or another emergency draft.

Then, one March night five months before Surrender, everything changed. The sky filled with American B-29s, and the city was in flames, his neighborhood gone, his home indistinguishable from the sea of rubble spread in all directions, charred carcasses indistinguishable from other carbonized flotsam, the whole world black and blistered and peeling like the parts of his own face and body that had caught the gale, its whipping heat gouging his nose and decimating his lungs while chemical sparks, like a phalanx of bees, attacked his body. Worse had been the pain afterward, the hell of his body fighting the necrotic invasion, and the horrendous thirst that raked his throat, the dry clicks and clacks of his esophageal muscles driving him insane. He was found and treated by self-organized survivors, as much as treatment was possible in that context; by the time new skin patched his body, welding its contiguous parts, his world was dotted with white soldiers. And for the first time, remembering his father's secret desire for defeat, the boy had felt a prickle of what he identified as vindication, a tentative hope.

And now?

He'd point at the ruins, the spill of tin shanties flapping with laundry, a cruddy

efflorescence of life reclaiming itself. Look
around, he'd say, voice inflated with visions
of a true democracy not yet born. Over the
last two years, those who'd chosen to survive had survived, despite the odds; now
it was time to rise and live. The Americans
had strode in with their big guns and white
ideals, visionary but also deeply patron-
izing, selling liberty with one hand while
suppressing rights and freedoms with the
other. How long did they expect them,
the devastated, to foot the bill for their lavish lifestyles and housing projects when
millions were still homeless and starving?
How long must they participate in the farce
of a capitalist democracy that subordinates
human lives for a healthy profit? Look, he'd
say. The moment for revolution was beginning to blow over; history was beginning
to write itself, smoothing over the cracks,
building over the rubble, erasing all traces
of the destruction, the raw amniotic space
that had been rent at the cost of eighty million lives. Everywhere cranes were appearing, their metallic arms reaching for the sky,
while pile hammers pounded the earth, lay-
ing the foundation for a country soon to

be encouraged to forget this moment, this interregnum where everything lay in suspension, the known world sundered, the unformed future challenging everybody to reassess themselves, reimagine their lives, refracted by grief but not lost. Already, on the heels of the pacifist constitution ghostwritten by the Americans to safeguard the interests of the Western world, Japan was being urged to remilitarize; ex-soldiers were being mined for their combat experience in China and Korea. Soon the corporate beneficiaries of the war, still sucking on the bones of the dead, would feast on a new war, and Japan's recovery would begin this way: supplying the American demand for combat vehicles and equipment that would further split and burn the countries across the Sea of Japan.

Despite everything, his parents had believed in the possibility of a new future; he too had wanted to believe—to wrest from the destruction the seeds that might still make their lives count.

WITNESS #6: FURUKAWA TELEPHONE CALL, TOKYO METROPOLITAN POLICE DEPARTMENT, APRIL 30, 1947, 10:00

Like my men told you when they dropped off the kid at your station: he showed up at the press. I was out; when I got back, my pal Ōtsuka was . . . Well, you saw the body. Tied to a chair the way you pigs like to do it. A real blow to our Party. Ōtsuka had been complaining about the kid coming around, demanding information—where MacArthur went at what time, that sort of thing. Never thought he'd actually attempt anything. Then again, kid has it rough, with that face. He must hate our Liberators who slaughtered his family. So, listen, I did you a favor; I found the kid before he made his attempt. In return, it'd be nice if you released some of my comrades who were only exercising their democratic prerogative to protest. I'd come give this testimony in person, but I assume you won't guarantee my safety or my rights as a free citizen to leave your pigsty once I step in, am I right?

Also, I'd keep an eye on that kid's friends. I wouldn't be surprised if they put him up to this in the first place . . .

Q. Who's Furukawa to you? Who else is involved? Look at me!

In his dream, he walks with her in a city that's both this city and not. He's older, she's the same, strolling alongside him with a little torque dimpling her clomping gait. The city is quiet; purple clouds gather in the indigo evening, rain bruising a sky that never weeps. Always a storm is brewing, dusting the sediments that have fossilized the bones of all the cities that have come and gone, wrecked by their failure to imagine a viable future.

This city, built on the ruins of others, is hatched with scars, and as they walk they wade their fingers through the green and yellow grass sprouting in the grafts.

At the city limits, they come to a wall that has cycled through eons of demolition and rebuilding. Today it lies in destruction, marking an end—or is it a beginning?—they cannot decipher. As usual, they climb over the wall to rest beneath a tree, its leafless tines offering only the memories of past canopies that have sheltered others who, like them, have lain here, spine to root, and because it is his dream, she lets him trace the topography of her body, disfigured by the same chemical that had seared his face and annihilated his home, welting those parts of his world that had refused to burn. By now, she, like him, has adjusted to her new self, the alien grip and pull of her skin, which she feels most keenly on her lip, trembling the muscles that inevitably blind her, an icepick headache every three days. Once upon a time, she, like him, had taken her body for granted; now she's resigned to a cohabitation in which she's housebound, servile to a self that had always served her. He touches her drooping lips; her face clears. But even in his own dream he cannot undo what has been done; he can only hope to salvage his dream when he awakes.

In another part of the city, twelve kilometers away, his hero who has used him is hunting his comrades, unable to distinguish peace from war, friend from foe, past from present, because for him, nothing has changed, one oppressor replaced by another, and there is no end to the storm of frustration blinding the eye of his fearful heart.

WITNESS #7: THE RŌJIN TOKYO METROPOLITAN POLICE DEPARTMENT, MAY 3, 1947, 14:00

Eh? Covered in boils, you say? There are hundreds of him in the Heavenly Curtain House of Dump, all mottled-faced Jean Valjeans, Product of a Defeated Japan. I myself may not be much to look at, with all but my two front teeth missing and half my nose restored with this piece here whittled from the finest spruce, but I've traveled to and fro, lived my share of tragic lives, seen my share of tragic sights, heard my share of tragic stories—from murder to love-suicide to the great fires dropped from the sky, forever transforming us into centipedes, wrapped in our foreigners' castoffs. **High**

in the sky, there is a chirruping bird . . .
Know that song?

It's from forty or fifty years ago, before our country embarked on this stormy path that elevated war to page one, money matters to page two, relegating vital affairs such as gardening and women's topics to page four. But you say you want to hear the true goings-on in the streets today? For a small donation, I'll tell you the latest about a lonely bean sprout biding his time while two students and a woman bicker about the fate of a locked-up boy fabled to have attempted the life of a foreign general come to lead the people with counterfeit coins.

Big waves, small waves endlessly rolling on
Ceaselessly echoing the sound of the sea

From time to time, that tune drifts in through the holes in my brain, its refrain like a message from another world where I was surely a priest or a great judge or an important town crier . . .

Q. I'll ask you one more time. What were you doing on the afternoon of April 29, 1947?

On April 29, he'd woken in the predawn, curled against a concrete step, spine pressed against the back door to a restaurant he didn't recognize. He wasn't hurt, just stiff, his shoulders and hips locked, his toes a clump of marbles. A pinprick pulse ticked above his eye; later, the pulse would root and bloom, beating like the heart of a bulimic flower disgorging its scarlet petals, but right now he was functional, better than functional, the day soft and pliable. Around the corner, a shutter lifted, the ruckus of metal and keys evicting the night. In five hours, he'd greet the roaming rōjin; in six, he'd visit the students; in seven, he'd meet Furukawa. But right now the day's, the night's, the week's, the month's logistics were not yet a concern. Across the street, someone muffled a giggle. At this hour, night still loitered in the streets, children were still pimping their sisters for the Occupation troops, used condoms still floated in the gullies, but the sun was leaking over the horizon, the panpan prostitutes were collecting their mixed infants, the patrolmen were rousing the drunks. It was early, and he'd been woken by a dream. It was his first proper dream in months. Kiyama, Sato, and Konomi with his parents at his old home, waiting to surprise him. He never got to see the surprise, but he'd felt their warmth, a white cocoon that continued to cocoon him now as he walked down the half-lit street toward the Sumida River moving like a serpent, its oily back spangled orange and yellow, the ghost of the fire that had once raged over these waters leaping to lick the bodies that had tumbled toward it. Usually, he beat at these sparks of memory that threatened to consume him, but today he let them flare, a conflagration of feelings.

That March night, just before the air raid, he'd been restless, hunger and irritation goading him to leave his house after curfew to knock, like his peers, on his rich classmate's door. Nobody had liked that classmate, an arrogant brat who'd sailed on the coattails of his military father, but since the air raids began the brat had surprised them, siphoning food from his parents' pantry and doling it out to anyone desperate enough to break curfew and risk arrest. Word was the brat wept the whole time, jumping at every sound, but he never confirmed this, his first and only foray cut short by the air raid siren, its red wail, like a sinking foghorn's, mourning the coming end. In many ways, he never left that moment, halfway between his classmate's house and his own, his stomach frozen midplunge as he realized what was happening. Of course he'd run, thoughts of his parents blotting the map of the air raid shelters they'd taken pains to imprint in his brain. But he never made it home; the whistling sky opened faster than he could run, and his neighborhood erupted. And for the first time he witnessed the calculus of the universe express itself with an algebraic simplicity even he understood: in his selfishness, he'd disregarded his parents' one rule—never leave after curfew—and they'd been taken from him.

He'd never questioned this logic, not until this edge of daybreak, with the reddening sky, reminiscent of another time, stopping him in his tracks. Because he'd

gone there, hadn't he? Weeks later, when
he finally had the strength, through the
charred streets to his old school, his family's emergency rendezvous point. The largest concrete structure in the area, the school
was still standing, its battered face encircled
by a necklace of rubble. Oddly, the gates
were intact, the metal grates swung open,
a lone woman absurdly directing a line of
survivors through them.

At first he didn't recognize her, her fraz-
zled hair standing on end. Then he did, the
gentle tilt of her head giving her away. For
a moment, he was riveted, the mirage of his
pretty teacher springing his heart. When
she looked up, her eyes leapt, her yapping
hands turning apologetic as she detached
herself from the gates to hurry toward
him. But something was wrong; there was
a shadow on her face, even though there
were no trees left, nothing to cast shade. She
smiled, and her hair lifted, an unlikely flash
of summer, just before he saw what it was:
a split in her face, her left side as lovely as
ever, her right denuded of eyebrow and eye-
lash, her skin, once the envy of every girl
in class, wormy with welts. She was a few

steps away when her mouth opened. What words, what news, would she impart? His world narrowed to the shape of her lips, the sound of his parents' fate held there; his body jerked back. One step, two steps. Then he was running, his teacher's confused shouts dissolving into a commotion of noise before they had the chance to cohere in his ears. But what had she said? He strained to hear the ghost of her words tunneling back through the static of time. Because she'd said something. Her urgent voice lifting not in pain, he realized now, but wonder, perhaps even joy, as his body retracted and his mind swiveled, away from her face, away from the school, away from the line of survivors emitting a putrescence he'd finally, finally, recognized as death.

FOUR

THE VISITOR

He came around noon, this man, this soldier, who called himself Murayama. At first I thought he'd come, like so many in those months after the war, to beg for food, or inquire after the whereabouts of someone I may or may not have heard of, but this soldier, this Murayama, had come clutching a piece of paper, looking for our son, Yasushi.

I did not **not** trust him, my eyes wandering from the scrap of paper he'd apparently followed here to the gaunt face lowered in a deferential manner rarely seen these days. Gripping his satchel, he spoke politely, and as flooded as I was with questions, I did not immediately ask them, his presence like a beaten dog's, weary and shamefaced, his whole shrunken person so darkened by what

I assumed was the tropical sun that he appeared like a photographic negative backlit against the bright street. Instead, I told him that Yasushi hadn't returned from the war, and though Murayama's eyes flashed at this news, he never once attempted to peer past the wooden gate I had opened just wider than a crack despite my husband's parting caution each morning, and after a moment I found myself leading him into the front room, excusing myself to rummage for some tea leaves and a small bowl of millet noodles, which was more than I could offer. Whatever this man could tell me about our son I wanted to know—or so I told myself. Turning him away was unbearable.

The paper was brown, shiny with wear, and I resisted looking at it as I poured the tea, embarrassingly weak, and urged the noodles, taken from my evening portion, toward him. In this room, softly lit by the midday sun sifting through the osmanthus tree rustling outside the sliding glass doors, he seemed less shrunken than coiled, his muscles humming with such nervous energy I began having second thoughts. Calculating the time I had before my husband's return in the evening, I focused on how I should nudge him out. For even then I knew I would keep the visit to myself. In retrospect, I can only say that it was a guarding instinct at work, though I cannot say for whom.

Murayama did not speak right away. Instead he gazed around the room, bare now except for the pale ornamental vase my husband had sent from Harbin during his tenure there. Like everything else, I did not expect the vase to stay, its delicate color soon to be given up for a sack of grain or a few stalks of vegetables, but for the moment it cheered the room, its quiet shape attracting the eye and settling the soul, though it did not seem to have this effect on Murayama. Seeing that he'd withdrawn into himself, I got up and slid the glass doors open.

The air outside was still, the sky abuzz with cicadas clamoring as though to convince everyone it was summer, a hot one, to be appeased only by kites and watermelons, both of which had been conspicuously missing from the season for some time. In fact it was hard to believe it was already July, almost a year since surrender, and yet the stream of returning soldiers and refugees seemed only to be increasing, bringing new hopes and difficult tidings to those in perpetual waiting. Until now, I had been repeating to myself that even if Yasushi had survived, he may not want to return to this house he'd once found so intolerable as to run away. But now? I sat back down and glanced again at the creased paper placed at the edge of the low lacquered table.

Murayama, for his part, seemed to have forgotten me, and again I urged the tea and noodles toward him. To my surprise, he met my gaze. This man, this soldier, knew Yasushi, and the knowledge, like a sudden clap, shifted the curtain of air between us, and for a moment I could feel my son's presence, his shape, his face, almost visible, until Murayama moved, and the moment released itself.

Picking up his chopsticks, Murayama bowed and began to eat, chewing the noodles, sipping the broth, his movements measured as though heeding the advice of someone who'd once told him to slow down, eat with care, and he confessed as much, explaining that his mother had enforced it. "The good thing is it helps with the hunger," he said, adding that the last time he'd eaten properly was two days ago, when he discovered that his home, indeed most of Nagoya, had been razed by the firebombs.

"Did you find your family?" I asked, blotting my face with my handkerchief.

Murayama looked away. He'd searched for them in the shanties that had cropped up in the ruins, but nobody had seen or heard from them. "That's when I decided to make my rounds, see who I could find. Shizuoka was the closest, so I came here. I didn't think I'd find you—seems like this city too went the way of Nagoya." He glanced about appraisingly this time, taking in the vase, the wall, the view of the narrow garden. The house, unrefreshed for years, felt indecently opulent.

I dabbed my face again. "These are troubled times—I appreciate you coming all this way. Yasushi would be upset he missed you." Again I caught that flash in his eyes. I quickly went on. "Did you know each other long?"

Murayama explained they'd started out in different units. "As the war went on and we lost more people, units got merged.

I was stationed in Luzon. That's where I met Tanaka—I mean, that's what your son called himself: Tanaka Jirō. I don't know if you were aware." His gaze slid toward me.

Tanaka Jirō. It was a name I recognized. It belonged to the kenpeitai officer who'd once come to this house to interrogate my husband about his "antipatriotic" views—an unimaginative catchall accusation the government launched at whomever it fancied, even a respected doctor like my husband. That Yasushi had hung on to the name— this was a shock; he'd been so little, and we never spoke of it. But Yasushi and my husband had always had their differences. Still, it was a cruel snub. "Murayama-san, please excuse me. We've had no idea about Yasushi's whereabouts since he ran away from home seven years ago. He was only in high school, but he was committed to serving, so we assumed he'd found a way to enlist, even without my husband's consent. We made inquiries, of course, but found no trace of him. Now I know why. Did he say why he chose that name?"

Murayama, listening keenly, shook his head. He explained that the two of them had spent only the three months they were stationed in Luzon together. "Just before we were deployed, I got pulled from my unit because I had mechanical skills they wanted to retain. I went straight to my commander—I **asked** to go with them."

"But you were kept back," I said, my voice thin.

Murayama nodded. "When I knew I was staying behind, I offered to, you know, take care of anyone's effects, if it came to it. At first Tanaka wasn't interested, said he had no one he needed to send anything back to. But the next day, after they were gone, I found that." He gestured at the paper.

The revelation struck me, its bluntness leaving no room for interpretation: as far as Yasushi was concerned, he'd severed himself from us. But the implied subtext was worse. "What kind of mission was this? When was it?"

Murayama shifted in his seat. "Two years ago. The unit was assigned to garrison an island. Given the state of the war . . ."

"And you never heard anything? There was no news?"

Murayama lowered his gaze. "I got

shipped out right after. Last I heard, they'd lost contact. But that doesn't mean anything," he added. "Strange things happen all the time."

This was no doubt true—it was the source of so much painful hope—but my fears seemed confirmed. I began to shake.

"Listen." He set down his chopsticks. "No one knows for sure—that's the real truth. And these days you never know who's going to turn up," he said, alluding to all the soldiers who'd returned only to find their names etched into tombstones in the family lot.

I nodded, but I felt numb. Outside, the leaves of the osmanthus tree were shimmering like coins, the cicadas chorusing to an emulous screech. I glanced at the vase. Its demurely fecund shape, once so expectant, now only emphasized its hollow interior. "May I?" I gestured at the paper.

Apologizing, Murayama handed it to me.

The paper was softer than I had expected, the worn folds releasing a leathery smell, and I saw at once that it was my son's handwriting, his gruff script, stabbingly familiar, still slouching to the left despite his early determination to correct it. This evidence, along with the other—the two names he'd written: his given one relegated beneath the hideous one he'd chosen to assume— pierced my chest, and my heart swelled, hurt and grief cresting before breaking into gratitude for this scrap of Yasushi that had made it back.

I was about to say as much, thank Murayama for the care with which he must have carried the paper, but when I looked up, I saw a strange expression cross his face, an odd detachment as though he'd been noting the moment—a lone middle-aged woman in slow undress—and my stomach clutched. He was a soldier, I reminded myself, the shadowy rumors that had been circulating in the streets suddenly murmuring close to my ear. What did it matter that he was polite, that he had known Yasushi, that he was someone's son? I glanced at his hands, toughened by mechanical work and who knew what else. As his blunt fingers fingered the teacup, I found myself shifting toward the vase, though I knew I'd be no match for a soldier, even a starving one like this.

Murayama did not seem to notice my alarm. Once again apologizing for his presence, he thanked me for my hospitality and repeated that he'd only come here hoping against the odds that Tanaka had made it back. "I didn't know where else to go—where else to be. Us soldiers, we're pretty unpopular these days."

I did not reply. Instead, I stood and slid the glass doors wider.

Outside, the day had mellowed, a light breeze loosening the air, the cool shadow cast by the eaves beginning to elongate on the ground, evoking the shape of the awning we did not have but had always wanted, a generous one, ample enough to cover the stone step we'd placed at the foot of the sliding glass doors. Even Yasushi had smiled at the idea, probably thinking that it would let him sneak his cigarettes during a rainfall, and for a while, encouraged by his approval, my husband had put considerable energy into seeing it constructed, the two of them tentatively tolerating each other until, one afternoon, Yasushi failed to come home from school. That evening the cicadas had been relentless just like this, and the pang of that memory cut through me. I returned to my seat. "People are just tired. They're looking for justification—some way to make all this make sense. You mustn't let them bother you."

This time it was Murayama who did not reply. Instead, he swirled the teacup, watching the dregs rise to the rim, and I noticed that a sheen had come to his forehead. Why was he here? The question, contained until now in the back of my mind, effloresced, and a new fear fanned across my back. Given the circumstances, he must have known Yasushi wouldn't be here. The realization swept through me; I could not move. After a moment, I repeated, "You really mustn't take these things personally. People are nervous. And you had orders to follow."

Murayama had apparently heard me the first time. Looking up, he brusquely told me that he appreciated my sympathy, but he was tired of people, so-called civilians, rolling out the carpet when there were things to cheer about, only to whip it away when the going got tough. "What makes you think you have the right? It was our lives you risked."

"Well, if we had known, if we'd been properly informed—"

"Then what? What would you have done?"

"Someone would have put a stop to it."

"Like the Emperor?" He laughed. "Truth is, none of you wanted to know. And now you want us hanged."

"That's unfair. Nobody faults you for following orders," I said.

"Orders?" Murayama looked at me.

"Please." I glanced at his hands again, grubby with dirt brought back from Luzon and wherever else. "In a few months, we'll all see things more clearly. Would you like one more cup of tea?" I moved to comply, even though I knew there was none left.

Murayama slapped his palms on the table, not hard, but with passion. "I know what people are saying. All the things we supposedly did, the slaughter and whatnot. What I want to know is, do **you** believe it? Do you believe your son—"

I seized the neck of my blouse. "What? Do I believe what?"

Murayama licked his lips. Then his face slackened. "Forget it. Tanaka was a stellar guy. A model soldier." His voice was dutiful and hollow.

I picked up the paper and again examined Yasushi's script. There was nothing to betray him, but, having assumed myself a mother of a soldier, I hadn't been immune to the whispers, the hushed anecdotes with their grisly suggestions, and these details, powerful in their obscurity, had collected like secret pearls in the back of my mind. Was this then why Murayama had come? To confess, to be absolved? "Please," I insisted. "What were you saying about Yasushi?"

Murayama peered at me, his furrowed face dubious but full of desire. He glanced at the vase, the green color almost blue where the sun had drawn its shade. When he turned back, he reassured me that Tanaka had been an upright soldier, well loved by everybody. "We just had a job to do. Sure, we heard **stories**—starving men losing their heads and even eating each other—but those guys were in remote places. I mean, don't get me wrong, Tanaka was on an island, but his island had villages—I mean, sure, he would've had to secure his position, but the point is, if people just cooperated, told us what we needed to know, but those natives . . ." He laughed nervously. "Would you like to see my album?"

It took a moment for my mind to catch up. When it did, my heart jumped. Of course, the album. I had been shown these books before while visiting bereaved neighbors; that I might one day see my son's had not registered. I searched Murayama's face, oily with sweat despite the breeze that had begun to visit the room, and I could smell his body, a seeping acridity. I gripped my handkerchief. Yes, I nodded. I wanted to see the album.

Murayama wiped his forehead and reached for his satchel. Explaining that Yasushi, originally from a different regiment, was not actually **in** his album, he assured me that military life was similar everywhere. "See this?" He pointed at the first photograph. "That's me." Little more than a schoolboy, his face, like the others, was braced against uncertainty, his ardent resolve only betraying a notion of who he still believed he could be. "That guy there?"

His first bunkmate. Page after page, he picked out key figures, rattling off facts about his division, the commanding officer, the number of battalions, platoons, and sections that made it up, his voice rising as the photographs showed fewer rows of soldiers, their individual faces becoming clearer, the background changing to show slivers of fields, runways, harbors. Coming to a portrait of his own unit, he told fond anecdotes about the hardships of camp life, how training, meant to harden them, only made them feel more exposed, more penetrable, their quickest reflexes always plodding against the speed of bullets. "At some point you realize they're just trying to beat the fear out of you." He recalled each slap, each punch, how the humiliation pumped him up. "The worst was when some idiot screwed up, we all got punished. So much for team spirit; most days we wanted to kill each other." He laughed. "Or kill **them.**" He jabbed at a photograph of decorated officers.

"Were there incidents like that?"

Murayama smiled. "Not in our unit. That would've been suicide." He flipped through the pages, looking for images of the more colorful characters known for their petty rebellion, and again the feeling of Yasushi's proximity seized me. How much had I longed for this? I had lived with a notion of Yasushi as a grown man, but without any context he had defied imagination. Now I was glimpsing his world, the details of his surroundings supplying a hint of his voice, his face, his life, and the experience was so beguiling I found myself giving over to this reunion with my son.

At five o'clock, my husband's Gustav Becker chimed, its sonorous report startling us. Seizing the moment to comment on the yellowing sky, I noted the quickening traffic flashing through the gaps in the wooden fence foretelling my husband's return. To my relief, Murayama flipped to the album's last pages, where he had pasted in his own snapshots. He lingered over these, locating each one—Singapore, Malaya, Philippines—identifying all his closest friends, explaining that Yasushi would've been in some of the images had anyone been able to coax the camera from him. "He loved that thing, thought he could be a photojournalist.

These were his favorites." The images were
of small, sentimental things—an ant on a
cigarette butt; a fish in a puddle held by an
empty crab shell—but they'd captured what
his eyes had seen and moved him to record,
and I breathed, swallowing the lump that
had come to my throat.

Murayama, noticing this, hastened to
cheer me. He described their friendship,
the epic arguments they'd enjoyed, sparked
by their disagreements over the quality of
an image, their technical points turning
like empty spits in the heat of their rivalry.
"What did we know about photography?"
He laughed. "Still, by the end, he'd learned
something," he said, pointing out a few
more of Yasushi's photographs, mostly por-
traits, some exhibiting a clear development,
a growing promise I could hardly bear to
witness. I touched the album. Murayama all
but leapt up. He slammed the album shut,
his gaze darting from my hand to the wall,
settling on the vase, the pale shape now
burnished by the afternoon sun, and again
I saw that peculiar look, cool and assessing but almost guilty now, and it struck me
that he **had** come for something, perhaps

to burgle me after all, and I quickly apologized, explaining that I had meant no harm, that his visit had been a gift, one for which I wished I had something to offer. "It's nothing, but would you like to take some of Yasushi's clothes?"

Murayama blinked. Then his face creased, stricken. Shaking his head, he muttered an embarrassed apology and stood up. Stuffing his album into his satchel, he thanked me again for my hospitality. "You never know," he told me as he pulled on his gaiters and hoisted his satchel, his voice edged with a chattiness that rattled the house. "Tanaka was famous for pulling things off." In fact, when he **did** show up, would I mind letting him know that he, Murayama, had looked him up?

I promised I would and unlatched the gate, asking if there wasn't anything more I could do. Telling me that he'd already inconvenienced me sufficiently, he bowed deeply and stepped away, turning once to wave before dissolving into the evening crowd.

Returning to the room, I hastened to straighten up, gathering the chopsticks, nesting the teacup in the bowl. I wiped the table, swept the tatami, gently slipping the paper into my pocket. Closing the sliding glass doors, I locked them, vigorously testing the latch. On my way out, I stopped to wipe the vase. There in the depths of its womb was a photograph, its white shape stenciled against the dark, and a chill snaked up my spine. I picked it out. In the foreground was Murayama, his open smile revealing a sunny boy not yet browned by the tropical sun. A field spread out behind him, a few shrubs in the distance, the open meadow bisected by a diagonal line: a newly dug trench. Along the trench was a line of people, roughly clothed and blindfolded, their legs folded under them, their ankles and wrists bound by ropes tied to stakes hammered deep into the earth. Though diminished by distance, their faces were crisp, the ends of their blindfolds flapping around their open mouths contorted by their anticipation of the soldiers standing several meters behind them, bayonets unsheathed. Like the prisoners, the soldiers' faces were also diminished but crisp, and as I stared, my eyes darting from the ferocious faces of these boys gripping their bayonets to the runny faces of the prisoners twisted in desperation, I realized that their expressions were in fact identical, both parties bound by the same fear, the attackers anticipating the same moment of piercing anticipated by the victims, and it was then that I registered that what I was looking at was not, as I had first assumed, an execution, but rather a training session, the line of shrubs not at all shrubs but a row of chairs fattened by decorated officers observing the performance. Two questions sprang at me: Why had Murayama left this picture hidden in this vase? And was this, like the others, Yasushi's photograph? Then it dawned on me that perhaps this whole visit had been a ploy plotted perhaps by Yasushi himself to not only leak the incriminating image—wasn't that what photojournalists did?—but also signal to me that he, though uninterested in presenting himself, had in fact survived.

This last thought seized my imagination, and the more I thought about it, the more it seemed plausible. Wouldn't it explain Murayama's peculiar behavior, and hadn't he, at the last moment, been careful to prepare me for Yasushi's return? I brought the photograph closer, its faint chemical odor penetrating my nose. Yes, those were indeed officers, and that was definitely a row of training soldiers, one end eclipsed by Murayama's head, the other end cut off by the photograph's border, the last visible soldier a mere slice, one visible leg stepping forward, one visible arm raising the bayonet, his face, cocked and therefore visible, sending a bolt of shock through me. Yasushi.

Outside, the sky had cooled to a pleasant cobalt, and as the clacking footsteps of the passersby began to thin, one pair branched off to stop outside the gate: my husband. I gripped the photograph. Glancing about for a place to hide it, my gaze, like Murayama's, alighted on the vase. I carefully lowered it image-side up so that its gray face would blend with the vase's dark interior. I stepped back; my buckling knees folded me to the floor. Outside, the gate rattled, the rusty bolt catching as usual. Smoothing my skirt, I arranged myself, tugging my blouse, straightening my back, as the momentary quiet of the room, once again assailed by the cicadas, was swallowed up by the darkening summer sky.

TRAIN TO HARBIN

I once met a man on the train to Harbin. He was my age, just past his prime, hair starting to grease and thin in a way one might have thought passably distinguished in another context, in another era, when he might have settled, reconciled to finishing out his long career predictably. But it was 1939. War had officially broken out between China and Japan, and like all of us on that train, he too had chosen to take the bait, that one last bite before acquiescing to life's steady decline. You see, for us university doctors, it was a once-in-a-lifetime opportunity. We all knew it. Especially back then.

Two nights and three days from Wonsan to Harbin the train clattered on, the lush greenery interrupted by trucks and depots manned by soldiers in military khaki.

Despite the inspections and unexplained transfers, this man I shall call S remained impassive, shadowed by a dusky light that had nothing to do with the time of day or the dimness of the car's interior; he sat leaning against the windowpane, face set, impervious to the din around him. Later, I would come to recognize this posture of self-recrimination, but at the time I had barely recovered from our initial journey from Niigata to Wonsan across the Sea of Japan, and I was in a contemplative mood myself, in no condition to pause over the state of others, much less engage with my colleagues, who by now had begun drinking in earnest, liquor still being plentiful then, oiling even the most reticent of tongues. So I excused myself and must have promptly nodded off, for the next moment it was dawn, the day just beginning to break, the length of the train still shrouded in sleep. I was the only one awake, the only one woken by the sudden cessation of rhythm, which drew me to the window, still dark except for my reflection superimposed on it.

We had apparently stopped for cargo, the faint scuffling I could hear revealing a

truck ringed by soldiers, their outlines cam-
ouflaged against the paling horizon. Later
I would learn the significance of this stop,
but for the moment the indistinct scene
strained my eyes, and I pulled back, hoping
to rest for another hour.

Forty years later, this scene returns to
me with a crispness that seems almost spe-
cious when so much else has faded or disappeared. Perhaps it is simply the mind,
which, in its inability to accept a fact, returns to it, sharpening the details, resolving
the image, searching for an explanation that
the mind, with its slippery grasp on cau-
sality, will never be able to find. Most days
I am spared by the habits of routine. But
when the air darkens like this, turning the
windows inward and truncating the afternoon, the present recedes, its thin hold on
consciousness no match for the eighty-two
years that have already claimed it. If hindsight were less truculent, I might have long
ago been granted the famed view of belated
clarity that might have illuminated the
exact steps that led me into the fog of my
actions. But hindsight has not offered me
this view, my options and choices as elusive

now as they had been then. After all, it was war. An inexcusable logic, but also a fact. We adapted to the reality over which we felt we had no control.

For what could we have done? After seven years of embroilment and two years of open war, the conflict with China had begun to tax the everyday, small signs of oncoming shortages beginning to blight the streets, thinning shelves and darkening windows, so that even menus at the fanciest restaurants resembled the books and newspapers blatantly censored by the Tokkō thought police. Then, when officials began making their rounds of sympathetic universities, seeking candidates disposed to patriotic service, our director submitted a list of our names, eliciting more visits from more officials, this time escorted by military men. Were we alarmed? Some of my colleagues were. But the prospect of a new world-class facility with promises of unlimited resources stoked our ambitions, we who had long assumed ourselves dormant, choked off by the nepotism that structured our schools and hospitals. If any of us resisted, I did not hear about it. Flattered and courted, we let ourselves be lured, the glitter of high pay and breakthrough advancements all the more seductive in the light of our flickering lives.

So the day we set sail from Niigata we were in high spirits, the early sky heavy with mist, the hull of the **Nippon Maru** chopping and cleaving as the sound of rushing water bore us away from our coastline, leaving us to wend our way through our doubts and worries to arrive in Wonsan, stiff and rumpled but clear in our convictions. After two turbulent days, we were grateful to be on steady ground, overwhelmed by new smells and sounds, the bustling travelers and hawkers broken up by the young, bright-eyed representative dispatched to meet us. This youth was energetic, if brash, and perhaps it was this, along with the sudden physical realization that we were no longer in Japan, that reminded me of my son, but it plunged me into a mood that would last the rest of the trip. Of S I have no recollection at this time, not until a few hours' gap resolves into the memory of that cold window of the stilled train, my eyes pulling back from the soldiers and truck, their dark outlines replaced by the reflection of my face, above which I caught another face, its eyes watching me.

No doubt it was the hour, and the invasiveness of having been watched, but the shock colored all my subsequent encounters with S, so that even decades later I am left with an ominous impression of a man always watching as the rest of us adapted to our given roles and fulfilled them perfectly. Did we exchange words? I regret that we did not. For by the time I gathered myself, he was gone. Two hours later we pulled into Harbin, our Emperor's celebrated new acquisition.

From Harbin we were to head twenty-two kilometers south to Pingfang. But we were granted a few introductory hours in the famed city, and we set about familiarizing ourselves with the cobblestone streets flanked by European shops and cafés still festive with wealthy Russians and a few well-placed Chinese, all of whom politely acknowledged our entourage. If people were wary, they did not show it, and we, for our part, acted the tourist, taking turns deciphering the familiar kanji strung together

in unfamiliar ways on signs and advertise-
ments as onion domes and minarets rose
beside church steeples and pagoda roofs,
obscuring the city's second skyline: the
"Chinese" sector of this once Russian concession city. Once or twice unmarked vans
stole by, but overall our impression was of
wonder and delight as we strolled through
the crowd, the sun on our backs coaxing a
healthy sweat despite the chill in the October air.

If not for a small incident, Harbin might
have remained an oasis in my memory of
China. But our young representative had
irked me from the start, and the farther we
walked the more he chatted, pointing out
this or that landmark we **must** have heard
of, and soon his loud, presumptuous voice
began grating on me, and I snapped back
with an energy that surprised even me.

My colleagues were quick to intervene,
rallying around him like mother hens, cluck-
ing at my severity. But, you see, my son and
I had been getting into it just like this, and I
could not abide the youth's hooded eyes;
I lashed out, admonishing his temerity, his
misguided courage and naïve ideals—the

very things I believed had pushed my own son to run away, presumably to enlist. I would have lost my head then, save for the tether of my wife's pleading face, which appeared before me, reminding me of how, despite her terror, she had refused to blame me each day I failed to find our son. I dropped my voice and let myself be pecked back, the sun-dappled street once again leading us on, this time to our first proper meal in days.

The day's specialty was duck. Despite our meager group of thirty-one, the restaurant had been requisitioned, its large dining room conspicuously empty, its grand floors and walls echoing the stamps and scrapes of our shoes and chairs as we accepted the seats arranged around two tables set in the center of the room. S was observing us, his stolid face amplifying the garishness of our own as our tables began brimming with plates and bowls, flushing our cheeks and exciting our chopsticks. At last the duck was set before us, its dewy skin crisped and seasoned. For most of us, this was our first taste of the bird, and the pungent flesh, voluptuously tender, provoked our passions, prompting us to trade stories of our youthful lusts. But I for some reason found myself remembering the days I had spent toting my sister, who never tired of feeding the ducks that splashed in the pond behind our house. I earned my title as the group's sentimentalist that day, but I believe it was at this moment that we fell in with each other, our shared pleasure piqued by our unspoken guilt at gorging on such an extravagance when our families back home had mere crumbs to support the patriotic frugality demanded of them. Perhaps this is why Harbin has stayed with me, nostalgic and laden, edged with a hysteria I would come to associate with this time.

I BELIEVE few of us forget what we keep hidden in our memory's hollows. True, many of us are capable of remaining professionally closed-faced, tossing out facts of our wartime accomplishments the way we toss our car keys, casually and full of the confidence of important men who have worked hard and earned their keep, rightfully. But forgetting?

My two colleagues and I have been debating this point over our yearly meals taken here in the rural outskirts of this wintry city in northern Japan where we converged eight years ago. They claim that if not for these meals, they might have forgotten these memories stowed for so long, buried by a present that discourages remembrances so that trace feelings, occasionally jostled, may surface, but nothing more. For why dig up graves from a banished past, selfishly subjecting all those connected to us to what can only amount to a masochistic pursuit? Isn't it better to surrender to a world populated by the young, who, taught nothing, remain uncurious, the war as distant as ancient history, its dim heat kindling the pages of textbooks and cinemas, occasionally sparking old men with old grudges, but nothing to do with them?

I would like to disagree. But life did move on, the war's end swallowing us up and spitting us out different men, who, like everyone else, slipped back into a peacetime world once again girdled by clear boundaries and laws meant to preserve lives, not destroy them. And yet, for me, S has continued to tunnel through time, staying in my present, reminding me of our shared past, which we, with all our excuses, have been guarding as tightly as the walls that surrounded us in Pingfang.

You must understand something: we had always meant to preserve lives. A few thousand enemies to save hundreds of thousands of our own? I hardly think our logic was so remarkable.

What was remarkable was Pingfang. Its imposing structure looming in calculated isolation, its vast grounds secured by high-voltage walls, its four corners staked with watchtowers overlooking its four gates armed with guards whose shouts were regularly drowned out by the clatter of surveillance planes circling the facility. Approaching them for the first time in jostling trucks, we watched the walls of the compound unroll endlessly before us, each additional meter contracting our nerves so that our faces, initially loose with excitement, began to tighten, eliciting a lustrous laugh from our young guide, who turned to remark, **Of course, we don't bear the Emperor's emblem here.**

Sure enough, when we stopped for authorization at the gate, we saw that the walls were indeed ungraced. In a world where even our souls were expected to bear the mark of the Emperor, the absence was terrifying, and perhaps this was when I **saw** Pingfang, its forbidding grandeur, cloaked by its unmarked walls, presaging what it was capable of. By then it was clear that the warning emanating from it made no exceptions, even as it opened its gates and saluted us in.

In increments we would become privy to the extent of Pingfang's ambitions. But first we were dazzled. Our days snatched away by seminars and orientation tours, we scarcely had time to unpack, our bodies as well as our minds collapsing into white sleep that seemed to flood always too soon with sunlight, so that even the hardiest of us grew weary, dragging from conference rooms to auditorium, the occasional outdoor tour whisking us off in rattling trucks that clattered our teeth and fibrillated our brains until we developed an aversion to Pingfang's astigmatized landscape. After a fortnight, we reached our threshold. We broke down, all of us mere husks of ourselves, our individual drives wrung out of us. Until then we had been accustomed to mild routines with little expectation; to be inducted into a life ruled by the exigencies of war proved transformative. We readjusted, our senses and sensibilities recalibrated to accommodate the new demand. After all, humans are remarkable in their ability to adapt. Time and again we would find ourselves reminded of this fact, which, I believe, was at the root of what came to pass at Pingfang.

HAD I understood what I glimpsed that night from the train window, would I have turned back, returned to the circumscribed safety of my home and career? I would like to imagine so; in my right mind I am certain of it. But here lies the problem: the issue of "transgression." In peacetime all lines are clearer; one need only assemble one's motives and evidence for the courts to make the determination. And even if proceedings are flawed and verdicts inconclusive, in one's heart, one likely **knows** if one has transgressed. But in war? Does transgression still require intent? Or is it enough for circumstances to conspire, setting up conditions that pressure one to carry out acts that are in line with, but not always a direct result of, orders? I do not know. Yet I find myself looping through memory's thickets for that exact bridge that let us cross our ambivalences to the other side.

My two colleagues believe Harbin was the bridge. They claim that, as tourists, we were set up to accept the exotic and so dismiss what would have been, in another context, obviously amiss. I do not dispute this view. Yet I wonder whether we hadn't been set up—inoculated—long before we set sail for Wonsan. By then the mood of war, long since gathered in the air, had precipitated into crackdowns, the once distant patter of the jingoists' tattoo literally pounding down doors to keep us spouting the official views. Even our mandatory participation in civil defense drills, as well as our patriotic duty to look the other way, had already become two more chores as seemingly unavoidable as the war itself. Resisting would have been foolhardy, the hardline climate a meteorological fact, its terrorizing power mystical in effect. Yet I am a man of science; I have never been swayed by weather's mystical claims. Nor have I been captive to its blustery dramatics. So, when I was a young man, still proud of my own mind, I was arrested. My son, Yasushi, was six then, a bright child already righteous, susceptible to grand ideals. He never mentioned my arrest, but I believe it shamed him. He became rebellious, his puerile disobedience erupting into full-scale mutiny by the time he was fourteen. My wife urged me to confront him; I did nothing of the sort. How could I? I, who had ultimately recanted my beliefs. True, I was thinking of them, my wife and son, their torturous road if I refused to cooperate. But finally it was that I could not bear it, the dark shapeless hours sundered by clubs, water, electricity: I gave in.

Four decades later I do not have reason to believe Yasushi is still alive, but every so often there is news of yet another Imperial Army straggler emerging from the jungles in Southeast Asia, and I am unable to let go.

The latest straggler, one Captain Nakahira Fumio, widely speculated to be the last repatriate, is currently on the run. His hut, discovered on Mindoro Island two weeks ago, had evaded detection for thirty-five years. The authorities finally released his picture.

What could I do? I charged into the news-stand. The image, a grainy reproduction of a school portrait, showed a hollow-chested boy with an affable face, generic enough to be any youth. Could Yasushi have taken his identity? Because, you see, back then, when Yasushi was raring to enlist, he'd been too young. Needing my consent, he'd approached me with the forms. I, of course, refused, citing the importance of his studies, and worried that he'd try to forge my signature. But Yasushi, single-minded, was a step ahead of me. Realizing that forms are traceable and therefore retractable, he opted to trade in his identity. What name he assumed we never found out. Even then the military was eager for soldiers, and I, despite my connections, had a record: an official charge of treason.

Comparing the images for quality, I chose several newspapers and hastened into the street still burnished with morning light. That's when I saw him—S—his now old man's shape bearing the shadow of his younger self, his ornithic neck bobbing forward, his once languid gait sped up to a near footloose shuffle. I opened my mouth to address him. But what was there to say? Had I been a different man, able to withstand the gaze of those who'd surely be quick to condemn me for what they too might have done in my position, I might have braved the attention of the one man who may yet have the right to judge me. But I am not that man. Humans may be adaptable, but that says nothing about our ability to change.

ALL TOLD, I spent twenty-four months in Pingfang. Officially, we were the Bōeki kyūsuibu, the Anti-Epidemic Water Sanitation Unit, Unit 731, a defensive research unit. Materially, Pingfang spanned three hundred hectares, its fertile land dappled with forests and meadows, its innumerable structures—headquarters, laboratories, dormitories, airfield, greenhouses, pool— luxuriously accommodated within its fold. Locally, we were known as a lumber mill, our pair of industrial chimneys continually emptying into the impending sky.

I remember the first time I stood beneath one of these chimneys. Having finished a procedure, we had followed the gurney out, the damp air white with frost, the bare earth crunching underfoot. S, like the rest of us, was in a morose mood; our work, bacteriological in nature, was making useful gains, but we had not succeeded in developing the antidote we had been after, and I, for one, had become increasingly restless. By then it was 1940; the war, gridlocking in China, was beginning to fan southward, and I was convinced that if Yasushi had indeed enlisted, he would end up in the tropics, where the fruits of our work would be most vital.

I do not know why I risked airing these thoughts. Perhaps it was my way of acknowledging my son. I approached S. Until then we had all been careful to keep to the professional, repeating stock answers, but S was sympathetic. He chatted openly, agreeing with my prognosis, adding only that the war might reach American shores before pushing farther south—an unentertained notion at the time. I was about to press him on the feasibility, indeed the audacity, of such a course, but just then a flare of heat drew our attention, and the gurney, now emptied of our maruta—yes, that's what we called them: **logs**—pulled us back to our duty.

Because, you see, that was what Pingfang was built for, its immaculate design hiding in plain view what we still hoped to control: the harvesting of living data. For how else could we compete? Our small nation, poor in resources and stymied by embargoes egregiously imposed by the imperial West. Our one chance lay in our ability to minimize loss, the most urgent being that of our troops, all too often wasted by war's most efficient enemy: infectious diseases. But war spares no time; again and again we found ourselves beating against the very wall that had always been the bane of medical science. In other words, our problem was ethical; Pingfang sought to remove it. The solution was nothing we dared imagine, but what we, in medicine, had all perhaps dreamed of. We merely had to continue administering shots, charting symptoms, studying our cultures—all the things we had always done in our long medical careers—except when we filled our syringes it was not with curatives but pathogens; when we wielded our scalpel it was not for surgery but vivisection; and when we reached for tissue samples they were not animal but human. This was perhaps Pingfang's greatest accomplishment: its veneer of normalcy. We carried on; the lives of our soldiers, indeed our entire nation, depended upon us.

I do not know who came up with the term "maruta." Possibly its usage preceded us. The first time we saw them we were in the hospital ward, where they looked like any patients, intubated under clean sheets changed daily. The second time we saw them it was at the prison ward, where they looked like any prisoners, uniformed and wary. Both times, I remember the hush that fell over us as we registered exactly what we were being shown before we were briskly ushered away. By the time we were given full rein over our research, we were using the term, counting up the beds, tallying our maruta in preparation for our next delivery. Indeed, I believe it was a cargo transfer that I witnessed that morning on the train to Harbin.

I was asked to inspect such a cargo just once. Woken abruptly, I was summoned by an officer waiting in an idling jeep. Throughout the ride, I was bleary, my mind cottony with sleep, and once I gleaned the purpose of the trip—a preliminary health scan—I shut out the chatter and arrived unprepared for the secluded station, the small squadron of military guards patrolling the length of the curtained train, the cargo's white tarp peeled back to reveal twelve prisoners strapped to planks and gagged by leather bits.

My first reaction was morbid fascination, my mind unable to resolve the image of these people packed like this, and the term "maruta" acquired a horrific appropriateness that struck a nerve. I began to laugh, a sputtering sound that elicited a disapproving glance from the officer who pressed me forward. How they managed to survive I could not imagine. Trembling with exhaustion, they lay in their thin prisoner's clothes, wet and stinking of their own unirrigated waste, until one by one they were unfastened, forced to stand, their movements minced by the shackles that still bound their hands and feet. No one protested, the only shouts coming from the guards as they stripped and prodded them, the tips of their knives shredding their garments, exposing them first to the cold, then to the water as a pair of soldiers hosed them down.

Had I been able to, I would have abandoned my post, and perhaps I made as if to do so, for the officer gripped my arm, his placid face nicked by repulsion, though it was unclear for whom or what. As the water dripped away, and the maruta were toweled off, I was led to the nearest plank, where four women, now manacled together, sat shivering. They were all in their twenties and thirties, their eyes black with recrimination and their chattering bodies so violently pimpled by the cold I could hardly palpate them. The second plank was an all-male group, each man, wiry with work, irradiated by a humiliation so primal my hands began to shake. The third and final plank was a mixed group, perhaps a family. One woman grew so agitated by my attempts to minister to a limp girl that I barely registered the man pulled from the train and added to the cargo. This new prisoner was my age, in good health and spirited enough to have risked the curtains to "spy" from the train window. He was brought to me to be tranquilized, and though I must have complied, I remember nothing else, only the leering heat of the soldiers snapped to attention behind me, and then, later, the vague relief that flooded me when the next day I stepped into my ward and did not recognize a single face.

Lumber mills?

I do not believe anyone was so naïve.

PINGFANG'S OPERATION expanded with the war, its defensive function superseded by its natural twin: the development of biological weapons. This offensive capability had been pursued from the start, mostly in the form of small-scale tests surreptitiously deployed as creative endnotes to our ongoing anti-insurgency missions, but it did not peak until the war took that fatal turn toward America. By then, many of us had been dispatched to newly conquered regions or strategic teaching posts back home, but news continued to reach us, mostly as rumors but sometimes through familiar details we recognized in news reports. As the war entered its final throes, Pingfang rose in importance. By the time Germany began its retreat, Pingfang, already anticipating a Russian offensive, had begun testing, for example, the human threshold for the northern freeze. How they planned to use the data I do not know. With so few resources and little infrastructure left, there would have been no way to manufacture, let alone distribute, any new equipment. Why these tests struck me as crueler I also do not know. Perhaps the obvious brutality of the method touched my conscience. Or perhaps it was simply a defensive reflex, the mind's protective instinct that indicts another in the attempt to save itself. After all, if I had been in their position, I too would have likely carried out these experiments, meticulously freezing and thawing the living body to observe the behavior of frostbite or assess the tactical viability of a thoroughly numbed soldier. While some of us still insist on our relative humanity, I do not believe we can quibble over such fine points as degree.

I, for one, return to the fact of the cargo inspection, and it was this that finally drove me from my practice, a quiet family clinic discreetly arranged for me after the war.

Until then, the setup had suited me. The clinic yielded enough to survive on, and I was able to keep to simple diagnoses and treatments. Even so, the body does not forget. A clammy arm, a quivering lip: my hands, once recruited for their steadiness, began to jump.

So eight years ago, following my wife's death, I moved to this city in northern Japan. At the time, China had just normalized its relationship with Japan, and my two former colleagues and I, having respectively come to a similar juncture, reunited at a small noodle shop known to connoisseurs for its duck. It was our first contact since the war, and it took us a moment before we could attempt a greeting, our old hearts fluttering like scattered chickens. Once again we ate with a greediness we dared not explain and parted with a gaiety that consoled us. But I believe we would have preferred to sit alone with our meals, if not for our curiosity and relief that this moment, dreaded and yearned for, had finally come to pass. Since then, we have had an unspoken agreement to reconvene on the same day every

October, the fateful month we boarded the **Nippon Maru.**

ONLY ONCE did S and I manage a sustained conversation. That day I had gone in search of a colleague, T, a surgeon of considerable talent, who had taken to visiting the female prisoners. Once soft-spoken and decorous, he had become the most unruly among us, his increasing notoriety forcing us to take turns restraining him. But T was not in the female prison ward that day, and I made my way to headquarters, thinking he had gone to request more "materiel," but nobody had seen him there either. I was about to retrace my steps when I glimpsed S emerging from a restricted office, slipping a sheaf of papers into his laboratory coat. When he spotted me, he paused but made no attempt to explain himself. Instead he fell into step with me, convivially opening the door to the underground passage that connected all the buildings in Pingfang.

"I don't know what will happen to T after this," I said, trying not to glance at the papers peeking from the coat.

"You mean after the war?" S shrugged. "Who cares?"

"He could still have a career—a future—if he's careful."

"Future?" S looked amused. "Where do you think this war is going?"

I lowered my voice. "We're just following orders."

"And you think the world will sympathize?"

"What choice do we have? T, on the other hand, is being excessive."

"And you think that makes you different."

"I'm saying the world will have to consider that."

"And if it doesn't?"

I was silent. It was true: the world had no obligations; what chance did we have in what was likely going to be a Western court? True, we were obeying orders, but we were the ones carrying them out; we could not look at our hands and plead innocence, dusting them off the way our superiors did, passing off their dirty work and expecting it returned perfectly laundered "for the sake of the medical community." From the start, this had been an untenable situation we were expected to make tenable; forced to be responsible for what I felt we should not be, I had become resentful. I began misnotating my reports. Small slips, easily dismissed, until the accumulation became impossible to ignore. Instead of 匹, the counter suffix for animals, I began writing 人, the counter suffix for humans. I worked systematically, substituting one for the other with a calculated randomness befitting Pingfang.

I glanced at S's laboratory coat, the stolen papers tucked beneath. "I suppose it'll depend on if anyone finds out."

S patted his coat. "We all have to do what we have to do, don't we?"

"After everything, they'll have no choice but to protect us," I said.

S did not disagree. "The matter may also interest others beyond our small military and government," he replied.

And he was right. That was more or less how it played out, with the cold war descending on the infernal one, and the Americans, fearful of the Russians, agreeing to negotiate with our lieutenant general for sole access to our research, the objective being the advancement of their own secret bioprogram stymied by medical ethics. The result? Our full immunity in exchange for all our data, human and otherwise.

FEW HISTORIANS have unearthed, let alone published, evidences of Pingfang's abuses. Those who have done so have been divided over the problem of numbers. At one end, Pingfang's casualty rate has been estimated at several thousand. At the other end, the number hovers closer to 200,000, mostly Chinese but some Russian and Japanese deaths as well. I believe both figures tell a truth. While our furnaces saw no shortage of logs in their six years of operation, our goal was never mass extermination. Our tests, contingent on the human body, its organic processes and upkeep, were costly, and even our field tests, aerial or onsite, were limited to small villages and hamlets optimally secluded for tracking our data. But Pingfang cannot be confined to its five years of operation. Its construction took two years, 15,000 laborers, 600 evictions; and afterward, when surrender triggered the destruction of the compound whose walls were so thick that special dynamite was needed, the final blasts are said to have released merely animals, the only witnesses to escape alive. And the gain? Militarily, history has shown the regrettable results, with rumors of biological weapons and unexplained outbreaks surfacing now and again, if only in the half-light of prevarications. Medically, it is harder to assess, our research having pushed our field to the cutting edge, landing many of us influential positions in the pharmaceutical sector, where some of us are still directing the course of medicine, or the money in medicine, in not insignificant ways.

The irony of it all is how well we ate within those walls, our maruta fed better than us to maintain optimal biological conditions. This prurient coupling of plenitude and death, so lavish in its complicity, has lent a kind of heat to my memory of Pingfang, compressing its eternity into a vivid blur coalesced around two towering chimneys, their twin shapes always looming, gone the moment I turn to look. These days it is this collusion of the mind with Pingfang's irreality that terrorizes me, the fog of the entombed past threatening to release a hand, a face, a voice.

My colleagues are more fortunate. Our annual meals seem to have done them good, churning up old soil mineralized by the years, the new exposure letting them breathe. I, however, find myself hurtled back to people and places lost to time but not lost to me. At my age it is time that is present, its physicality reminding me of the finality of all our choices, made and lived.

This morning they deemed the story of the straggler a hoax: Captain Nakahira Fumio, whereabouts irrelevant.

And so it goes, all of us subject to the caprice of time as it releases not what we hoped for but what it does before it closes its fist and draws back, once again withdrawing the past from the present. And perhaps that is as it should be. For what would I have done had Captain Nakahira been my son? Would I have shown myself, risking the eyes of ambitious journalists—risking those of my son? I have not even had the courage to face my wife at her grave.

———

I MENTIONED S to my colleagues for the second time last year. After the friction of the first time I should have known better, but the urge had taken hold of me again. Over slivers of duck prepared to our specifications, I once again gave my account of the papers he had stolen, the exchange we had had. As before, they listened patiently, commenting on his courage, his uncanny foresight and reckless integrity, wondering how they could have forgotten such a character. Again, I described his solitariness, the way he had observed us—quietly, persistently—until they remembered, not the man himself, but the previous time I had given this account. Should he have exposed the papers? I asked. As before, my colleagues turned on me, asking me why I returned to this, what stake I had in these moral questions, nothing but a masochistic exercise—was I sure I hadn't made him up?

I defended myself, reminding them that we had each mentioned at least one person the other two hadn't been able to recall, and wasn't the point to see if we **could** imagine it—another life, another self—because look at us, I said, year after year, three old men uselessly polishing stones.

The silence was prickly, and for the first time we parted uneasily, our forced gaiety failing to hide the rift that had been widening between us. Indeed, the last few times we convened, we had gone through our menu of memories rather mechanically, and despite our appetites, our bodies have grown less tolerant of the fowl's fattiness, and I am not sure that we haven't lost our taste for the bird now that we have exhausted our staple of remembrances. Perhaps at our age it is only natural to want a release, to move again in time with the clock.

As for S, he may as well have never existed the way things turned out, those papers he never exposed. Yet he had offered me a vision, a different way forward, and perhaps that is my final offense. I did not risk that chance. Instead, I carried on, watching as the world marched on—another war, another era—with fewer of us left every year to cast a backward glance.

Perhaps this is why I continue to spiral back, tantalized by those moments during which it might have been possible to seize the course of our actions. Because, you see, we all had that chance. That day, just before we walked to the chimney, we had performed a surgery. I was at the head of the table, logging the charts, while T glided the scalpel over the body's midline. Y, my future noodle shop companion, was tracking the vitals, the beat of the pulse measured against the ticking of the clock, as the body underwent all the characteristic spasms—the fluttering of the eyes, the shaking of the head—the once warm flesh rippling with tremors as the skin grew clammy, its tacky surface soon sliding beneath our gloved hands as we wrestled the mutiny of the body. Perhaps if Y had stuck to procedure. But, you see, Y was monitoring the vitals; he was looking at the body, its special condition, and it struck him that he should be tracking not one pulse but two—the second, unborn beat. So he pushed his fingers in; the maruta bolted up. Fixing her eyes on us, she opened her mouth, stilling us. Few of us had acquired the language beyond the smattering of words we kept in our pockets like change, but we did not need language to understand her, her ringing voice a mother's unmistakable plea reminding all of us of our primary duty: to save lives, not destroy them.

Needless to say, we did not save anyone's life in that room that day. Instead we went on to complete a record number of procedures, breaking down bodies, harvesting our data, the brisk halls and polite examination rooms only reinforcing the efficacy of omission as we pushed to meet the demands of a war that had heaved us over one edge, then another, leaving us duly decorated but as barren as the landscape we left behind.

As for S, his story began irrecoverably to diverge from ours the day he slipped those papers from the office. While the rest of us hunkered down, he continued to plan and plot, imagining a justice that seemed inevitable. When the war ended and the Tribunals began, he too must have waited, hoping and fearing that justice would find him. But the sentences never came, and he must have felt its weight doubled back on him. Yet he never disclosed the papers. Instead he stowed them away, perhaps planning to donate them someday, tucked among his old medical books, to one or another bookshop frequented by frugal university students who may have the courage to expose them. Then, eight years ago, he retired to a house in the rural outskirts of a northern city, where an old cedar gives its shade to a backyard visited by birds in the spring and blanketed by snow in the winter. There he spends his days tending to the saplings he has planted behind the shed, where he keeps the papers stashed in a crate of old textbooks. Now and again his mind wanders to the crate, and he marvels at the unrelenting human will to preserve itself.

But today, with spring softening the breeze and the birds abundant in the yard, he finds himself compelled to visit the papers. After all these years, it is a wonder they have survived, slightly yellowed but otherwise intact, and he places them on a workbench he keeps outside the shed. In this light, the pages are clear, and the famil-iar misnotations have the power to jolt him, once again invoking the face of the woman, her wide eyes and gaping mouth, silenced by the wet sound of the fetus slapping the slop bucket. For days he had smelled it, the sweet scorched scent drifting be-neath the common odors of cooking and laundry and disinfectant, and he inhales, filling his lungs, as he steps back into the shed, pausing to appreciate his rake and shovel, the long-handled hedge shears now corroding on the wall. Reliable for so many years, there is comfort in this decay, the evidence of a life granted the luxury of natural decomposition. He untangles a rope, empties the crate of his papers. The rope is sturdy, as is the crate. He drags them to a spot beneath the arching cedar and sets the crate's open face squarely on the ground. He briefly wonders if his colleagues will meet this year. He hoists the rope, faces the wall. Once again creepers have scaled it, their dark leaves ruffled by a breeze eager to spread the fragrance of the neighborhood's peach and plum blossoms. He grips the rope; the crate wobbles, and while I never tested the precise time it takes for air to be absorbed by the lungs, the brain to starve of blood, and the body to cease its struggle to save itself, I am hoping that, in that duration, I will be able to wrest from myself the snatch of consciousness necessary to remember once more my sister and those ducks that swam in the pond back home.

THE LAST BULWARK
OF THE IMPERIAL
EMPIRE

October 28, 1944, 09:00

A fly landed on his face. His skin, caked with mud, grime, and the occasional scab, offered plenty of options, and it climbed up his chin, pausing at the corner of his lips, assessing the sore that had ripened there, a soft puddle pooled in the crack chapped by the heat that had long since drained his canteen. He blinked; the white tropical sun swarmed his pupils; he heard the flap-scrape of the split-toed jikatabi dragging in front of him; and he was marching again, the smoking shoreline strobing behind him, specks of vultures circling the sky like kites.

October 28, 1944, 15:13

By last count, they were down to two thousand men, a quarter of their original regiment. And aside from the makeshift guerrilla units they'd left behind to stall the enemy, they were retreating eight kilometers inland, away from the coastline where they'd taken their stand nine days ago, when the sea, emerald and spotless, heaved up a city: a fleet of several hundred enemy warships abuzz with planes. There had been no warning, all communication having sputtered out more than a month ago, leaving them to carry out orders that may or may not have become obsolete. Their mission had been simple: to harness the energy of eight thousand men to erect a human wall so impenetrable that any invading force would shatter against it. In short, their task was to transform themselves into the fiercest Niō to guard the Empire's southernmost gate, and all they'd done in the six months since their arrival was dig, hammer, and hoist, the pride of being the last bulwark of the Imperial Empire forcing them to overlook even its latest broken promise: the thin meals, already reduced to twice a day, now cut to once as they endured the mockery of their shovels and pickaxes ringing high and hollow against the cold rocks and coral reefs. From the start, everybody had known the Empire would lose control of the sky and sea, but they never expected a city to appear, the approaching mass configured to not only defeat but obliterate them.

Their air unit was the first to engage. Forty planes, meticulously hidden around the island, rose to meet several hundred enemy fighters. Led by the last of the Empire's aces, the unit did well, each pilot downing an average of three enemy fighters before plunging, evanescing in the green-blue sea. An hour later the first wave of naval bombardment commenced, the unrelenting roar ripping the air, spraying up sand, hacking down trees, boring holes the size of craters well beyond their first line of defense. They couldn't believe the discrepancy, their carefully conserved rations of fuel and arms laughable against the barrage. The ground rocked, trees erupted, bodies plumed; he ducked and rolled, his body airborne one moment, tumbling the next, only the miraculous yank of a platoonmate saving him from the engulfing soil.

October 28, 1944, 17:25

Tonguing his canteen, he scavenged for moisture trapped in the grooves along the rim. In this heat, water did not stay where it was needed, and his heart thrummed, a low, darting beat. There was no wind, no clouds, the uninterrupted sun splitting his skin, agitating the soft creases of his armpits, the softer folds of his groin, the softest webbing between his toes. Many were discarding their footwear, preferring the searing earth to the wet abrasion of canvas on raw feet, while others retrieved them, unable to endure the rocks perforating their soles. Gripping his American M1 pried from a corpse, he leveraged his gait, fighting to stay with the men around him, aware that his life depended on his ability to keep up with military time.

At last they stopped to wait for nightfall. Now and again a Grumman fighter streaked the air, but it no longer roused the few hundred men collected here, under the shade of these trees benevolently scattering the day into scraps of insignificant sky. Until now, morale had been decent, all of them having unexpectedly held out on the coast, troubling the enemy who had had to make several attempts before securing a foothold on the beach. As the front edged back, its scraggly line began to crumble, but they'd still held together, shifting their attacks from day to night, dynamiting tanks, grenading encampments, plundering tins of enemy food. Now and again, thoughts of surrender floated up, but they were gunned down by chattering M2s. When the order to change course finally rippled through them, they'd heaved together and begun marching, dragging themselves to the edge of this clearing fifty meters wide, its shimmering grass dappling with shadows as schools of enemy scouts trawled the area.

Leaning into a tree trunk, he resisted the lure of the soft grass swaying below him. Many had already succumbed, bowing into the earth, while others slumped about eyeing one another's mess tins. In front of him, a large man with a broad back was picking at a wound, his knees jerking as he dug out bits of shrapnel welded to his flesh. Behind him, a teenager with a crusty face cried for his mother. Somewhere someone lit a cigarette, and the gray smell caused a small commotion. Caught in the babble, his mind flitted and twirled, alighting on ghostly faces he tried to push away—his anxious mother; his imperious father—the occasional shock of buckling knees jarring him awake. At some point, he felt his arms droop out of their sockets, his knuckles brushing the cool grass.

Then dusk: the narrow twilight bristling with mosquitoes. In the hushed sky, a damp breeze picked up, stirring the shapes of the living, who clattered over those who couldn't or wouldn't move. Up front, the highest-ranking officer took command, hurrying soldiers across to the intact line of trees, beyond which a mountain loomed, breathing darkly. One by one, the men slipped away. When his turn came, he hustled with his group; the trees closed in; night morphed around him. Fumbling for the shoulder in front of him, he tethered himself, projecting his senses outward. The dark slowly settled. Soon the men fell into a rhythm, their shuffling lull broken only by the snap of branches and the occasional voice of the lost and panicked barking out in the dark.

October 30, 1944, 01:59

They were met by gas lamps: the retrenchment brigade. Stationed here for their final stand, they'd readied a trough of water and packets of reserved rice. Ahead, a field table had been set up, two clean-faced officers squabbling over who should get credit for what portion of the battle, the Army or the Navy. Collecting his share of the last Imperial rations, he made his way to a tree, near which a fire was popping, a ring of men warming their mess tins. There were no familiar faces, but the men opened their circle and offered him what looked like lizard. Adding his food to the fire, he peered at the happy light flickering around him. As a child, he'd hated bonfires, the way they'd furrowed the faces of the people he knew, revealing something sinister. Only his mother had appeared unchanged, the wavering shadows merely crumpling her face, showing the pleading look she got whenever his father reprimanded him. It stifled him even now to think of them, though he wouldn't object to his mother's winter nabe, the fish and vegetables that had nourished the broth. He lit a cigarette. It had been five days since he'd last pampered his lungs, and it pleased him to discover that the Golden Bat, far inferior to the Mikasa, repelled the mosquitoes just as effectively.

November 2, 1944, 11:45

The enemy charged with a force unstoppable by makeshift booby traps and rigged 89s. The mountain quaked; a confetti of human limbs. In the scramble he took a hit, a white explosion midway between his ankle and knee. The pain was shattering. When he coalesced, he was surprised to find himself moving, his pumping elbows propelling him forward. Most landmarks were gone, but he spotted a cave occupied by three men thrown together by the fray. Having combined and recombined many times, the men did not refuse him, but it was clear that each man's survival had been thrust on himself. Still, a tentative companionship

developed, their brisk exchanges—enemy
position, changing weather conditions—
shifting to a cautious sharing of anecdotes
before he took the plunge and offered his
name: Tanaka. The other three responded
immediately—the brawniest, Yamada; the
handsomest, Maeda; the tallest and highest
ranked, Kimura—each taking turns sharing
the contents of his pockets: a puff of cigarette, a cap of water, a taste of dried squid.

"Where did you get this?" Maeda asked,
sniffing the squid.

"Granny's technique," Yamada replied,
watching them savor the miracle of pro-
tein and salt. Yamada, it turned out, was a
fisherman's son. "Bet the last time you had
anything decent is when we torched that
village. Or did you miss that banquet?"

Tanaka remembered the raid, the sludgy
dream of moving through the burning ham-
let weeks ago. He had no idea Yamada had
taken part. He himself had been recruited
for it in the middle of the night, enticed by
the lure of a meal, but he never figured out
who had organized it, or how many had
participated; it wasn't anything anybody
talked about.

Maeda swallowed the squid but said nothing.

Kimura peered out of the cave. "Gentlemen, clouds are gathering. Get ready to go uphill." Kimura had functioned as a scout when they still had a function.

Tanaka retightened his tourniquet. Nobody had acknowledged his leg.

November 3, 1944, 07:04

The enemy, refreshed, stormed. Bodies piled up. Sunlight punctured the treetops, and a drowsy haze drifted through the mountain depths, its canopies breached for the first time by light. Seizing the island's water source, the enemy tapped the villages, arming the men raging to avenge their plundered fields and wives and daughters. The Imperial Army staggered; banzai cries flared. Now and again, parallel cries echoed from the enemy's side, but nothing slowed its advance. The Imperial Army buckled and fell, scattering its men into a tunnel of caves soon to be smoked out or dynamited or buried. Those who escaped broke out in fever, while others lost themselves in the jungle maze. Biding their time in the scooped darkness beneath a cliff overhang, the four banded men discussed a rumor Kimura had heard about boats supposedly hidden around the island. They argued and strategized, Tanaka's fear spiking as his leg warmed and festered, a hot primordial pool.

November 4, 1944, 23:20

Night again, and his wound acquired a new presence, its glittery pain illuminating it like the inside of a geode. He was beginning to sweat, shivery ripples skimming his skin like a breeze. Outside, the wind combed through the leaves, shaking out sounds that scuttled across the cave floor. Occasionally, flares popped, machine guns tutted, but even these had become intermittent. By now they were all accustomed to the fact of death, but the thought that **he** would die, cease to exist, terrified him. Like everybody else, he too had pledged his life, bragging of the exploits that would earn him a spot among the heroes enshrined in Yasukuni, but his bluster, rousing at the time, mocked him now. In the nineteen

years of his life he'd never felt so **material.**
Beside him, his companions were remi-
niscing about the girls they'd liked, first at
school, then at the comfort stations, their
voices, initially soft, turning lurid as they
passed around stories, fondling details and
names, the words fluttering and combin-
ing. Haruko, Haruko, Haruko. The one
girl he'd slept with, a girl from the comfort
station in Luzon. Slight and shiny-eyed,
she'd reminded him of a grade school crush
he'd never got over, and, for days, he'd prepared himself, what he'd say and do. But
primed for deployment, he'd been so keyed
up, the longed-for sensation so new, he'd
failed to contain himself, the rapture coming too soon, the mix of surprise and embarrassment making him strike out. He'd never
hit a girl before, and the contact, blunt and
sickening, wobbled his gut, scooping up
his balls. He'd apologized right away, but
Haruko, probably beaten many times, had
shrunk from him, trembling his hands so
badly he couldn't do up his drawstrings.
He'd vowed to return the next day, and the
next, until he'd proved to her that he wasn't

like the others, but he'd been shipped out the next morning, an age ago.

November 5, 1944, 01:12

His leg was a pulpy larva the size of a ripe papaya. At one point, Yamada cradled his head and said, **Drink**. And he drank, the swampy water sliding down his throat like an eel.

Another time, Maeda pushed something warm and chewed into his mouth, and he ate.

Still later, Kimura brought his mouth to his ear, but by then he was going, then gone.

November 5, 1944, 03:47

The theater of war has many back doors. Sometimes they're revealed to a foot soldier, accidentally.

November 10, 1944, 18:00

He stood on deck, hazy islands rising around him. Ahead, Yamada and Maeda were leaning on the railing, their absent companion, Kimura, winking in the gap between them. So far neither had been forthcoming about what had happened, but he'd gleaned that Kimura had located one of the fishing boats indeed hidden around the island.

Turning into the breeze, he marveled again at his presence, his scrubbed skin and stitched leg surreal in the sunlight. Even his pain was contained, its borders clean, purified of all traces of the caves and of the long craggy hike he didn't remember to the fishing boat now lashed to the side of this cruiser, the sole survivor of a chain of battles that had recently expelled the Empire from the Philippine Sea. It was miraculous their boat had intersected the cruiser. Then again it was no more miraculous than the fact that he hadn't been left behind.

Trading places with Yamada, he raised his binoculars. Out here, the water was green, its shifting surface, at once monotonous and beguiling, advantageous to those who lurked beneath it. Every lookout devised his own way to resist the dazzle, but, even so, he found his attention slipping among the waves, the rhythmic lull drawing him back to the island, all his comrades left there to be slaughtered like dogs. As Imperial soldiers, they'd stood by their fate, the honor of saving their families, saving their country, saving Asia, entrusted to them; that he'd been plucked from this destiny was a humiliation he couldn't apprehend, and his anguish, riddled with the guilty pain of relief, wound a noose around his heart. Why had he been spared? The waves rocked and lapped; the faces of his former platoonmates iridesced, as delicate as soap bubbles. Like them, he should've become a god, not a ghost clinging to borrowed time. And yet, whenever his mind roamed to his leg, he felt his chest flood with the shame of secret gratitude.

November 12, 1944, 08:00

In the military hierarchy, power is absolutely asymmetrical.

December 4, 1944, 21:00

Off the coast of Formosa, they were transferred onto a merchant marine vessel conscripted by the Sixth Fleet, the Navy's submarine division. Destination undisclosed, they knew only that they were headed to a naval outpost in the bowels of the Bungo Strait. On deck, he fished out a cigarette, enjoying the open air and water still under Imperial jurisdiction. Three hours ago, enemy torpedoes had sunk two of their transports, a total of 1,000 men, 220 enemy prisoners, and 1,100 tons of irreplaceable fuel, weaponry, and food lost to the sea. Surely it was another sign that he'd been spared for a reason, everything he'd done— running away at fifteen and falsifying his name and age to enlist—part of a grander plan. In fact, thinking back, it was obvious the gods had ensured his passage, and he cringed at how he'd spent his adolescence cursing fate for giving him a father who'd disdained the military so absolutely he'd vowed never to sign the consent form Tanaka had needed to join up. Ironically, it was his father, a proud and vocal doctor, who'd ended up paving Tanaka's way, getting himself arrested for forgetting the omnipresent ears pricked to catch any unpatriotic inflection. Tanaka, only six at the time, never forgot the policeman who'd burst into their home and slapped his father blue before hauling him away. It was this policeman Tanaka had approached nine years later when his father refused to sign the consent form, and it was this policeman who'd presented him to the right recruitment officer. The policeman had liked that Tanaka, needing a new name, asked if he could take his: Tanaka Jirō. It was one of the best moments of his life, and Tanaka, remembering this now, breathed; peace spread around him like a summer skirt.

At last the sacred mountains of Kyushu, darkened by curfew, broke the monotony of the night. It had been four years since he'd last seen these peaks, and the vista, so different from the festive panorama he remembered, reminded him again of the war's advancing frontier. How had his parents fared? By now they would've given him up for dead, his mother heartbroken, his father cursing the blight that was his only son, and this thought, evoking all the years he'd lived under his father's disapproval, plucked a nerve and sent a melancholic twang through him. How often had he dreamed of returning, head held high, chest lavishly decorated for the years he'd spent crawling among jungle snakes and leeches to repel the white devils who, with their forked tongues, sweetened their cheapest promises while plundering Asia right under the nose of Japan, their ally in the Great War? What he would've given to see his father bowed, his father who'd always belittled his ambition to serve the world the way he, Tanaka, believed to be right. But by the time anyone learned of his contribution to the Greater East Asia Co-Prosperity Sphere, he'd be gone, reborn eternally in history.

December 5, 1944, 09:00

Their weapon was introduced to them fitted atop a transport cart, its long body tapered at the front, four fins attached to the rear. Measuring 14.6 meters, the Kaiten was an enlarged version of the Navy's own Type 93, the world's fastest and longest-ranging torpedo. Boasting a speed of 30 knots and projected to carry a 1.55-ton warhead, a single Kaiten was said to be capable of sinking an aircraft carrier. Walking them to the rear, the commanding naval officer, Sub-Lieutenant Nagai, pointed out the rudders, the two propellers blooming above them like caged flowers: the Kaiten's diving planes. Explaining its propulsion system, he emphasized its quick launch capability, its impressive range: 23 kilometers at maximum speed, more than twice the range of any enemy torpedo. He showed them the periscope—a 15-meter extension—and invited them to look underneath. There, on the underbelly, was a hatch just large enough for human shoulders to pass through. They straightened.

"Private First-Class Yamada, Maeda, Tanaka, do you have any compunctions?"

The soldiers gazed at him; nobody had ever asked about their compunctions.

"I know you've served the Army—no doubt you did so courageously. What I'm asking is, are you ready to join the Navy to defend not just our country but our race from extermination?"

The men lifted their chests. "Yes, sir, we are."

"Are you sure?"

They glanced at each other, then at the

Sub-Lieutenant. What difference would it make? Behind them, the transport cart creaked, and the Kaiten shivered, its black body awaiting its vital component. Tanaka closed his eyes; the jungle's interlocking hands reached to smother him. "Yes, sir," they said, almost in unison.

"Do any of you have familial responsibilities?"

Yamada sucked in his breath. "No, sir," he said. Maeda also replied in the negative, but Tanaka hesitated. He was an only child, his family's sole heir. It was a technicality, and the question no doubt a formality, but his throat locked.

Sub-Lieutenant Nagai recited the conditions for exemption every soldier knew by heart.

He lowered his gaze. "Sir, I apologize. I have no responsibilities."

Sub-Lieutenant Nagai nodded. For a moment, he looked sympathetic. Then his face emptied. "Training will commence at 08:30. You'll start in the simulation room and report to me until my own sortie is decided. Yes, that's right," he told them. "I'm an officer, but I've decided to sortie as well. Dismissed."

February 6, 1945, 14:30

One knock on the hull, and he counted to ten. Despite two months of simulation, live training had a different feel to it, and his hands faltered, the sensation of the moving vessel distracting him. Diving crank, seawater valve. He forced himself to focus. The Kaiten's golden depth was 15 meters, deep enough to avoid detection but shallow enough for the periscope to poke above the waves. He opened the valve; the Kaiten drilled down. Even here, in the bay's relative calm, his path was crosshatched with currents. He squeezed the crank, rode the bumps. At 15 meters, he leveled off. Checking his angle, he waited for the water to slacken, then accelerated. The Kaiten leapt; he gripped the lever, but the Kaiten raked the reef, disturbing the ghost of a private whose cracked skull and fractured cockpit had sunk him into irrecoverable depths. Tanaka hung on. The Kaiten hopped, skipped, then lifted. Grabbing his stopwatch, he began counting, sweat ribboning his back.

Ten minutes later, he raised the periscope. Gray-blue sea. He checked his compass: Where was his target boat? He had seven seconds to look and retract. He swiveled to the right. Nothing but water, white sparkles playing like seabirds. He swiveled to the left. Two warning shots. He swung the periscope. Rocks! He cut the rudders and accelerated. Waves slammed against him. He fought the controls; his tail slid, bumped once, twice, then cleared. Two minutes later, his escort boat found him. A quarter of an hour later, he was on the pier, vomiting, sour scraps of his breakfast pelting the water like flesh.

March 3, 1945, 17:00

Victory for the Empire! Four vital hits: a transport, a destroyer, two heavy cruisers. It was good, but everybody wanted an aircraft carrier. He'd pictured it hundreds of times, his dead-center hit blowing up the biggest carrier in the water. He'd imagined the headlines, his dumbstruck parents, his soul enshrined in tragic glory at Yasukuni. All he needed were the coordinates to turn the tide of history. Then there would be nothing: just the sun and sea, the empty waves pebbling an island, all traces of the war gone, only his memory, snagged by rocks, blown about by a forgotten breeze.

April 12, 1945, 13:00

In war, information management is paramount.

But inevitably rumors slip from mouth to mouth. Like the death of Ensign Noguchi, the only Kaiten pilot to return from his mission unlaunched. He'd been discharged honorably, his cause for failure a technical malfunction. But a week on shore, he'd dispatched himself, a soft, unshelled torpedo splayed like a starfish in the rocks below.

Yamada, Maeda, and Tanaka sneaked out to the cliff edge to keep vigil for Noguchi.

April 18, 1945, 06:30

Three cheers for the sortieing pilots! He willed his legs to straighten, snippets of the

previous night hurtling back at him. Un-
accustomed to the free flow of liquor, his
head had spun almost immediately, blur-
ring the hours between the first toast and
the pounding sunlight; he'd barely made it
to roll call, his head swollen to the size of the
largest temple bell in Kyoto. Every New Year
it took seventeen monks to ring that bell,
and he felt like that bell now, rung by seventeen monks wishing to awaken him. One by
one, they tipped back their sake cups. Bowing deeply, they received their short swords,
then they were marching down the pier to
the I-55, the last of the Imperial submarines
to take them out to sea.

April 22, 1945, 04:30

Underwater by day, above by night, they
zigzagged across the East China Sea, cir-
cumventing enemy fleets amassing between
Formosa and the North Pacific. Below
deck, the submarine crew tunneled through
hatches, calling out numbers—air pressure, water pressure, coordinates—as they
searched for the cluster of aircraft carriers

thought to be headed toward Okinawa. Confined to their quarters, a single cabin outfitted with shelves of bunk beds bolted to the walls, the Kaiten pilots read, played cards, wrote. Yamada stood for the hundredth time and paced. "How long can it take to find a whole **fleet** of carriers?"

Maeda, sitting with a book, banged the metal floor. "If you lose your shit now, there's no way they're going to launch you. You want to end up like Noguchi?"

Tanaka, lying in his bunk, stared at the metal ceiling inches from his nose. He was a side sleeper, and rest had become intermittent, his body waking him every time it tried to turn, his shoulders too broad for the space. "We might never find any carriers. Better get used to that idea too."

Maeda tossed his book. "Who cares. This war is over anyway."

"Yeah? So why are you still here, then?" Yamada toed Maeda. "Why didn't you surrender to the white man when you had the chance? They wouldn't have given two shits about you, but you might've made it; they might've sent you back home to your ma."

Maeda swiped away Yamada's foot as he stood. A Formosan, he'd been sensitive about his status, rounding up the colonial conscripts on base to fight for their collective respect. He'd gotten it too, brandishing his well-honed Japanese to outcuss anyone who challenged him. "Don't talk like you care about the war. I know what you are. You're an opportunist. Lots of guys went after those island girls, but you—you're actually proud of it. You don't care about anything except pleasing yourself."

Yamada smirked. "Those were some good parties you missed. I guess they reminded you of your sisters, huh, Colonial?"

"You're sick," Maeda said.

Yamada laughed and flung an arm around his neck. "Come on, I'm an asshole. But don't say I didn't tell you. You should've surrendered to the white man when you could. As for me and Tanaka?" He drew a finger across his throat.

Tanaka closed his eyes. What they needed was a cigarette, the feel of fresh wind blowing down the conning tower.

April 27, 1945, 08:03

At the edge of the Philippine Sea, 75 meters deep, they picked up a signal moving rapidly toward them. Two escorts, and an unidentified vessel, possibly a cruiser. Unable to accelerate, the captain, risking sea pressure, dived deeper. Through the open density of water, they heard the faint sound of engines; each man gripped the nearest stationary object.

The first explosions rocked the submarine. The next snapped off the lights. Clinging to the railing, he listened to the shouts, the long list of damages barked over the shockwaves. Another boom, and steam hissed into his face. He dropped to his knees as the floor batted him into a cage of bolted table legs. Scrambling to latch on, he fought the swing of his body, but the floor pitched, and his head rattled like a sack of beans. He let go. A hand caught his wrist, and Yamada, moving like the fisherman he was, reeled him in. Minutes later the depth charges stopped. Two hours later, they surfaced, risking detection for air. On deck, all three Kaiten were astonishingly intact. The crew broke out a bottle of sake: one sip each to celebrate the miracle.

May 12, 1945, 15:21

At last the radar lit up, a microexplosion of lines: two long dashes followed by a third, a giant, flanked by many shorter ones. The captain descended to their cabin. With three Kaiten missions under his belt, the pilots' emotional threshold wasn't a mystery to him. He tapped the doorframe, and in a gentle, sturdy voice he described the state of the war, the risks and benefits of their options, the flaws and wastefulness of all except one. "Do you understand the importance of your task?" he asked. Yamada clenched his jaw. "We do," he said. When no protests followed, the captain gripped each of their hands. Three minutes later, the standby sounded.

May 12, 1945, 15:24

Stopwatch, flashlight, sea chart. Tanaka took them from his maintenance man. Flipping the light switch, he shimmied up the hatch into his seat. As usual, the air, cold and still, was faintly sour with rust. He buckled himself in. Diving crank, rudder controls, compass. Water grazed his metal skin. He checked the gyroscope, the start bar. All set: he rapped three times. The hatch below him screwed shut. He breathed, letting the first wave of panic break over him.

At last the captain's voice echoed through the earpiece. "Kaiten One, get set." Tanaka raised his periscope to look at Yamada, his long nose prehistoric in the green-black water. Yamada had wanted to be the first to pass Yasukuni's gates. Tanaka pumped his periscope three times, but Yamada didn't return the signal. Ten seconds later, Yamada's engine ignited; bubbles erupted from his tail. Then he was gone.

"Kaiten Two, prepare." Tanaka swung his periscope to the right. In the dim water, he could make out the tip of Maeda's vessel latched just aft of him. Before Noguchi's suicide, Maeda, a student conscript, had often fought with Noguchi, also a student, about a people's revolution that would or wouldn't come out of the war. It had seemed pointless, two Kaiten pilots passionate about a future they'd have no part in, but it had made everyone dream of a different life. He wasn't sorry when the talk stopped. The cables released, the engine whirred, and the glittery sound of bubbles carried Maeda away.

"Kaiten Three, prepare. Angle: forty degrees left. Range: ten kilometers. Enemy speed: eighteen knots. Course: two hundred forty degrees. Your target is a destroyer. Run full speed for twenty minutes, then check your position. Good luck. On your count."

Ten seconds later, he gripped the start bar and pushed it back.

May 12, 1945, 16:15

The ship was enormous. Even at 500 meters, it filled his vision. He panned to the left: no ships, no debris. He panned to the right. Where were they? He could've sworn he'd heard the detonations. He straightened his periscope; the destroyer streamed back, larger than a moment ago. He glanced at his stopwatch: time had vanished. He steadied his hands, adjusted his angle. In less than two minutes he'd blast through Yasukuni's gates. Fear aerated his veins. But out here, in the middle of the ocean, there was only one way to go. He flipped the activation switch and fired the engine to full throttle.

May 12, 1945, 16:17

Green sea; sparkles of light; the receding keel of the destroyer. He sat for a moment, staring at the depth meter. 17.5, 17.6, 17.7 . . . He rattled the diving crank; its empty glide plunged his stomach. 18.1, 18.2, 18.3 . . . He slammed the controls. A minute later, he flipped the self-detonation switch.

May 12, 1945, 16:55

The Kaiten continued its lonely descent, its one-and-a-half-ton nose towing it down. He pounded the hatch, jiggled the detonation switch. 35.1, 35.2, 35.3 . . . His legs began to twitch, a riot of muscles and nerves. 35.6, 35.7, 35.8 . . . The Kaiten's estimated crush depth was 400 meters; at his angle and speed, how long would it take to reach it?

The water crackled and swayed, gently letting him pass.

May 12, 1945, 17:35

A soft bump. He looked at the depth meter: 78.9. He pressed his eye to the periscope. The Kaiten had obviously hit a shelf, but with evening inking the water, it was impossible to see. He rattled the rudders. 78.9 meters. He banged the walls. The light blinked off. Shouting, he groped for his flashlight and snapped it on. The dark air swallowed its meager light, and a new fear studded his chest. He thumped the walls, shifted his weight from side to side. 78.9 meters. Outside, the water was a thick black curtain. It shifted and swayed but revealed nothing. A sob welled up in his throat. Then his bladder released.

May 12, 1945, 18:30

Submarine I-55, three Kaiten hits! Two destroyers and one transport. Banzai for the Shōwa Emperor!

Banzai
Banzai
Banzai

May 21, 1945

As they came to bloody grips with their exotic enemy, Americans were beginning to realize that to the Japanese mind (an entity utterly alien to them in culture and almost as uncontemporary with them as Neanderthal man), the Emperor Hirohito was Japan. In him was embodied the total enemy. He was the Japanese national mind with all its paradoxes—reeking savagery and sensitivity to beauty, frantic fanaticism and patient obedience to authority, brittle rituals and gross vices, habitual discipline and berserk outbursts, obsession with its divine mission and sudden obsession with worldly power. . . .
                              —TIME

August 6, 1945

"There was a terrific flash of light—
even in the daytime. . . . I could see
a mushroom of boiling dust . . . up
to 20,000 feet. . . ."
—Cpt. William S. Parsons,
weaponeer, ENOLA GAY

FIVE

PASSING

Once upon a time, there was a fisherman named Urashima Tarō who lived with his aging parents. One day, on the seashore, he came upon a gang of boys bullying a sea turtle and rescued it. The next day, when he returned from fishing, he found the turtle waiting with a gift: to take him to Ryūgū-jō, the Dragon Emperor's Undersea Palace. Clambering atop the turtle, Tarō journeyed deep into the ocean to a wondrous paradise where he was greeted by the enchanting princess Otohime. Time passed blissfully, but on the third day, Tarō, unable to forget his parents, asked to be returned home. Otohime was heartbroken, but pained by his unhappiness, she pressed a keepsake tamate-bako into his hand and, cautioning him never to open it, summoned the turtle. When Tarō arrived ashore, he saw immediately that something was different: he recognized no one. Rushing into town, he found everything changed. For days he roamed the unfamiliar streets searching for his home, but nobody knew anything. Eventually he came to a graveyard and learned the truth. Three days undersea had been three hundred years on land, and everyone he knew was dead. Devastated, Tarō flung the tamatebako to the ground. Out poured smoke and ashes, transforming him into an old man.

LUNA WHEELS her carry-on down the branching road to her grandparents' house. It has been more than two decades since she last visited this rural town in Kanagawa, and despite nine hours aboard a plane across the Pacific, she feels unprepared, the dusty road disorientingly familiar, the winding curve still blind with coniferous trees that incrementally reveal the shallow peak of the roof, the tinted top of the carport, and the quiet face of the house itself, with its sidelight window and stately door, the blue umbrella crock, faintly mossy from years of rain, holding the keys left there for her. The last time she faced this door, she was six and visiting her grandparents with her parents and sister. It was 1986, her grandfather was ill, and despite the tension between her parents, no one—not even her father, Luna believes—knew he'd end up staying behind in Japan and leaving them. Now, twenty-three years later, following a phone call from a Mr. Watanabe notifying the family of her father's death, Luna, the only one in her family who bothered to learn Japanese, has decided to return to sort the house before demolition.

On the surface, the two-story home has changed little. A patina has darkened the hardwood corridors and stairs, and a deep creak has settled into its bones, but otherwise everything seems unchanged, the corded telephone, the rack of guest slippers neatly in their place, all the windows, half-frosted for privacy, still dressed in 1980s elegance. Even the linens, though spotted and frayed without her grandmother's upkeep, appear not to have been replaced. It is as though her father, the sole occupant of the house for well over a decade since his parents' deaths, left no mark. It unsettles her, like walking into a wax museum of her own memory, its staged perfection emphasizing its barrenness, all its inhabitants departed, the silent walls and corridors turned against her trespass. Switching on the heater, Luna ventures down the hall to the only door left closed. Once her grandfather's sickroom, it has since been converted into her father's study, and it is here that Watanabe, her father's closest friend and colleague, has assembled a temporary altar to hold the urn. In the morning, she and Watanabe will inter it in her grandparents' grave at the nearby temple.

The altar is plain, just a white sheet covering a squat platform, the urn and a large monochrome portrait sharing space with a vase of flowers and two offering bowls, one holding rice, the other water, along with an incense burner, several sticks of incense, and matches—an allegedly unorthodox setup for which Watanabe has apologized, though he has done this for Luna, postponing the urn's interment and instead stopping by to

refresh the food and flowers for almost three
weeks while Luna completed her teaching
duties at Berkeley. She is grateful, of course,
though it is the photograph that transfixes
her, her father's face older than she has ever
imagined it but peering out with an expression she instantly recognizes: a temporary
seriousness breaking into delight. It loosens
a lid she has forgotten. Unlike her mother
and sister, her resistance to her father has
softened over the years, but so much about
him was buried by her parents' transpacific
separation, then divorce, the weekly international calls dissolving into annual birthday
cards that conveyed little of his personality.
It pains her that she never visited him—
something she considered several times in
recent years, prodded by her career (litera-
ture of the Japanese diaspora), tethered, as
she is well aware, to her absent father, her
illusory home. But like many things in
her life, she put it off, the immediacy of
the present unfailingly easier to prioritize.
This fact digs close to her bones, and as she
stands in the kitchen rinsing the offering
bowls, two things come to her: the mellow

timbre of his voice even when he scolded her, and the unrelated fact that her period is due and she is unprepared.

It is later, after she returns from the convenience store and calls Watanabe to inform him of her arrival, that Luna sees the boxes.

THIS IS what she knows about her father: Born sometime in the spring of 1945, he, like many of his generation, spent his life captive to the Second World War, his research, the initial reason he crossed the Pacific to the United States, taking an unexpected turn when his parents confessed that he was an orphan—a Korean war orphan—they'd adopted during the American Occupation. Her father, an exacting academic, would've objected to the term "war orphan," arguing that he'd been orphaned not by the war but by Japanese colonialism, which had forced his biological parents across the Korea Strait. Either way, what gripped him was the document his parents had shown him: a registration card bearing the name of his birthplace, Matsushiro, a small castle town in central Japan where, during the war, a labyrinthine underground bunker complex was built. Comprising miles of interlocking tunnels and designed to include a subterranean palace, the complex was never finished, but months before the war's end, certain of Japan's defeat, this was where the emperor expected to hide, negotiating the terms of surrender regardless of the human cost. Most records were destroyed, but historians estimate that five to ten thousand Koreans had toiled there, digging into the mountains with picks and axes, hundreds killed by dynamite blasts and cave-ins as well as malnutrition and other diseases Japan knew it had no resources to treat. Many who survived were abandoned, some executed for schematic secrecy, and among the incriminating sites excavated, several showed proof that military sex slaves had been housed there. Does this mean her father was a child of a forced Korean laborer, perhaps of a sex slave? All Luna knows is that his discovery of Matsushiro and his adoption spiraled him into a maze that catalyzed his return to Japan. The question is what he found at the center, the end of his trail.

———

WATANABE ARRIVES the next morning with containers of homecooked food. An unfussy, earthy man, he fills her father's fridge and assesses her warmly, pointing out her family resemblance: same chin and mouth; same thick hair black enough to shine blue. Which is fair: Luna has taken after her father almost entirely, a fact that has already caused confusion here, her American accent hiccupping her interactions because, visually, she passes.

"Ready?" He hands her the urn and carries the portrait to the backseat. A social advocate with a legal background, he met her father four years ago while poking around an old Imperial naval base for demographic information about the suicide pilots stationed there during the war. By the time they left the crumbling base, they were strategizing ways to protect and preserve neglected war sites and their stories. Luna could picture their partnership right away, their skills complementary rather than overlapping, both men interested in grounded activism. It corroborates the image she has carried of her father.

The drive is pleasant but disquieting.

Luna has anticipated changes, but this is a different town, with cookie-cutter houses sprouting in the backwoods, the bamboo and Zelkova groves corralled to a patch of community park. So different from what she remembers from her childhood visits, the winding footpaths and weedy shrines passed out of local memory, "local" now being a collection of outsiders, mostly suburbanites and retirees deposited by the economy's ever receding tide. Gone too are the neighborhood pharmacy, the shadowy stationery store, the bank of rice vending machines she once begged to operate. There was also a dank tunnel used, if she remembers correctly, as an air raid shelter during the Second World War, but she finds she can't ask. It's ridiculous, this place that figured so little in her life, but it prickles her throat, the erasure of her past made concrete by this evidence of change and the foolishness of memory that has clung to what was always a chimera, a tantalizing echo of the mind's desire to preserve an ephemeral moment.

"Everything's different. I feel like Urashima Tarō," she says, taking in the new hair salon, the chain convenience store, the renovated produce mart with stacks of instant food boxes out front. She is reminded of the boxes she found at the house. "Was my father thinking of moving?" she asks, watching the road curve into a pretty mountain forest. Her father's death, she knows, was unexpected: a heart attack.

"Not that I know of. Why?" He squints at the tip of the temple roof emerging above the trees in the distance.

She tells him about the boxes, seven in all, shoved into inconspicuous corners—under the coffee table, behind half-open doors—as if left there by a forgetful child. "They're full of paper—research, I think, but they're random." Since graduate school, Luna has followed her father's career, periodically running his name through academic search engines, thrilling at the discovery of a new article, the proximity of his views to hers a secret pleasure she wants to resent. But last year, three changes hijacked her attention: she finished her dissertation, got a job at Berkeley, and got married. The next time she searched her father's name was after Watanabe's phone call; heart stuttering, she combed through the results, but there was nothing new. Last night, seeing the boxes, she felt the same apprehensive excitement, but when she slit the tape, all she found were typed pages, the topics ranging and unrelated to any of his previous output, many of them fragments with no beginning or end, the dropped punctuation and missing citations eerie, like looking at a featureless body. She turned on all the lights in the house. "It's odd—I remember him being meticulous."

"Maybe they were meant to be recycled?"

"They were sealed, as if for a move—or maybe storage."

Watanabe has no reply. Following the signs to the temple lot, he parks, and they sit for a moment. Then, gathering the urn and portrait, they climb the shady steps to the main hall.

THE SERVICE is simple, with the elderly priest and his son taking turns to recite the sutras, the rhythmic beat of the mokugyo fish drum overriding the regiments of progressive time, transporting her to an adjacent sphere that seems harmonized with her jet lag. Rocked in the hammock of sound, hypnotized by her father's monochrome gaze observing her from the altar, she almost misses her cue to offer incense, and the hour vanishes, the final silence releasing her to earth, but barely. She carries the feeling with her to her grandparents' grave, a square plot with a stone pillar. She never thought this would be how she'd see them again, their names carved into granite, their two urns stowed side by side in the shallow chamber beneath. She feels curiously uplifted to see her father's urn join theirs, his a lighter gray but with the same domed lid. It is a pleasant day, the sun burning the morning chill, and it is only when Watanabe hands her the portrait retrieved from the priests that the finality hits her. And maybe this is true for Watanabe too, his face bereft beyond sympathy. She is glad the proceeds from her father's house will fund the initiative he started with Watanabe.

"When my father left our family, he was looking for his biological parents," Luna says as they wind back down the mountain forest. "Do you know if he found anything?"

Watanabe shakes his head. "I know he went to Matsushiro a few times."

Matsushiro. The last time she heard the name was through the static of the telephone straining to bridge the distance of the still new divorce. Now, hearing it come so readily from Watanabe's mouth, it registers sepia-toned and slightly bitter, like oversteeped tea. Almost sixty-five years after the end of the Second World War, the battle over the narrative of history and who might control it—her father's lifelong concern— seems to be intensifying, not lessening, with regional stability hanging in the balance as the world, strained by old frustrations and new restlessness, creaks and shifts, exposing unresolved fault lines normally buried under market priorities. In fact, Luna has arrived to find the whole of East Asia focused on whether the new Japanese prime minister will visit the Yasukuni shrine, home to two million uniformed war dead, including Class-A war criminals from the Second World War. During the American Occupation, authorities proposed burning down this emblem of nationalism and building a dog track—a perfect encapsulation of American democracy if ever there was one—but the shrine, permitted to survive, has endured as a symbol of Japan's refusal to face its war responsibilities. Most prime ministers, under heavy media scrutiny, have distinguished their personal pilgrimages from their official ones, often refraining from the latter for diplomacy, but several have made visits amid international outcry and even made noise, despite popular opposition, about revising the country's pacifist constitution—a move continually encouraged by the United States government, which started pushing for it almost immediately after ghostwriting that very same constitution during the Occupation. Luna recalls how upset her father used to get reading his Japanese newspapers in the living room of their Victorian nestled just off campus in Urbana. She cringes to remember how urgently he tried to explain, but it seemed so distant, utterly irrelevant. It was the same when he discovered his roots. "So he talked about it? His identity, I mean," she says.

Watanabe, catching the shift in her tone,

glances at her. "Not really. But his commitment to the Korean people's stories during the war touched a lot of people. You should've seen the funeral wreaths."

To be a product of a history—to feel the weight of that legacy—Luna feels a flash of envy. It gave her father a clarity of purpose she feels she lacks. With fewer people left every year to tell the lived stories, she can understand why he invested in the past—to expose not just the buried roots of history but the fragile bedrock of the future vulnerable to the human propensity not only to forget and repeat but to be ignorant and led. "It must have been fulfilling," she says, modulating her tone. "These days the past gets buried so quickly. People don't see the relevance, or they don't want to. Even my students get defensive about things that happened two hundred years ago. A country like Japan can be at the forefront of a peace movement, but that's not what's happening. I can see why he came back."

Watanabe flicks the turn signal and joins the midday traffic radiating from the town center. "Like your father, I became politically aware during the sixties and seventies.

Your country had your movements; we had ours, and one of our flash points was the future of your military in our country. I'm proud that most of us continue to be allergic to war, but will that change? Will our government force that change? What will people do?" He talks about China and North Korea, the logjam with South Korea. "The truth might be that we've all come to rely on this history. It's the perfect narrative. It helps our neighbors nationalize, which helps our government rally its base, the voters who want a stronger Japan. Your father was tireless, but his frustration was real. It took a toll."

Luna, chastened, swallows her own sense of futility infecting her heart. "It's such a bind." She tells him about an article she read about a Japanese scientist working on an irrigation system in a Chinese village. His happiest moment hadn't been his project's success but the villagers' acceptance of him after months of hostility and mistrust; they couldn't believe the Japanese could be kind. "Of course, we've hung onto our version of the narrative too, in America: World War Two was our last 'unambiguous' war.

It still gives us leverage. It's easy for us to tell others to move on, get along, not drag around old issues."

"It's not so different here, thanks to our economy," Watanabe says. "In very different ways, I think for countries like yours and mine, the issue is that war has become a metaphor. There are real wars, real costs to wars, but they've largely been outsourced, and daily life is peaceful."

And this, she thinks, is true. The perfectly paved streets flanked by perfectly unlittered sidewalks fluttering with festive bargain banners: even here, beyond the cities' cosmopolitan polish, there is little to remind people of the war. At the same time, the war is omnipresent, rearing up in conversations not just as history but as current event. This morning, she found herself riveted to a news program discussing the problem of American military misconduct in Okinawa. It was just a segment among the day's topics, but it was a jolt. Murder, drunk driving, burglary, with rape and battery of women and children leading the list. In Italy and Germany, the American military respects national laws; here, quite literally,

it gets away with murder, disrupting cities
and neighborhoods in other ways too: sonic
booms at all hours of the night; new tactical
vehicles no doubt too unstable to practice
over American cities routinely careening
out of the sky, loose parts sometimes striking school grounds. She knows there have
been protests, but the daily congregations
around American bases have been a surprise, little of it picked up by the media
back home. If yesterday her accent made
her self-conscious, today she feels ashamed.
She has never felt so American. "Everything
feels so volatile; it's an eerie peace. I find it
remarkable that people here aren't more resentful of America." She wonders if resentment too can be outsourced, and to where,
but doesn't ask.

THEY SEE the woman standing by the
gate when they come around the curve
toward the house. She is short, maybe in her
fifties, dressed in a style not of this town.
Watanabe doesn't recognize her, and Luna
catches herself matching the woman up with
her father, surprised by the twinge of pos-
sessive suspicion that constricts her chest.

"I'm sorry to bother you," the woman says when they emerge from the car. "I'm looking for Masaaki-san. He—oh." She stares at the monochrome portrait.

"You knew my father?"

"Your father?" The woman's eyes leap to Luna's face. "I didn't—"

"I live in America," Luna says, perhaps a little brusquely.

The woman nods slowly. "I'm sorry. My name is Yagi. I run a boardinghouse in Tokyo." She rummages in her handbag and produces a business card: HOUSE OF HOPE. The address is unknown to Luna, but Watanabe homes in on the area, and in a moment he and Yagi are discussing land-marks. Luna, unsure what to think, invites them inside.

The house is messier than she thought, the stacks of paper taken out of the boxes edging into the hall. As she ushers them into the kitchen, she notices Yagi, clearly a stranger in the house, looking around with quiet curiosity. Luna can't decide if she's relieved. When they settle, Yagi tells them about the boardinghouse and Luna's father's weekly visits since the summer. "Miyagi-san really looked forward to it. So when your father didn't come for three weeks in a row . . ."

Luna turns to Watanabe, who looks equally blank. "I'm sorry. Who is Miyagi-san?"

Yagi assesses them for a beat. Then her gaze slides to the portrait propped on the counter, and a look of disappointment crosses her face before grief covers it over. "Miyagi-san is one of our residents. He's been with us since my father started our place right after the Occupation. Miyagi-san is your grandparents' biological son. Your father's brother."

Luna stares at her. "You mean, he's my uncle?"

"He never mentioned a brother," Watanabe says, equally stunned.

"They only met about a year ago," Yagi says. "Miyagi-san was separated from his parents during the air raids. Back then, my father managed a welfare shelter. The Heavenly Curtain Hotel's House of Hope. It was literally stitched together with tarps." She smiles. "Miyagi-san was just a teenager then, and my father liked him right away.

I was born toward the end of the Occupation. Miyagi-san is like an uncle to me."

"So he was in Tokyo all this time?" Luna asks. "I didn't even know my grandparents ever lived there."

"As far as I know, Miyagi-san was born in Tokyo," Yagi says. "Like many after the war, there was no way for him to prove his identity, so he took odd jobs, mostly day labor, and helped my father around the shelter. He was involved in those peace protests too, but he was vague about his activities. He was always secretive."

"How did they find each other?" Luna asks, trying to absorb the details.

"Miyagi-san volunteers at a nonprofit called Sanyūkai, an organization that helps the homeless. A couple of years ago, he got very sick and started talking about finding his parents' grave. Most people ended up in common graves after the firebombing, so I don't know what he expected, but with Sanyūkai's help, he eventually found your father."

"And they had no clue about each other."

"Your father knew—your grandparents told him at some point—but his shock

when he opened the door to see him alive—
that's a story I've heard many times."

Luna tries to picture it: two men, unrelated but related, meeting for the first time
at the threshold of their parents' house.
"I can't imagine," she says. "Did they get
along?"

"Oh, they were always yakking on about
something. I guess they had a lot to catch
up on."

She likes the image: the companionship
of two orphan brothers. Then she pictures
Miyagi in the corridor of this house, peering into the rooms, the lived spaces his parents had inhabited without him. "This is
just so strange. How often did they see each
other?"

"Maybe a couple of times a month," Yagi
says. "Until Miyagi-san got sick again this
summer. It's his lungs—from the firebombs.
It was the same with my father—he was
about your father's age when he died." She
looks sorrowfully at Luna.

"How is he doing now?" Watanabe asks.

"He has good and bad days. Actually"—
she brightens—"if you have time, maybe

you can visit. I don't think Miyagi-san ever imagined meeting his niece."

Luna feels a stab of panic, the flutter in her throat not excitement but closer to fear. "He probably doesn't know I exist."

Yagi reaches across the table and touches her hand. "Let's see. I know Masaaki-san has two daughters. You lived in the state of Illinois. I've seen a picture of you. You were probably nine or ten. There was a house in the background. I think it was your house in the town called Urbana."

Luna feels a spiraling. "I don't remember this picture."

THAT EVENING, as she sorts more paper in the boxes into proliferating piles, a familiar twinge in her uterus propels her to the bathroom. Not yet.

When she finally lies down in the guest room, she dreams of an undersea journey to the Dragon Emperor's palace, but when she gets there she finds herself in a windowless room, lit by a missing bulb, a cord dangling from the empty socket. There is no sound, no sign of life, and when she reaches to pull the cord, she realizes that even she isn't in the room and wakes herself up. It is the first time she has had a dream in which she isn't there.

Unable to fall back asleep, she lies in the dark, watching the moonlight stencil the guest room window on the floor, and finds her thoughts drifting back to the last time she saw her father. After four years of separation, he'd returned to the States to make the divorce official. Like most of her childhood, the memory has survived largely voiced-over by her sister's rehashing of all the incriminating things their father had said and done in the two hours they'd spent with him, but recently Luna's recollection has been quieter, the years having peeled back the noise, baring the moment in starker detail, starting with Katy's refusal to tolerate him in their house. They ended up at a restaurant, Luna oppressed by her pasty chicken dinner with its mound of mashed potatoes inexplicably shaped into a cone, and the way her father kept mushing it down as he chatted on, asking questions and encouraging answers, his face flickering, then dimming, going out all together when he got up to pay. They drove back to the house and stood in the yard while his face slid into a watery mess so disconcerting even Katy conceded to his snotty anaconda hug. Luna too conceded, but a peculiar numbness had slackened her body, and she found she couldn't move, not even to accept his gift: an illustrated, bilingual edition of **Urashima Tarō**, which, with its cartoonish colors, Luna could tell was meant for a child much younger than her. Now she sees the point had been the dual-language feature probably meant to invite her to learn his language. As it happened, Luna did learn, and the fairy tale became a kind of epigraph to her career, but of course her father will never know this. It must have been then, just before he climbed into his rented sedan, that he snapped the photograph Yagi had seen, but that moment, like many others in her life, is gone, curated out of her memory by the great adjudicator of experience.

THE HOUSE of Hope is a short walk from the station. A historically segregated neighborhood of tanners, butchers, and executioners, the area has since been integrated into neighboring districts, its

myriad workers' lodgings now attracting
foreign backpackers increasingly conspicuous among day laborers, the unemployed,
and the homeless, almost all men, many of
them once part of the postwar workforce
recruited to rebuild the country. Watanabe
points out Sanyūkai. The building looks
derelict, but there is a lively throng outside
gathered by the organization's outreach ef-
forts and its lifeline services. Farther down,
among a boxy coterie of illuminated signs,
they find Yagi's boardinghouse, its tinted
glass doors busy with notices advertising
rooms in Japanese and English.

Yagi warms and rises from behind the
counter when she sees them. "Miyagi-san
was hoping you'd come," she says as she
retrieves a set of keys from the pegboard
and leads them through the hall, past the
kitchen, the toilet, the communal bath,
then up the stairs to a corridor crowded with
doors, the occasional murmur of the television brightening the hall. Miyagi's room is
at the far end. Knocking gently, Yagi listens,
then inserts the key.

The room is tiny and as dark as the
curtains allow. In one corner there is a

nightstand with a myopic black-and-white TV; above it, a shelf with a few folded clothes and several books. A futon takes up most of the tatami floor, Miyagi's body indistinct under the covers. Luna can just make out a hospital mask covering his face, and she is reminded of her grandfather, his sudden presence warping her sense of time, folding the two halves of her life into a single dimension of space. The experience is dizzying, almost exhilarating. Yagi shakes off her sandals and kneels beside the unmoving man.

"We don't have to wake him," Luna says from the doorway.

"At some point, everyone has to eat, do their business, see a few faces." She checks Miyagi's forehead. "He was excited to meet you."

Luna wonders if this could be true; luminously pale, Miyagi looks unearthly. Watanabe, perhaps sharing her thoughts, catches her eye. She wonders how well Miyagi was the last time her father saw him. She wonders if he knows about his brother's death.

Yagi turns down the covers, refills the water cup, her movements practiced and unflinching. Miyagi, discomfited, directs an uncertain voice into the room. "It's just me, Miyagi-san." She touches his hand. "You have visitors today, remember?" She introduces Luna and Watanabe, repeating their names several times before helping him sit up. In the gloom, he looks diaphanous, a black cutout.

Yagi molds his hands around his water cup and changes his mask before gathering the laundry and the water jug. "He should be fine for about a half hour," she says, shuffling into her sandals and nudging Watanabe to follow her out.

Suddenly alone, Luna tugs off her shoes and sits at the foot of the futon. Propped against the wall, cup tipped on his chest, Miyagi looks asleep again. In the window, the curtains ripple, the cold slip of air carrying the tang of smoke. She wonders what her father must have felt coming here, to this world Miyagi has been relegated to spend his life. The curtains flip; light splashes the wall, and Luna sees a photograph tacked up near Miyagi's head: a family portrait of a grade school boy flanked by his parents— her grandparents? She cranes to look and startles to find Miyagi observing her, his eyes alert.

"I'm Luna," she says. "You knew my father—your brother."

Miyagi continues to observe her. Then he raises a shaky finger and draws down his mask, revealing a narrow chin, an old man's mouth, a face gripped by keloid scars. One rarely sees such disfiguration here, the culturally unsightly still often hidden, and she wonders if this is also why he kept to the margins. "Is that you?" she asks, pointing at the photograph. Miyagi doesn't respond, and heat rises to her ears. She finds it hard to reconcile his eyes with the rest of him, their lucidity belonging to another time. "You must be standing with your parents—my grandparents."

Miyagi continues to stare, and Luna finds herself searching for an exit strategy. Then his mouth moves, and again she feels the pull of his gaze. She leans closer. She catches the wheeze and rattle clotting his chest, the phlegmy reek wafting from his mouth, the acridity of medicine mixed with something organic. She picks out a sound—a word: konomi. Preference. For what? Then there is a thud in the hall, the clatter of shoes as Watanabe returns, and when Luna turns to greet him, Miyagi grips her wrist. The contact is so sudden Luna flinches, but Miyagi doesn't let go. Trembling, he lifts himself, a muscular energy moving him, anger and alarm transfiguring his face as he begins to shout. From down the hall, she hears Yagi running. In a moment she is at the door, scattering her sandals, directing Luna to step back as Miyagi convulses into a violence of coughing.

THE TRAIN is quiet ahead of rush hour, and they glide the few stops to the office her father shared with Watanabe, the aftershock of the afternoon vibrating between them. Several times, Watanabe has mentioned a folder he feels she should have, but Luna knows it's also his way of inviting her to the place where her father spent most of his time before his death. After the boardinghouse, the office, a single room in a five-story walk-up, feels almost spacious, though with little more than a table, two chairs, and a bank of filing cabinets, it resembles a low-budget TV police interrogation room, marginally improved by the dorm room fridge, the small hotplate and kettle, a crown of American mugs ringed around a plate of bagged tea. Her father, she remembers, was never without a mug, nursing it close to his chest as he chatted up a neighbor or colleague, throwing out incorrect playground slang whenever Luna and her sister Katy drifted within earshot. It made Luna laugh but drove Katy mad, the difference between them encapsulating the family divide. Luna never knew where she belonged.

Watanabe scrapes back a chair. "This was your father's spot."

Luna assesses the foldout, its gunmetal frame and vinyl seat. When she sits, she finds it comfortable, the sun pressing on her back, the practical tabletop spread in front of her. Her father must have enjoyed it here, but all she can picture is his stiff back peeling away from the chair, his clammy forehead smacking the corner of the table. She stands.

"Do you think my father was planning to ask Miyagi-san to move in with him?"

Watanabe turns, hands poised over the file drawer. "That could explain the boxes."

"Does it? There's plenty of room in the house; he didn't have to pack. Why do you think my father never mentioned him?"

Watanabe pauses again, then shakes his head. "Your father never did anything without a reason, but I admit it was a surprise."

Luna pictures her father in Miyagi's dark room. Orphans from opposite sides of history: it's as though the war had swapped their destinies, catapulting her father into what might have been Miyagi's life, and Miyagi into what could easily have been her father's life had he not been adopted. She can't imagine that the irony was lost on her father: he, the son of the colonized, living the life of the colonizers' son, while Miyagi labored on the fringes, building structures that would never benefit him. It's a grotesque reversal, and there should be no room for resentment or guilt, but feelings follow their own paths. She thinks of the photograph on Miyagi's wall, its odd placement, as though tacked up to be seen—by her father? She banishes the image of Miyagi's outrage.

Watanabe finds the folder and secures it in a manila envelope before handing it to her. Luna is curious, but she's glad for the excuse not to look.

"I have to say, that was strange back there," he says, watching her wedge the envelope into her tote. "Right before Miyagi started yelling, he looked at me. It was like he knew me."

Luna feels a quiver in her belly. "Actually, just before you came back to the room, he said something. 'Konomi,' I think."

"As in 'preference'?"

Luna nods. "All of a sudden he was so present—just **there.**" It feels unfair to think she just met her last known relative on this side of the world, only to find him across a crease in time she can't reach. "I can't believe I actually met my uncle."

Watanabe watches her rub her wrist still garlanded with the memory of Miyagi's fingers. "There's something I've been meaning to ask. Did you ever try to contact your father?"

Luna has braced for this question. She tells him about her first year in graduate school, where, for the first time, she found herself among people who, unlike her sister and mother, recognized themselves in her.

It was an empowering experience, desolate in the end, the inelastic limits of community banishing her for those parts of her that didn't fit. She thought of her father. A simple correspondence, maybe a scholarly one: weeks of false starts and tangled emotions, she gave up.

"Back then I wanted too much too specifically, and I was afraid of being disappointed. I was twenty-one; I assumed I had time," she says. "It's what happens when your life is shaped by someone who isn't there. My father was who I thought of when my family and friends fell short of understanding me. And he felt **real**. That's the thing about absence. It retains the possibility of a return even if it's not probable. And it made a lot of things possible. It let me imagine another place where I might belong. It helped that I look like him." This, she realizes, is true. Funny how the ties of blood, expressed physically, have the power to seduce you into believing the bond is real, elemental enough to transcend the gulf of time and distance, when, really, it's likely nothing more than a mirage granted the force of reality by mundane evidences habitually reinforced, like the tension that used to crimp not only her mother but also their neighbors whenever they saw her father's shape lurking in her face. "I guess he's gone," she says.

Watanabe is quiet for a long moment. "It's complicated for you," he says, finally. "For what it's worth, I know he always assumed you'd visit."

IT IS past seven by the time Luna returns to the house. Settling at the kitchen table, she slides the folder from the envelope and spreads its contents, sweeping the receipts to one side. She spent her whole train ride learning her father's lunch habits: noodle sets (¥990); curry specials (¥1090); the occasional bookstore purchase, including, curiously, a translation of Jorge Luis Borges's labyrinthine stories. The rest of the folder is more personal. She couldn't face it on the train.

The least complicated is the registration card. Time has buffed it to a featureless shine, but the name of the town, Matsushiro, is still clear, as is the year of issue, the twentieth year of Shōwa, along with the red lacework of stamps pressed into the surface like lipstick.

What pains her most are the glossy brochures from the 1980s collected from various international schools around the city. All her life Luna was led to believe her father's departure was unilateral; now, it seems that at the very least he'd envisioned their life here. At most there had been talk between her parents that failed. Useless now to reassign blame, if there is blame to reassign, but she feels her world tilt, the story of her life poised to change.

The third item is mysterious: an address in Niigata scrawled on a notecard. A friend? A colleague? Another family member? All she finds when she looks it up is an unremarkable dot in a region famous for its rice production.

The final item is the most haunting: a sheaf of stapled pages containing a smattering of newspaper clippings, retrieved, it seems, from microfiche. The scan is good, preserving the analog texture of ink on newsprint, each article, just two or three lines, a variation on the same theme: unidentified women of "dubious" ethnicity and profession found murdered in red-light areas during the Occupation.

The last stapled page clarifies nothing: a block of text copied, Luna will later learn, from a zuihitsu written by a Japanese American poet. Floating in the center of the page without context, it provokes a strange feeling, like falling into a chasm, the white gap between languages, where there is a sensation, tip-of-the-tongue, but no words to attach to it.

When nuns interviewed Koreans in Hiroshima after the bomb, the survivors drew a blank. When inadvertently questioned in Japanese, one began to wail and recall the horrors. Others could also recall it in Japanese, but not in their mother tongue.

What does it mean to remember in one language, but not the other, the mother tongue?

What does it mean to survive, witness to an attack so negating of life it gutted your brain, eradicated your voice, leaving you blank-faced with a mouth that opened only when prodded by the colonizer's tongue?

Why did her father file all this here?

SHE SEES Watanabe one last time. She is out back, the contents of the house up-ended in the yard, when he stops by with her father's favorite mug.

"Sorting the recycling?" He eyes the piles, rolling up his mental sleeves. "My wife and I are free tomorrow."

"I'm pretty much done," she says. And this is true. Her father has left little in the end: just shelves of books, a few clothes, and the boxes. The rest are leftovers car-ried over from the previous generation: the duct-taped rice cooker, pots with miss-ing handles, an assortment of supermarket plates and bowls. It seems paltry, these in-herited things he'd adapted his life to, living among them as though he were a bracket, a temporary graft in the family genealogy. Yet there is also something appealing about a life stripped to the essentials, everything in the process of being used up, its whole lifespan spent.

She says as much to Watanabe as she

changes her shoes for what will be her last walk through the neighborhood. It is a clear day, the sky an opulent blue, and she can see that on a day like this the town does boast spectacular views of the country's famed mountain.

"I suppose I do see what the fuss is about," she says. "It's surreal."

Watanabe glances at the specter that has loomed over his entire life. "That mountain makes it too easy to believe we're one big homogenous family."

"I always thought that was a Western stereotype until I learned it's also what this country sells. It's a convenient narrative. Japan the homogenous; America the diverse. We can look at each other to confirm our own fantasy image of ourselves. It's a flattering mirror. One in which minorities either disappear or are cloned."

"Well, you've clearly inherited your father's cynical streak," he says. "From my vantage, America **is** diverse; unlike here, people can **become** American in America."

Luna shakes her head, frustration rising. "America is black or white. I can't tell you how often I'm asked where I'm **really** from.

Most of the time, we're not part of the national conversation, unless we're needed as a model, the proof triumphant of the American Dream, or as faces for People of Color campaigns—or that's how it can feel. Right now, we're not the ones fearing hate crimes and roundups, but it's easy to imagine— it's not like it hasn't happened before. All it takes is a war. It gets old figuring out where I belong."

Watanabe considers this, the permutations of her grievances rooted in a history so umbilical to her identity as an American. "When your father discovered his Korean roots, he said it changed his relationship to his work. But did it change his sense of himself? I can't answer that for him, but I know that, by the time I met him, his concern wasn't where he belonged but how **he** wanted to fit in."

"That's an interesting distinction," Luna says, feeling the loss of one more conversation she'll never have with her father. "Not everyone has that choice, though. Being here, I keep thinking about **Urashima Tarō**. My father told us that story so many times my sister and I started dreaming of evil magic boxes." She laughs. "It wasn't until I read it for a class in college that I saw it as a cautionary tale about leaving home. It's how I've been teaching it: as an allegory of exile. Now I wonder if it's actually the opposite: a moral about being too attached to our roots."

"Because Urashima Tarō could have stayed in paradise?"

Luna nods. "There's also a price for staying, though: he has to give up his ties to the human world. He has to forget his roots— forget who he is."

"Is that wrong? Can people never have a new life?"

Luna doesn't answer right away. Is forgetting a prerequisite for a new life? "I suppose it depends on if memory is a choice. In Tarō's case, he **couldn't** forget because he's human."

They are quiet as they concentrate on climbing the road corkscrewing up the slope, staggering houses, wrinkling walls, mocking the developers who had to concede to these mountains despite the technologies that brought them here. At the top, they pause to catch their breath before continuing through the backwoods where the houses are older, more resplendent, separated by stone walls above which Luna can see the domes of ornamental trees hinting at gardens often replicated on a grander scale in botanical parks. Next time—if there is a next time—will these be gone too, sold off by their inheritors to make way for the new?

"The thing I like about fairy tales is the variation," Watanabe resumes. "In every version I know, Urashima Tarō suffers for his attachments and returns to shore. In every version, he opens the tamatebako. But I don't think he's punished for being human. The tamatebako is a mercy."

The interpretation is generous, she thinks, but one that doesn't change the known story. What if, she thinks, Urashima Tarō **had** remembered Otohime's warning and not opened the box? Because in all the versions, that's the unexplored story. She is reminded of her father on that last family visit here, how intent he'd been on showing them the sites, not the big established attractions they wanted to see, but the vulnerable local ones, trying to impart something of his own lived story. At the time, it was hard to understand. Now she finds herself gripped by what will happen when she leaves Japan with no ties left to return to.

"I always felt strange in my own country, even my own family," Luna says. "But I feel strange here too. It's strange to feel connected to a place you've only visited a handful of times as a child. It makes no sense. What does America or Japan—or, god, Korea—mean to me? What did it mean to my father? What should it **mean** in our world? Because as far as I can see, all it does is create destruction." She swipes a fallen branch off the path. "I think I'm pregnant."

Watanabe turns to her, surprised. Then he looks pleased, then mournful, then somber, as he shares this new weight of her father's death. Luna is glad when he doesn't sentimentalize it. "I like how in America people keep their ethnic roots, either as a middle name or with that convenient hyphen in your language," he says. "But you never changed your last name."

Luna remembers the decision, the agonized waffling before the wedding, the fear of untethering that seized her. "I suppose if I'm really pregnant I'll have to sort that out.

It's funny. I've always pictured myself with a boy, but I've always been set on the name 'Erin.' I had a childhood friend with that name. My father made it sound so pretty the way he pronounced it. I used to wish it was mine."

IN THE end her father's roots are indeterminable. The Korean laborers, accounting for seventy percent of the workforce at Matsushiro, were indisputably the majority, but there were also three to five thousand Japanese workers and officers present, and it is ultimately unclear who had access to the ten or twenty women kept there to satisfy and subdue them. It is also unclear whether all the women were Korean, or whether, as in many "comfort" units, there were Japanese and maybe Chinese women as well. The biggest mystery is how a newborn had managed to survive the mountain site so prohibitive of life itself.

Her father might have come to a similar conclusion, judging by the most recent manuscripts she has found in the last box she discovered, hidden the whole time by the white sheet Watanabe had spread over it for the altar. The manuscripts are all dated this year, the newest not a week before his death, each an attempt to write not his history, it turns out, but his own story, beginning with the lacquered box his mother produced from the closet, the sealed lid hiding the registration card that would change his life—then nothing, the paragraph and sentence abandoned, sprouting question marks underlined twice, a particularity that chills Luna, who recognizes her own habits there.

Like all the rooms in this house, the study is bright, lit by a wide window below which sits his desk, now clear of the laptop and hard drive and the jar of pencils he'd kept there. Like the pencils, the laptop and hard drive were well used, but when she booted them up she found not a single file, each reset to factory condition. What finally undid her, though, was the plastic bag she found in the filing cabinet stocked with hanging folders that still hugged the shape of the documents her father had boxed up and scattered around the house. It contained picture frames, all empty, and a single scrapbook started in the 1950s that held photos of her grandparents and also, surprisingly, the one of Luna, Katy, and their mother stenciled like bright cutouts against the dim backdrop of their house in Urbana, but none of her father—just rectangles holding the places where he'd been. She found no letters, no postcards, not even one of the birthday cards they'd stamped and sent, and these are the things that will haunt her at odd hours throughout her life.

Yet in less than a day, Luna will wheel her carry-on up the aisle of the plane, jittery with exhaustion but anticipating the moment she will see her husband and tell him the news. It'll be a portentous moment, the flash of excitement and fear awakening a restlessness inside her. For just hours before her flight, after declining Watanabe's offer to see her to the airport, she'll rush around her grandparents' house, shutting off the gas and electricity, locking doors and storm windows, knowing she'll be the last family member to set foot in it. It'll be a peculiar moment, already imbued with nostalgia, the once cold rooms, warmed by familiarity, reminding her of the hours she spent rooting for answers and finding only traces

of a man seemingly bent on evicting himself. Or at least that will be what she'll be
forced to conclude, the walls and corridors
now forever incontestable in their silence.
And for the first time she'll feel herself surrender, the old hurt and budding regret
crushed beneath the weightier sorrow of departure and the slow panic of the uncertain
future opening her chest.

What, for example, should she do with
the boxes?

When Luna calls Watanabe, he will offer
her his shed, and she will eagerly accept,
even though it will make no sense. In fact, it
would be satisfying to see her father's boxes
gutted and broken down, the piles of flat
cardboard cut to size and bound for recycling. For her part, she will take only three
things: the scrapbook, the folder, and the
mug. By then it will be clear there is no one
there in that house. She has waited too long.
They waited too long. They had already
passed each other in the night.

PAVILION

Isolated more than twenty miles beyond the gate of Dugway Proving Ground [in Utah] . . . lie the remains of German-Japanese Village, where replicas of German and Japanese buildings were constructed . . . to test incendiaries for use in World War II. Even today special clearance is required to get to what remains of the testing site, and locating it amid the interconnecting labyrinth of seemingly nameless and featureless roadways is difficult.

—DYLAN J. PLUNG, "THE JAPANESE VILLAGE AT DUGWAY PROVING GROUND"

"It's funny," Seiji said when Masaaki walked into the cloistered room billowing with light blown in through the cheap powder-blue curtains. "Here you are, coming in from the sunshine to visit me in the dark, but we're not all that different, are we?" A statement iridescent with—was it mockery?

Masaaki closed the door, cutting off the light from the boardinghouse hall and leaving the man before him backlit, his oval head and craggy shoulders looming like prehistoric cliffs. In the last month, Seiji had declined alarmingly, his spindly frame bereft of flesh, his head, once vigorously snowcapped, as threadbare as a combed beach. The war, concluded almost sixty-five years ago, had ravaged his throat and lungs, leaving the peaks and valleys of his health chasing each other unpredictably. The boardinghouse manager, who'd been renting to Seiji for decades, claimed she'd seen him worse, but it was clear that for him the peak had never seemed so far. From here, there would only be valleys.

Masaaki leaned his satchel against the wall and sat in his usual spot at the foot of the futon, the worn tatami faintly sour: the imprint of generations of sweat. "How are you feeling?" he asked.

Seiji ignored him, and for a moment they listened to his wheeze, the shuck and whistle steady in the loom of his chest. In the window, the curtains settled, the light folding its glittery wings, and the gray room revealed itself: the tidy sketch of the overhead shelving, the rounded cube of the analog TV as anachronistic as Masaaki's bottle-bottom glasses in the twenty-first century. Masaaki unzipped his bag and extracted his water.

Despite everything, here he was again in the poorest heart of Tokyo visiting this man, his brother, who he'd met only a year ago when Seiji turned up at his house in a rural pocket of Kanagawa, looking for information about his parents. The meeting had been sublime. Seiji, separated from his parents during the American firebombing of Tokyo in the spring of 1945, had learned of his parents' survival only weeks before he found his way to Masaaki's door. And Masaaki, who'd discovered Seiji's existence only as an adult, when he learned that he himself had been a war orphan adopted by their parents during the American Occupation, had only a blurry impression of Seiji captured in the one photograph that had survived the war: a tattered family portrait commemorating Seiji's first day of school, framed and crowned with a black ribbon designated for the dead. The two men had spent hours that first day pinning down dates and events, endlessly circling back to confirm this or that detail—**So, your biological parents were Korean, that's all you know? So, our parents were in Tokyo until at least July 1945?**—as though afraid to let the timeline rest. Masaaki wasn't sure when their excitement had turned shackling. Seiji's roving gaze, which had lingered over the cut glass ashtray, the dusty turntable and record collection, had fixed on him.

"I'm sure you noticed too. The coincidence," Seiji resumed now. "The two of us thirteen years apart and utterly unrelated, but orphaned by the same war and sharing the same parents. It never crossed my mind they'd survived and adopted a child. What's interesting is that, all along, you were just on the other side, growing up in the bright world you inhabit, advocating for the future in your world of front doors and windows, while I advocated for it in mine crowded with back doors and alleyways, out of sight of yours. I keep returning to this fact, like a fly to light, or maybe a rat to water in a drought."

Masaaki said nothing. The parallels had struck him too, their biographical corre-spondences a fortunate convenience, their antiwar commitments a shared interest they could huddle around over coffee on inter-mittent afternoons. And for months they did huddle over bottomless cups in one or another hole-in-a-wall kissaten, Seiji regal-ing him with tumultuous tales of his early activities, the historic clashes with the riot police through the sixties and seventies over the ongoing American military presence in Japan. Masaaki, who had followed these events on television, found the personal perspective riveting. But over the weeks and months, the stories, even the man himself, began to feel oppressive. Beneath the pat-ter, there was always an undercurrent. It was nothing concrete—a pause over the rim of Seiji's coffee cup, a catch in the slice of his setting gaze, as elusive and as beguiling as an eel. It worked on him. He began to dream, figments returning to him in milky flashes until he had it, reconstructed, in his head. The backdrop changed as often as he and Seiji changed kissaten—an old habit of an old militant, Seiji liked to joke—but the scene was always the same: two men facing each other, one older than the other, the younger poised with a question he never asks, the opportunity cut off by the older man's quicker draw. The words varied—sometimes a comment, other times a question—but the tone never did, and a louring sense of inevitability would pin Masaaki as though to a script. When the scene played out, it would end these visits—that was the assumption, perhaps his hope, admitted only in his dreams.

"It was strange to find out my parents survived," Seiji continued. "Over the decades, I dreamt up hundreds of scenarios to allow them this outcome. Almost always, I was the linchpin, the crafty son who'd lead them through the bombs to safety. I rehearsed this again and again, as if repetition could change reality." He chuckled, a chalky scratch that rustled up a mess of coughs. Masaaki offered his water bottle, but Seiji

waved it away. "In the times I didn't play
the hero, it was my parents who'd find me,
weeks or months or years later. At no time
did I imagine you. But it's you I found. It
was like turning a blind corner I'd spent
years forging and finding a figure I didn't put
there. I kept asking myself, which is worse:
to never know your parents, or to discover
they'd adopted a new child and moved on?"

Masaaki cracked open his water bottle;
the warm liquid rolled down the desert of his
throat. He too had weighed this question.
An orphan who'd never known his parents,
he'd nevertheless grown up with a mother
and father taken, as it happened, from the
very man sitting before him. Objectively, it
was nobody's fault except humanity's violence, but it was a fragile comfort. The same
war might have orphaned them both, but
their differences were stark, Seiji's face and
body mottled by incendiaries while Masaaki
lived his entire life in comfort, cradled by
the very country whose imperial ambitions
had subjugated and killed his biological
parents. Now Seiji's appearance only deep-
ened his guilt, amplifying the anxiety he'd
lived with since he learned of his adoption:

that his life, even his identity, had been borrowed. And not only borrowed, it turned
out, but usurped from someone who'd been
relegated to society's fringes to dream up
blind corners around which he might find
his parents. The irony was that Seiji could've
found them if he'd looked twenty, maybe
even fifteen, years earlier—an easy thought
for Masaaki, with his laptop and Internet
and the benefits of mainstream life he'd
been accorded. Instead, their parents had
left Masaaki the house and the family plot,
its chamber spacious enough to accept him
when his own time came. It had seemed an
inevitable conclusion: to rest with this family history had cloven. Now he wasn't sure
he belonged.

"Obviously, I wasn't surprised they were
gone," Seiji went on. "Still, my disappointment was proportionate to the hope I felt
when I first learned they'd survived. To find
out so late—would it have been better if I
never found out at all?" He chuckled again,
a brief sound he confined to his throat
this time. "At least I know they were well
cared for. It didn't escape me that my father
died the same year that puppet Hirohito

died, may His Radiance rest in perpetual remorse. So, I should be grateful. Don't get
me wrong. I am." He lifted a jug Masaaki
hadn't noticed and poured himself a cup of
water. In the half-light the jug trembled and
the water sloshed, but Seiji was no longer
fussy. "What I'm trying to work out is what
we ultimately mean to each other."

Masaaki watched the cup tip, a pale moon
against a craggy summit, and the room
filled with the ugly sound of a discordant
body slaking itself. Since Seiji's confinement
to this room, Masaaki had insisted that he
move in with him—into what was, after all,
their parents' house—but Seiji had refused.
Rather than relieved, Masaaki found himself miffed. He and Seiji had no obligations
to one another, but hostage to each other,
he had come to find Seiji's presence uncomfortably anchoring. Masaaki had been in his
forties when he'd learned of his adoption—a
midlife cataclysm that had sent him lurch-
ing from a family life in the United States
to a solitary one devoted to tracking down
information about his biological parents.
Nothing had come of it except loss: loss of
time; loss of his wife and two daughters;

loss of all tether. Was this so different from the vanishing Seiji must have experienced, banished behind a one-way mirror through which he could see the lit world in which he didn't exist? Masaaki didn't think so. There was comfort in that.

Across the room, the curtains rippled, bubbles of sunlight spitting their bright coins. It was a cool afternoon, the breeze busily shifting its cargo of sounds and smells—the tinkle of a bicycle, the burnt tang of yakitori gristle—before collapsing in the gathered shade like a sulky smoker. Seiji adjusted his pillow and interlaced his hands. "Months ago, you gave me a book by a famous Argentinian writer. In it, there's a story about a Chinese spy, working for the German Reich, who must convey the location of a British artillery park before an Irish captain, working for the English police, silences him. The story opens just after the spy discovers the artillery park, and in the gathering shadow of the approaching Irish captain, the spy finds himself paralyzed by the problem of how to relay the information to Germany. I assume you know the story."

Masaaki not only knew the story but remembered the trouble through which he'd
gone to purchase the Japanese translation of
the book he'd read in English, itself a translation of the original written in Spanish. In
his former life as an academic living in the
United States he'd found the book, and especially this story, provocative, with its themes
of duty and dislocation, war and empire,
loyalty and betrayal, and the unavoidable
perversions that twist the actions of the subjugated who are pitted against each other
in self-abnegating violence. He'd been curious what Seiji might think. When the book
went unmentioned for weeks, Masaaki had
presumed it forgotten. Now Seiji was bringing up the very story he'd hoped to discuss,
but his tone was bladed. "You mean 'The
Garden of Forking Paths,'" Masaaki said.
His own voice, thin and cobwebbed, floated
in the dimness and vanished in the shimmer
between the curtains.

Seiji nodded, his hands a rock in the still
pool of his futon. "To reach Germany, to be
heard above the din of war, our spy knows
his message must transmit as precisely as
a gunshot. He decides to murder a man

whose last name is identical to the name of the town where the artillery park is located; his own name, coupled with his victim's, in a news article would unequivocally reach the German chief. But first, he, a conspicuous Chinese man, must reach his victim, who lives a train ride away in the English countryside." He paused, sipped his water, then continued.

"Luck favors our spy, and by a hair-raising margin he eludes the Irish captain. And following a set of cryptic but oddly familiar directions given to him by some children milling about the station—**take a left at every crossroads**—he arrives at his victim's house: an oddly familiar pavilion spellbound with Chinese music. There, he meets his victim: a tall, elderly Englishman who greets him in Chinese. Their meeting is sublime. While the two men have never met, their roots turn out to be entwined: once a missionary stationed in China, the Englishman is an aspiring sinologist intimately familiar with the works of the spy's great-grandfather, an illustrious Chinese man of letters with a passion for mazes, especially the garden mazes for which he'd been renowned. Sitting together in the cloister of the sinologist's pavilion, discussing the great man's work, the two men discover they're kindred. Yet the decision to kill hangs over the spy like the noose that awaits him, unavoidably, in his future."

Masaaki leaned back, the cool wall reassuringly uncomfortable. The summary was faithful, but he could feel the edges of a new story moving beneath the skin of the familiar narrative, and he dreaded what would emerge. "You make it sound like the story is about limited choices," Masaaki said. "As though, from the beginning, our spy, arriving at the sinologist's door, has one choice: whether or not to carry out his murderous intent. It's as though you're saying our antihero is trapped, confined to his assigned parameters."

Seiji tilted his head. "Antihero? I like that." Behind him, the curtains flapped shut, and his face disappeared into darkness. "What we need to remember is that what binds our spy and his victim is an unreadable novel about the nature of time written by the spy's illustrious great-grandfather. The reader is never told why the sinologist devoted him-self to this novel, a literary disaster by most counts, but it had captivated him, just as it had captivated generations of the spy's fam-ily who wanted it destroyed. It's this novel that initially stays the spy, who decides to spend his last hour before the arrival of the Irish captain listening to the sinologist's exegesis."

Masaaki uncurled his legs, feeling his blood rejoice. The novel was indeed the story's central mystery. Begun under per-plexing circumstances, with the spy's great-grandfather renouncing his worldly position before retreating into a pavilion to write an infinite novel about time and create an infinite garden of forking paths, the project was terminated a decade later under circumstances equally perplexing: the great-grandfather's inauspicious death at the hands of a stranger. Chillingly, when the family entered the pavilion, all they found were piles of contradictory drafts and nothing, not even a sketch, of the garden maze. To the spy's surprise, the sinologist claims to have cracked the mystery.

"The novel, as we said, is unreadable," Seiji continued. "Characters die in one chapter only to reappear perfectly alive in another. In this novel, time, as our sinologist explains, doesn't **progress;** it doesn't flow linearly in one absolute direction; a decision at a fork in a plot doesn't 'logically' eliminate all other paths not taken. Instead, **all** paths fork off and continue on, each invisible to the others but existing concurrently, each forking again and again at every crossroad, diverging, converging, crisscrossing, or simply running parallel across a vast, endless labyrinth of time. In some of these times, our spy might exist but not the sinologist; at other times, neither exists; in the times in which they both exist, sometimes they're friends, other times they barely cross paths; in yet other times they miss each other completely. Then there are times in which they meet as enemies. In the story we're discussing, the spy and the sinologist are strangers; war brings them together, exposing their roots tangled by the same history that left them exiles: the spy, a dislocated Chinese man working for the German Reich, finds himself a fugitive in imperial England, the empire he has come to sabotage, while the sinologist, technically at home in England, is equally dislocated, living in isolation in a pavilion uncannily reminiscent of the spy's great-grandfather's pavilion in China, where he'd retreated to write his infinite novel. Their meeting benefits them both: the sinologist offers the spy a chance to reconnect with his culture, language, roots, while the spy offers the sinologist the opportunity to present his theory and prove himself an expert, an intellectual heir—a **familiar**—of the great Chinese man he so admires and identifies with. All futures are possible at all junctures, but despite their sympathies and mutual gratitude, the spy shoots his kindred victim."

Masaaki uncrossed his legs again. He appreciated Seiji's attention to the subtext of imperial history he himself found integral to the story, but the implied fatalism troubled him. Why was Seiji insisting on it? He didn't like the parallel Seiji seemed to be drawing. He rubbed his knees, ashamed of his discomfort in front of the sick man.

"Again, I have to question your view of our characters' choices," Masaaki said. "It's true, the spectrum of our options isn't always perceptible, and clarity is a luxury for this spy trapped in enemy territory, but does it mean he has no choice? The reader is told he has one bullet in his gun. Could a Chinese spy working for the German Reich, to whom he has his worth—the value of the Chinese race—to prove, choose not to fulfill his mission? The pressure is extreme. But the spy is a rational man."

Seiji loosened the collar of his sweatshirt. On the wall, just to the side of his head, there was a small rectangle, a tattered snapshot tacked up by a pin. In this light, the image was murky, but Masaaki was sure it was the family portrait taken on Seiji's first day of school. Months ago, when Masaaki had brought it for him, Seiji had been quick to put it away, and Masaaki had feared he'd upset him; now he was relieved to see the photograph displayed. In the window, the curtains were still, the thin press of light like an incandescent thumb.

"You're right," Seiji agreed. "Our spy has

one bullet, and, logically, he has three possible targets: the sinologist; the Irish captain; himself. A learned man himself, the spy **chooses** to spend his last hour discussing his great-grandfather's novel with the sinologist he intends to kill. That he, immersed in a conversation about time and its innumerable forks, remains blind to his own forking options is curious. The Irish captain arrives; the spy has seconds to use his bullet. How differently things could've turned out. With a shift of his hand, he might've spared the sinologist; Germany might've never bombed the artillery park; history might've forked differently; and a different future than one of perpetual remorse might've been available to the spy. But remember: while all futures are possible, it's time, embodied by the Irish captain, that our spy feels he can't escape. Trapped in its stream, racing his impending capture, our spy arrives at the sinologist's door. Their paths cross, and so do the strands of their entwined past. In that past, the spy's great-grandfather was murdered by a stranger; in the present, the spy and the sinologist are also strangers."

The words hung portentiously. "You're not saying there's a correlation. That the one murder is related to the other?"

Seiji unlaced his hands. "Why not? Maybe there are patterns we can't escape."

"It's one thing to say history narrows our choices, but it's another to say there are scenarios that repeat over generations, that we're scripted to repeat."

"What makes you so sure there aren't? Like our spy who misses the story he's being told, maybe you're not positioned to know the script we're enacting."

In the window, the curtains puffed and, with a thwack, sucked outward; the men startled. Caught in the mouth of the half-lowered window, the curtains strained, a concave sail. Masaaki drew his knees into his arms, passing a hand across his forehead. On and off, he'd been experiencing a dot of pain halfway between his sternum and spine; now his body was coated with a clammy film. In the window, the curtains loosened; their corners flipped; ribbons of light blew back in.

"You're not serious," Masaaki said, rubbing the afterimage of the pain. "To say our lives are scripted is like saying we live in a play, that our choices are futile, that the roles we fancy we play in life and in the world are just that: a fantasy. I thought you believed in self-conscious action, the importance of exercising our agency."

"You shouldn't assume I'm aligned with the story," Seiji said. "We're talking about a piece of fiction."

Masaaki felt the jab. "You're right. What I should've said is that even if the spy missed the story, he could've honored his roots, shifted his loyalties, at least respected his sympathies. I can't accept that that wouldn't have changed the outcome. All futures are possible; we happen to be reading the version that forked this way. As for repeating patterns, the spy's great-grandfather was murdered by a stranger. Here, it's the great-grandson who murders the sinologist, a stranger."

Seiji slid his hands over his cup. "All futures **are** possible. The future in which our spy doesn't kill the sinologist also exists. But if **all** futures exist, every future is predetermined. I'm saying that in our version, there was no other way the path could've forked.

By the time our spy shoots our sinologist, his choices have narrowed to one." He paused. "Do you remember what prompted you to give me this story?"

Masaaki recalled traipsing all over town, leaving one bookstore for another in search of the book, but the context was gone. He admitted it, uneasily.

Seiji nodded. "I know you read the story many times; I read it many times too, and each time I've been plagued with the feeling that I missed something. Like time, words marshaled into a narrative are relentless; they drive on, talking over gaps, bridging contradictions, eloquently covering everything up. But once in a while a moment opens in the narrative, and we can seize our thoughts. Like you, I believe we have options, but only if we know where to look. You remember how the sinologist connects the unreadable novel to the lost garden of forking paths, right?"

Masaaki remembered the detail, crucial to the story. Through the rigorous assertion of reason, the sinologist deduces that, far from being a work of an eccentric or an infirm mind, the novel is itself a maze mirroring the labyrinthine nature of time. "Our sinologist concludes that the Garden of Forking Paths was never a physical structure," he said. "It was always only a symbolic one, forking across the pages of a novel. The garden and the novel are one and the same."

Seiji didn't move. In the window, the curtains flapped, offering flashes of illumination, but he alone occupied the position benefitting from its trajectory. "I've been laid up many times, but it always takes getting used to," he said, finally. "Time lures you places you wouldn't have gone otherwise. The last few days, I've been drawn less to the story's central parable about forking paths than to its peripheral details. For example, after our spy's great-grandfather renounces his worldly position, he retreats to what he calls the Pavilion of the Limpid Solitude to construct his labyrinthine novel. When he dies, his family discovers that he entrusted his literary estate to a—and I quote— 'Taoist or Buddhist monk,' and thereafter every descendant of the great-grandfather has cursed the monk for faithfully ensuring the publication of the questionable novel. Tell me something." He leaned out of the shadow. "Do you believe in curses?"

Masaaki felt his heart turn. "I suppose I haven't given it much thought."

"Because there's something I'm trying to figure out. As you said, in the present, it's the spy who murders the sinologist, while in the past it's the great-grandfather who is murdered by a stranger. At first, the inverted symmetry appears to reject any correlation. But what if, in the Great Labyrinth, we cross paths not only at various times but **also in various forms**? Details click into place. Just as the great-grandfather lived in seclusion in a pavilion amid a garden maze, the sinologist also lives alone in a pavilion reached by turning left at every fork. Just as the great man's library must have been filled with all manner of textual and other treasures, the sinologist's library is filled with exquisite artifacts and tomes from West to East, including silk-bound volumes edited by a Chinese emperor that the spy instantly recognizes but knows were never printed. So, who is our sinologist? He's elderly, tall, with a Westerner's gray eyes. He's the definition of a stranger in the context of China."

"Are you suggesting he killed the great-grandfather? That he's some sort of an imposter?"

Seiji opened his palms. "We know the sinologist is elderly, but is he old enough to have crossed paths with the great-grandfather? The story offers no clue, nothing about a theft of irreplaceable tomes alongside the murder. What it offers are other clues. For example, the references to 'Taoism or Buddhism.' Then the description of our sinologist as looking 'immortal.' We also can't forget the replicated pavilions. Maybe we're being asked to consider the possibility that the sinologist, in another time, in another form, **maybe in the form of an illustrious Chinese man of letters,** was murdered by a stranger who'd one day visit him in the form of a Chinese spy."

"You mean the sinologist is a reincarnation of the spy's great-grandfather?"

Seiji smiled. "Besides the pavilion, the other correlation between the long-ago murder in China and the current murder in

England is the presence of the infinite novel about time. It's as though it too has traveled through the Labyrinth and, in a coalescent time, bound two apparent strangers, prefiguring not the murder but its precondition. Like a curse, it's as if its appearance revived in the strangers a sleeping dynamic that **had** to play out in that cloistered room full of illustrious texts and objects deeply familiar to both. It's as though the spy and the sinologist have been nudged into what turns out to be a recurring trap to which they're inexorably drawn, like two captive rats who, trained to take a left at every crossroads, irresistibly fork their way into the center of a hall of mirrors filled with endless replicas of the pavilion, inside which the spy always, inevitably, encounters **as if for the first time** the sinologist in his different guises. You see, a curse is nothing more than a trigger. It can be anything. For some, it's an unreadable novel about time. For others, a photograph. For still others, a story by an Argentinian writer. Or maybe a shared set of parents."

The light flickered, the breeze like a passing truck; the curtains arced, and the room fluoresced, the afternoon sweeping across Seiji's damaged face, flooding the dark aquarium of the TV; the neat pile of clothes on the overhead shelf; the tacked-up family portrait of a boy not yet mangled; the plastic jug the color of American mustard set beside the diminished man Masaaki now realized he'd soon lose. The walls shimmered; the air pulsated, a luminous agitation Masaaki would experience again only in the final moments of his own life, which would unexpectedly precede his brother's, seizing him abruptly in his office one afternoon, eight weeks later. Lying on the floor, heart sputtering like a sparrow, he'd remember this light, the way it had teased the curtains all afternoon, simmering, then bubbling, then finally pouring in, a white vibration so pure it distilled every object into its glimmering essence, the golden beads tapping the air before releasing upward into a radiance where everything was as yet undifferentiated, where something and nothing were not yet opposites, where form, as yet unformed, had not drawn the jealous attention of time, with its corrosive wrath. This light, like the dizzying light of a maze, would feel familiar, its luminescence redolent of summer and childhood and their halcyon dreams where people, never lost, returned, like his ex-wife and two daughters and, these days, an image, like a memory, of two figures in a room.

Across from him, Seiji turned, his attention caught by a passing noise. Transfigured by light, the family resemblance was unmistakable, their father's blunt features refined by their mother's to unique but recognizable effect, and Masaaki, despite his envy, strained to remember him this way, in the bright eternity of this second before the curtains swept the air and the room gathered once more like an umbrella.

"Strange how light can obscure more than illuminate," Seiji said. "We've been talking about the curse of patterns that repeat over generations; what I know is that patterns also repeat across a single lifetime. My first foray into politics, as you know, was right after the war. There was a man, legendary in the radical world. During the Occupation, I got a chance to meet him. Things didn't go as planned. I arrived at his headquarters, an underground printing press. I knocked. No one answered. In retrospect, I should have left. Instead, I turned the knob. The first room I came to was dark. Blackout papers still covered the windows, a chink of light dribbling in like weak tea. I didn't see the body right away; there was no movement left in it to catch any light. That was the context in which I met the Legend." He lifted the jug, poured more water, and drank it.

"I was framed for that murder," he continued. "I wasn't guiltless. I should've respected the body that had served a life, but instead I helped the Legend. We bound the corpse, lashed it to a chair. We stuffed its mouth with cloth. It never occurred to me that I was helping him construct a crime scene meant to trap me. I was charged with murder and worse. I should've been sent to juvenile but wasn't; I thought I'd be old by the time I got out. Three years later, I was dumped on the street. No explanation, but even a kid like me had friends. I looked for them, but in an interregnum three years is a long time; the world had changed, everyone had disappeared into new lives. I started from scratch. Several months later, an article appeared in the newspaper. The Legend had been found dead, bound and lashed to a chair, his mouth stuffed with a cloth. The killer was never caught."

"You're saying this is your pattern—your curse? Betrayal and revenge?"

Seiji rotated his cup. "The thing I admired most about the Legend was that he had the voice to mobilize millions. Granted, we were motivated by hunger, but the resonance we generated when we came together to demonstrate was revolutionary. Bodies have power. It just happened that the Legend and I met in the shadow of a dead one, its stillness as powerful as the resonance of bodies in a march, but instead of jostling us into solidarity, its presence obscured our alliance, distorted our choices, narrowed them to one."

"So he had no choice, you had no choice, is that it?"

"The thing about betrayal is that it comes in many forms. Some are planned, others accidental: accidents of folly, accidents of circumstance. Then there are accidents of good intentions." He met Masaaki's stare.

"The problem is that the body, the visceral self, doesn't distinguish forms of betrayal; it registers only the fact, the blunt impact, the blinding locomotion."

"That doesn't mean revenge has to follow betrayal," Masaaki said, the words rolling across the floor of his stomach. "We're more than our bodies, our feelings."

Seiji drained his cup. "I always assumed that the worst thing about betrayal would be the injustice. In fact it's the disappointment. But to be disappointed there must've been an expectation, a hope. In my case, the corpse set the stage, but the spell was cast long ago by a magazine profile I read the spring I turned thirteen. I learned that the Legend and I shared a number of things. We lived in similar neighborhoods; our parents were of a similar political persuasion, which similarly cost us during the war. Like me, he was an only child, and that spring, housebound by curfew, I pictured us as brothers. So you could say it began with that magazine profile—that it was the journalist, the writer of the profile—**our father**—who set it in motion."

Masaaki felt his whole body clutch. "What are you implying?" he asked. "Our father didn't betray you."

"As I said"—Seiji smiled—"patterns repeat across a single lifetime. Sometimes all it takes is an accident of good intentions." He unpinned the photograph on the wall. "This was in the book you gave me."

Masaaki felt the electric plunge as he reached for the image that he suddenly realized was the family portrait commemorating not Seiji's first day of school but his own. He'd dug it up to show Seiji: the identical composition, the identical discontent on his own face as he stood flanked by their parents. He thought he'd misplaced it. "The key word is 'accident,'" he said. "Bodies might be blind, but you're too conscious— you can alter the pattern. I wanted you to see it. We look like we could be brothers— that's all I meant."

Seiji's smile broadened. "Are you sure?" He put down his cup. His lips trembled. Then he laughed, a sudden bellow, the purity of his pleasure cut short by a choking sputter, a chaos of new coughing. Masaaki could hear the blood in it, the salt and metal. He stood to help, but Seiji waved him away.

"You should've seen your face," he said, wiping his mouth. "I admit I was jealous when I saw the picture. But like the spy, my time is running out. I'm too sick to do anything except read stories written by an Argentinian writer who is compelling me to learn a thing or two about Taoism. Did you know some Taoists believe in heredity, the passing of, say, a curse, from one relative to another through the bloodline? The question is whether curses, like viruses, can transmit through other means, other hosts—an object, a figure, even a jealous heart—and, like that, cross from one to another, as from a stranger to a stranger, a familiar.

"The first time I read the story, I was annoyed; I thought it offered nothing but a fatalistic cosmology. Now I see that it's in fact about agency, how our actions can alter not just our personal trajectory but the larger one. You asked me once if I thought it was possible for humans to act for the benefit of the species, not just the interests of a nation, a culture, a religion. This is the conversation that prompted you to introduce me to that story.

"To his credit, the sinologist understood one thing: that the unreadable novel, more than a rhetorical experiment, is an alternative theory of the universe to stand against such luminaries of the Western Enlightenment as Newton and Schopenhauer. But like the spy's great-grandfather, who was murdered before he could complete his great novel, the sinologist's life is also cut short, maybe depriving him of another kind of enlightenment. A product of a whole tradition of Western thought, the sinologist rationally decodes the unreadable novel, deducing, convincingly, that the Garden of Forking Paths is not a physical place but a symbolic structure. But what he fails to grasp is that while time doesn't unfold across a physical place, it unfolds across a space, the space of time. And it's this failure that costs the sinologist his life and prevents our spy from altering the course of his action and the trajectory of history. Because it's only in the space of time—the space of a moment, the space of the present—that choices are born. Ironically, the spy, the direct descendant of the great novelist, understood this. Forking through the idyllic countryside toward the sinologist's pavilion, he momentarily forgets the war and the encroaching Irish captain, and his thoughts twirl on the fact that while the present moment is a speck in the vast history of our civilization, it's only in the present, the moment of the now, where everything happens—where anything **can** happen.

"Like you, I put little stock in blood and bloodlines and other such notions that pass from generation to generation, shaping our loyalties. We've seen how effectively these notions, these scripts, given the force of culture, can be marshaled for national interest and preservation. But even culture, broken down into small daily acts we habitually perform—here lies the space, brief but capacious enough for us to seize the spectrum of our choices. We Japanese, for example, have many rituals to acknowledge space: the physical space of a place, the space of a threshold, as well as the shared space of a meeting, the social space born in a moment of an encounter. We mark this space with a bow. I've never given it much thought, except to defy the practice which I saw as one more subjugating custom of polite society. But since meeting you I've come to see this as a gesture not of self-abnegating obeisance but of vital self-negation, as we each pause at the threshold of our common space and lower our heads in deference, so that we might, together, even under the eternal augur of a curse, ceaselessly start anew in light."

SIX

CROP

The crop had done well. Rows of vibrant green shoots knuckling out of the mud, springing like little children at the school bell. It would still take several seasons, but the transplant, Masayuki was sure, would eventually take, the best qualities of their rice, cultivated for generations at home in Niigata, given the chance for new growth here in California, all the way on the other side of the world. Until his cousin Mitsuru left for these shores seven years ago, in 1906, Masayuki had never imagined making what was for most a once-in-a-lifetime transpacific journey, and here he was crossing back and forth for the third time to help Mitsuru nurture these sprouts. It was gratifying to finally see the progress now, in 1913, and on this point Masayuki had no regrets, the excitement of working alongside Mitsuru worth almost any exorbitance. He and Mitsuru had always shared a passion for discovery, and Masayuki had grieved when his cousin left Niigata. Now Mitsuru went by Bob, and though Masayuki never learned whether the name had been chosen or issued to him, what was clear was that Bob, who answered only reluctantly to his original name, was determined to stay. This land had space, vast and unencumbered by primogeniture, the grip of old roots—or so it seemed.

Like most of Mitsuru's projects, the odds hadn't been favorable, and it had been a feat to coax their grain to thrive in a new environment that was, in many ways, hostile to transplants, despite the similarities they saw between Northern California and Niigata. Now, after six seasons, their crop was showing promise. A futurity.

Masayuki could report at least this much when he faced his wife, Taeko, who, in three weeks, would journey with their infant son from Niigata to the port of Yokohama to greet him when he disembarked the steamship **Hikari,** currently docked on this pier, waiting to depart this California bay. By then it would be five months since he'd last seen her, and the thought filled him with longing and apprehension. In all their years together, Masayuki had done little to draw Taeko's scrutiny; if anything, it was this lack that sometimes provoked her exasperation. In the case of his months in California, it was her interest in Mitsuru's health and romantic life that prompted her to do a little fishing in the memory lake of his heart, where, according to her, all the fish, bored by inattention, lay dormant. He was always curious what she'd dredge up, the slipped feelings and details she'd hold up wriggling between them for analysis. This year all his fish were wide awake, and it would not be Mitsuru she'd be concerned with.

At the ship's entry, Masayuki looked up at the gleaming hulk thrumming with an ever more efficient engine he could feel in his legs. Indeed, **Hikari** was an apt name for a ship that carried the shine of the future.

He was the first to arrive at his cabin, a tiny room stiff with cleaning. Other than the bunk beds set up on opposite walls, there was only a common night table, above

which a round window peered cataracti-
cally. He wondered if he should've stuck
to steerage. As it was, he'd splurged on a
second-class ticket, thinking he'd appreciate
the company of a few bunkmates over the
intimate anonymity of a constant crowd.
Perhaps he'd misjudged. Sliding his luggage
onto his mattress, he rejoined the bustle in
the corridor. His legs often felt heavier on
the return; this time, they felt numb, his
whole body dragging anchor.

Above deck, the day was clear and getting clearer, the sky and sea differentiated by
texture rather than color, each half meeting
at the horizon beyond which lay the frontier of the next epoch. Masayuki, born in
the previous century, knew he'd never live
to see the advances that would penetrate
earth's outer borders. Yet, just over a decade
into the twentieth century, technology had
brought the continents closer, science feeding and curing a world that would surely
one day want for nothing. Like his cousin,
Masayuki believed in humanity, its intrin-
sic propulsion to evolve, and the coming
ages' limitless capacity to progress; he too
was a born agronomist, impelled by life's

miraculous vigor to contribute to its vitality. Ultimately, he was a pragmatist, which was both his strength and weakness—and useful to his pioneering cousin, who'd tapped him for his own pursuits. Masayuki never regretted this exploitation, as others in his family called it; Mitsuru elevated him, Mitsuru who always dreamed in excess, reaching into a future that did not exist to seed an unborn world he'd insist was gestating in the air, in the water, in the soil, germinating across the earth.

But it was one thing to dream and another to be naïve, and Masayuki took care never to be naïve. As he saw it, there was a difference between blind faith and hope, and it was in the gully between the two that he always set his heart. It was the only way he could see to meet the future squarely. Taeko, like Mitsuru, valued his judgments, trusting their innovative sparkle. But he'd never before risked anything potentially irreversible.

ON DECK, Masayuki threaded his way to the railing, undeterred by the elbows and shoulders turning to resist him. Across the water plashing between the ship and pier, the crowd had slackened into listless clumps, and it took him a moment to find the spot where, moments ago, he'd shaken hands with his cousin, then with Edward, the once scraggly mop of a boy who used to come around with his father, the sympathetic white man from whom Bob leased his land. Now a head taller than Masayuki, Edward was no longer a boy—he'd made that clear. Looking back, Masayuki should've seen it coming, Edward's grown-up face pinking at the sight of Ayumi, Masayuki's fifteen-year-old daughter, when they'd disembarked at the beginning of this summer.

Summoning his strength, Masayuki let his gaze drop to the shape beside Edward. Not her usual trenchant self, his daughter was scrunched between several doleful families, her pale face sullen and averted. He was glad she wasn't looking, his child, no longer a child, who'd sat beside Edward in Bob's parlor the previous week, back straight, letting Edward talk like a grown man about the merits of Ayumi making a life in California with him, an aspiring **American** agricultural scientist. What could he do? Ayumi, a rambunctious child, had always trailed after Mitsuru, reaching for the world beyond their town; his wife, far from discouraging it, had indulged Ayumi, raising little resistance when she first clamored to sail to California with her father. But this—this was different, he knew. And yet he also believed a part of Taeko would understand. In the past year Ayumi had become subdued and restless, her thoughts often elsewhere as she chewed her dinner or swept the hallway, snapping at anyone who interrupted her. Masayuki had thought it had to do with her brother, two years older and about to leave home to pursue his medical studies. But Taeko had been convinced it was her own pregnancy, so late in life, with their youngest son, the unexpected event burdening Ayumi with more household duties and perhaps a glimpse of her own future in Niigata. Despite the help she needed with the baby, Taeko, not a soft woman, had made arrangements with her own sister, who agreed to stop by twice a day so Ayumi could travel again with her father. No doubt Taeko, upon his return, would demand to know what the prospects were of a Japanese girl in America, but it was the image of his wife's pity that had opened his mind as he listened to Edward and watched his daughter's face radiate a hopeful ardor he hadn't seen since she'd been a little girl. He'd consented. Ayumi, elated, had flushed, a vibrance that filled his chest, tickling every corner of it. It was only later that something heavier had tugged at her expression, and now this weight hit him full force, the pang like a prophecy of loss, his struck heart suddenly too large in its cage.

The horn bellowed; everyone surged and waved. In the ripple of hands, he saw his daughter lift her face. The horn bellowed again; the crowd around him pushed and shouted, the frantic swell crushing him into the railing. Of course, there was no way to know what future he'd opened by leaving her here; but there was also no way to know what future he'd averted. What he knew was that Ayumi's sights, like Mitsuru's, had always been set farther than his own—how could he refuse her this growth? He thought about his eldest, how tentatively he'd proclaimed his interest in the surgical science, fearful of hurting his father's feelings—which, naturally, were hurt, but not enough to blind Masayuki to the possibilities; he knew his son would go on to do good in the world. He thought about his youngest, an active infant who'd opened his eyes to stare at him moments after his birth. Perhaps someday this child too would leave them. All week, he'd wished his wife were here, with her clear-eyed ability to dowse where he could not, feeling with her own heart for answers beyond his purview. But maybe the times called upon one to place one's trust in one's fellow man and bet on mankind's collective potential. After all, the world was bound to get better, he told himself; he was already looking forward to his next return to California. In the meanwhile, there were always letters; in fact, he'd write the first one aboard this ship.

Craning over the railing, he looked across the widening strip of water cleaving the ship from the pier. Hands open, the crowd was yearning toward them, but where was Ayumi? He scanned the diminishing faces, his chest squeezing, then sprouting, as at last he caught sight of the running speck now calling to him, arms aloft, a kernel of new life he hoped would grow and bear fruit, a burgeoning cornucopia that would go on to nourish and shelter all his unknown descendants in ways that perhaps he, an unextraordinary man born with one foot in the old world, may fail to.

SEVEN

THE GARDEN, AKA THEOREM FOR THE SURVIVAL OF THE SPECIES

"So the world's deconstructing," Erin said. It was day three of their senior year of high school. He and Anja were sitting at their usual table in the cafeteria. "War's breaking out on all planes of existence. We're, like, the last human generation still holding out any chance of survival. What do we need to do?"

Anja, looking up from her phone to read Erin's lips, tapped her pen against the notepad she favored. Tap, tap. Tap, tap. Erin loved this about her, the tick of her brain pulsing through her body, tapping out a syncopated rhythm as she raced her thoughts to their possible ends. He adored her. Probably had from the moment he saw her three years earlier, her beetle-shaped headphones clamped to her ears, long blunt hair, straight as her back, dropping anchor in what he, a month into freshman year, had come to think of as **his** seat, two rows from the back. He'd strode over, plucked the headphones off her head, and was walloped, his homeroom watching. Worse, though, had been the distress on her face, her hands fluttering to cover her naked ears.

She flipped her pen, wrote, Planet's salvageable? Humans are salvageable?

He nodded, and nodded again.

Flip, tap. Flip. Cause of World Event?

He thought for a moment. "Anthropocene."

You mean Neoliberal Self-Destruction?

"Call it whatever."

Anja narrowed her eyes, her pupils pulling into pinpoints before releasing their javelins of light. Her dad, a drinker, loved to hold forth on America's dream of Empire, crudely laid bare over a decade ago by the triumph of the yellow-haired duck. Remember, kids, he'd say. That Duck wasn't some random nightmare; he was The Neoliberal who didn't bother with civil liberties.

"Okay, okay. Point taken," Erin said. Close to the end of the 2020s, it was clear where the world was headed. Cemented by the long-ago wars of the 1930s and '40s, the United States still had leverage, with its vast market and military umbrella, but along with the Russians and Chinese, it was now just one of three empires competing with varying degrees of subtlety to divide up the world, indenturing the poor and incentivizing countries rich in resources but stingy with cooperation. As the empires rubbed up against each other, physical wars, increasingly fought by drones and AI, still erupted in convenient third-party territories, but the bigger war was largely invisible, taking place in the underlayers of a cyberspace trolled by rogue entities targeting networks and individuals who thoughtlessly uploaded their lives. As their history teacher, an Iraq War veteran with a silvery beard, often said, a stylus pinched between his prosthetic fingers: **The enemy is everywhere; where's the real war?**

Anja resumed her tapping, the plastic rhythm quickening to a drum roll. She stopped, wrote, Did we get approved???

Erin grinned and held up their permission form. The principal's swooping signature had joined those of their English, biology, and computer science teachers. "We're on," he said, his own nerves leaping now, her neural rhythm jumping the synaptic gap between them. He took her pen. E+A Project #1, aka The Garden.

IN MANY ways, that project, their joint high school senior "thesis," as they'd ostentatiously called it, had been an ambitious bust, "ambitious" being the key word and maybe why their principal had approved it. Anja had done much of the coding while he refined the concept, the two of them camping out in his basement after school, Erin cranking his mother Luna's vintage goth band CDs, Anja occasionally surfacing to sweet-talk his sister Mai whenever she thumped on the door, her ninth-grade sensibilities affronted by Robert Smith's unearthly wails. It was rewarding work. While the project had to satisfy the agreed-upon requirements of AP English, AP Biology, Environmental Science, and Programming, they got to build a computer program inspired by Mozak, a Web-based citizen-science "game" created in the early 2010s to aid medicine. Anyone with Internet could participate in Mozak; all you had to do was look at images of neurons spidering across your screen and identify shapes, the idea being that humans were still more adept than a computer at complex pattern recognition. The data then helped scientists create 3-D images of neurons. It was brilliant. When he and Anja first stumbled across it over summer break, they'd played it obsessively. Then they'd moved on, but the idea had burrowed into their brains, eventually effervescing out of their many conversational rabbit holes like a rich, fermented substance. How, they wondered, could they tap its potential? Could they, for example, build a climatological Mozak to tackle their most urgent crisis driving all wars, fueling all economies, pushing humanity ever closer to extinction?

You mean a crowdsourced weather pattern recognition program? Anja had written. Like make weather predictable further and further in advance?

Erin nodded. "All we'll need is a virtual replica of our world. Superimpose a weather model. Then invite people to ID weather patterns. Like when pressure drops this much in the morning, it means snow in the afternoon, or whatever."

Then we add more layers. Space model. Ocean model. Pollen. Pollution. Etc.

"Eventually, we'll have an Earth model, a complete real-time replica of our planet. Progress it forward a decade or two, and voilà: it'll predict the future. We'll be rich!" Erin said.

We can do so much more, Anja wrote.

"Fine, we'll save the world. After we get rich."

Sometimes you're so small, E. Think Species. Think Climate Control.

"And that's how we attract the wrath of the gods," he'd said, laughing. "Didn't you learn anything in English?" But the idea, luminous with destiny, stuck, and they'd spent the rest of the summer drafting a proposal, detailing the steps they'd take, the teachers they'd consult. The final product would be a Web-based virtual reality program that would utilize humanity's collective effort to track Earth's changing climate and its effects on the human species, while participants recruited to identify weather patterns would also, eventually, be invited to design survival tools—new habitats, new gear, new farming methods—in response to the planet's changing environment. In maturity, they'd concluded, The Garden would be more than a game; it would be a tool capable of not only predicting Earth's weather but crowdsourcing solutions to the climate crisis in real time.

THE PROJECT, obviously wax-winged, had been preposterous, but no one had denied it had spark and engine, and in daydreams, Erin still believed they might have pulled it off—if Anja had stayed to graduate from high school. Instead, she'd left him with a buggy pre-alpha app and a "thesis" paper, written solo, describing what could've been. And it had hijacked the next seven years of his life. Now, midway into the 2030s, he had a full-blown virtual reality weather prediction program with the kind of real-world application they'd envisioned.

At his desk in his recently rented one-bedroom, Erin opened his laptop and raised his hands for the blue eye to scan his face and fingerprints. It was a split-second procedure, but the irony was never lost on him: he, the human subject, held up by his electronic tool.

"Messages?" he said.

No messages. And unlike the previous day (and the day before that, on and off for almost two months now), his machine appeared uninfiltrated. No animated serpent coiling up a bookish Tree of Knowledge. No winged Lucifer flashing his feathered trench coat.

"Last installed file?"

A window bloomed: his document folder. And there she was, though "she" was a dangerous designation, like naming a phantom, a cipher. He examined the new file: a seemingly benign Word document. Not that it mattered; "she" respected no walls. He clicked it open.

The world is deconstructing. You're the last human generation with any chance of survival. There is a Garden in the desert of time. You alone know the coordinates. Enter your move.

The words, an echo from long ago rendered in the language of twentieth-century adventure games, prickled his scalp. Was his intruder soliciting a response? He stared at the cursor, its anticipatory blink almost human. He typed, **Anja?** His nerves leapt; his fingers fluttered above the Enter key before pressing down, connecting the circuit.

The cursor skipped, blinked, then continued to blink: a regular Word file, not a Trojan horse. Exhaling, he deleted his keystrokes and clicked the green icon on his desktop.

NOTHING HAD changed in The Garden since he'd last logged out. The virtual planet was still pockmarked; storms were still pirouetting around the globe, whipping wrecking balls of wind, rain, ice, and snow, bursting pipes, drowning subway lines, disconnecting entire neighborhoods, winding back quadrants of civilization a century or more. Along fault lines, earthquakes rocked, buckling buildings, upending roads, heaving waves that redrew the coastlines. Everywhere temperatures thrashed and sea levels rose, shrinking beaches and exhausting marine life, submerging chains of islands, further spreading toxic material seeping from abandoned military bases no longer frozen by icecaps or quarantined on solitary atolls. Inland, rivers dried up and deserts expanded, denuding jungles and sparking fires that devastated towns, habitats, ecosystems, leaving the sun to irradiate the earth like a microwave. Erin zoomed into his last saved location: a bench outside a dog park in a city neighborhood, an exact virtual replica of the bench outside a dog park in his own real-life neighborhood—except progressed fifteen years into the future.

He felt the twinge every time he opened this world he'd envisioned with Anja. Anja would deem it lacking—the blunt details, the stutter in the rendering—but this was the best he could do, with investors coming and going, the fluctuating funds making a committed team difficult to retain. Just establishing the fundamentals—which weather models to use (ongoing dilemma); how far to progress the world (fifteen years); and to what end (disaster preparedness; damage minimization; maybe, ultimately,

climate control)—had been a titanic mile-
stone. Now The Garden was live, had been
for a year, and was beginning to produce results: breakthrough accuracy in weather prediction and an ever more complete virtual
replica of the world, all of it expanding the
program's usefulness, magnetizing all kinds
of people and, increasingly, companies—
just as they'd anticipated.

Snapping on his VR headset, Erin entered The Garden and was immediately surrounded by the sound of snuffling dogs in
the dog park, the yapping blur, rendered
from his avatar's POV, bounding and coiling, their low growls quivering at the edge
of play and aggression. He couldn't remember who had worked on these details—
Fernandez? Parker? Liu?—but they'd done a
good job. He stood, appreciating the drag
of his shadow as it slid off the bench, and
rounded the fence to the sidewalk. Traffic
had increased in recent months as more
users participated in the project, but at the
moment the cars were stopped at a light,
and he crossed toward an old ornate magazine building that had so far withstood the
wind, rain, snow, and corresponding floods

that had condemned several surrounding blocks—a worrisome trend that had also begun to manifest in the physical world, where worsening weather conditions were crumbling the oldest neighborhoods around the globe.

At the building's entrance, he glanced at the blackened vent on the wall. Erin himself had added that detail, reproducing the scorch mark left there by the electrical fire that had almost destroyed the actual building in the physical world in the late 1800s. The mark added no practical, or even aesthetic, value to The Garden, but it was a piece of history, a record of something lived. Erin had never cared for dioramas and living museums, never worshipped at the altar of authenticity obsessed with hyperreal preservation; what he wanted was to conserve the evidence of humanity, which The Garden, as populous as it was (a million active avatars at any given moment), seemed devoid of the longer he was here. More than anything, it was this—the progressive erasure and dismissal of history—that foretold for him humanity's eventual disappearance. Just fifteen years behind The Garden, the physical world was already beginning to empty itself of human presence, leaving carapaces of civilization in varying stages of extinction. Most corporate buildings were dead, fluorescent offices having reached near obsolescence in a world gone online, with the few remaining factories, largely automated, overseen by fewer and fewer people. The only structures that lit up any more were residences and small commercial buildings like this one, its occasional vacancies quickly filled by boutique companies that valued its high ceilings and tall windows in a location outside, but accessible to, the darkening museum of downtown.

Erin, who passed the actual magazine building on his daily jog in the physical world, had made the virtual building his team's virtual office. The first time they'd all assembled there in avatar form, he'd been struck by how many of them had created recognizably enhanced versions of themselves—a trend consistent in The Garden at large, where there was the occasional mythical creature or anime-inspired character or something wholly other, but the majority were straight-up humanoids.

As the world digitized, people seemed increasingly invested in their human identity, though investment in the species as a whole remained consistently low. Back in high school, he and Anja had spent hours recreating themselves from photographs they thought most accurately captured them. Now, seven years older, Erin had considered aging his avatar, but he had reasons to keep himself recognizably embalmed at seventeen.

At the building's virtual glass doors, he punched in a passcode and crossed the lobby to a bank of gold mailboxes. This was a nostalgic touch, but every so often he'd find a virtual letter or a postcard, and it would remind him that it was also this pleasure that kept people in The Garden, not just their planetary concerns. He pressed the elevator button and punched in a second code. The doors slid closed, and the elevator dinged to the seventh floor.

The office was quiet, the sweep of windows a liquidy obsidian reflecting a row of worktables, their bare wood surfaces lonesome for the storyboards and architectural drafts they'd once been designed for. At one, Mortimer, The Garden's co-developer, was hunched over an antique-looking map. A former college roommate, he was the only person who knew something of The Garden's origin story. Mortimer swiveled his half-robot, half-human face toward him.

"How's Gale?" Erin asked, surveying the weather panel taking up one wall of the virtual office. Off the coasts of North America, the sky was beginning to spin cotton candy, waves beginning to peak and roughen. If Gale Inc. proceeded as planned, it would be the fourth lab to virtually test its climate technology since The Garden introduced the Test Your Tech feature several weeks ago. From inception, the feature had been a win-win solution, giving them a revenue source while companies like Gale gained access to a no-risk testing ground for their beta programs. Unsurprisingly, suitors looking to buy The Garden also began approaching them, pleasing their investors but dividing the team. How much control were they willing to cede? One consensus was that nobody wanted to negotiate with their biggest, most aggressive suitor, Titan, a cybertech engineering company with ties to the military, who wanted them to cede everything. Then, five days ago, they received a threat. Titan had learned the location of their virtual office—known only to the team—and dispatched a representative: an avatar with rimless glasses who keyed in random passcodes until it tripped the alarm. Mortimer arrived first and, as in a B-movie, was greeted with a handshake and a message: a gentlemanly suggestion that the team accept Titan's offer and take the money while they still could. Erin called an emergency meeting; the team scoured the system but found nothing. How had Titan located their office? Eventually, someone suggested a leaker in their midst, and the office had gone still. Erin's mind leapt to his laptop "visitor," who never left digital crumbs Erin wasn't meant to find, and it jangled all the bells in his nerves. But he'd said nothing.

"What about the space suits?" Erin asked now.

Mortimer rotated the map toward him.

"These popped up about an hour ago, but otherwise no changes," he said, pointing out the new pairs of white space-suited avatars with the now familiar double-arrowed red triangle emblazoned on their chests. A couple of weeks back, they'd spotted the first pair in a nearby street, their identical look prompting them to speculate whether they were twins—or soulmates? Illicit lovers? Since then, replicas of the pair had proliferated in alarming succession around the globe. Mortimer had begun flagging them, but so far they'd done little except multiply and mill about. Erin had run a logo search, but there had been no matches, at least not in any existing database. The team hadn't known what to do. Were they Russian bots? Or some kind of Trojan horse—maybe ransomware? The insignia reminded everyone of the recycling symbol enforced on every product, except for the color, emergency red, and the direction of the arrows, double-pointed, like a process that could go both ways. So maybe they're a biohazard crew, someone had suggested; biohazard containment was a rapidly expanding industry. Or maybe they're here to combat a pandemic we don't yet know about, someone else had said.

"Are they still logging weather patterns?" Erin asked now.

"Half are," Mortimer said. "But what does that tell us? That they're legitimate participants? Look at them." He pinch-zoomed out to show the thousands of flags covering the globe like scales. "They look like Storm-troopers."

The proliferating insignia was ominous, each iteration like an insistent sign whose significance they ought to be grasping but were not. Users had begun contacting them too, their concerns still friendly rather than alarmed (**What's with the patrols? Adding surveillance or something?** ☺), but the disquiet was there.

"If this is a threat," Erin said now, "we better hope it's someone like Titan, not a government—or terrorist."

Mortimer didn't reply. Instead, Erin heard his physical phone in his apartment ping. He lifted his VR headset. A text message from Mortimer: **re titan. talk later. outside G.** "G" being The Garden. **Smart,**

Erin texted back, a dose of dread flooding his pulse. Back in The Garden, Mortimer headed for the elevators. "We'll keep tabs on the wind. Gale's hoping for seventy, eighty miles an hour to test their windbreaker prototype."

Hoping, Erin thought. Even in the physical world, the question wasn't if there would be storm winds but what category. "We'll see everyone tomorrow," he said to the closing elevator.

ONE ADVANTAGE of being the smartest kid in school had been, for Erin, security: that certainty of being special, like he was meant for something, a destined life. Anja, gifted at a completely different level, could've taken that from him—or, worse, brought out that Darwinian edge he hated in himself: a hard, wily pugnacity that bared itself like a set of overwhite teeth whenever he felt threatened. But Anja didn't do either, and that was probably what he missed most when she was gone: the feeling of being two against the rest in an overpopulated planet going to shit. Where they diverged was how they thought they should

fight the dissolution. It was their one active
fault line.

"Do you think The Garden's a bad idea?"
Erin had asked halfway into their senior
year. They were preparing to present their
progress to their teachers.

Anja had shrugged. At this point humans
have one way forward: Climate Control, she
wrote.

"Okay, but you know people are going
to use it for world domination, not human
preservation, right?"

If you think people are going to weap-
onize G, Anja wrote, That's so BCE. Before
Crisis Era.

"Anja, if a crystal ball told us Earth would
collapse in fifty years, do you think people
would make clouds to water crops or use
The Garden to control resources?"

Anja, shaking her pen, unbuckled
her backpack, a beat-up roll-top she carried everywhere. He knew she was stall-
ing. Lately, she'd begun calibrating her
responses, taking her sweet time to process
whatever she felt she had to before putting
pen to paper. Erin couldn't tell if it was a
sudden trust thing or some weird need to

baby his feelings, but it drove him crazy. Everything about her drove him crazy—her mixed signals, their nebulous relationship, and the way she made him second-guess not just her words and gestures but his own. Just the day before, while walking to clear their heads, they'd stopped at the grassy playground where his sister liked to sit with her friends. Mai wasn't there, but they'd stood for a while, watching the chirruping kids, Anja's arm slung around his neck. The first time she'd done this, he'd brought his arm around her waist, but it had felt wrong. Now he kept his hands in his pockets, trying not to focus on the warm lean of her weight. As heat migrated across them, collecting exactly where he didn't want it to, he hastily turned to update her on the news they'd been following—another cyberattack by the untraceable hacker that had been targeting the federal government, this time replacing the names of the politicians on Congress's website with those of their biggest donors—when she touched her lips to his, briefly but softly. By the time he realized what had happened, she was licking her lips analytically, and that was it. They'd walked back, debating the attacker's identity (Anonymous? Or that new one, Bakteria?) and the merits of such an attack (did consciousness-raising work anymore?), the moment—or was it non-moment?—gone, swept from her mind and dumped into his.

Anja uncapped a new pen. No risk, no future. If we don't make G, someone else will. Is that more scary or not.

The question was rhetorical, but these days he'd been oppressed by a vision: an infernal Earth where all nine circles of hell had overlapped, producing one endless refugee camp while the powers that be competed for climate control, the prevailing state lording it over the muck of the whole human species. In no way did he want to contribute to that.

"Fine, but we need to build The Garden in a way that we **have** a future," he said.

So we're building a mirror world to see which futures to weed out. If we can show people, if they really **see,** they'll want to avert the worst. Even rich people are still stuck on Earth.

"I just know people'll capitalize on it,

use it to spread doomsday shit and justify whatever."

You sound like my dad. Every garden has a snake, E.

That night, in his basement, Erin embedded a self-destruct mechanism into The Garden that could be triggered by the simultaneous activation of a code, nuclear-weapon-style. He felt childish, but he wanted a way to remind them of their partnership at critical crossroads. He built a synchronized random code generator app for himself and Anja. When he showed her the next day, she gazed at the app, trying to—decode its meaning? decide what to do? And with heart-stopping clarity he realized that for him, more than anything altruistic or humanitarian, the thought that there could be a universe in which he might never have met her, where a boy named Erin and a girl named Anja might never have existed, or might never exist again, hollowed his heart, a yawning cavern with no one to spelunk it. The feeling was so visceral it flipped a switch, a primal mechanism coded deep in the brain to reject any notion of a universe in which the human species didn't exist. Anja, though, was hardwired differently, and maybe this was what they'd understood as she dutifully installed his app on her phone.

LEANING AGAINST the virtual office window now, Erin half-expected to see the top of Mortimer's head emerge from the entrance below. But nobody had added that flourish to the logout process, and the glossy glass revealed only a dusky panorama beaded with city lights scattered above chainlinks of street lamps warming some neighborhoods while bleaching others. He appreciated this detail, not just its faithfulness to the physical world, where floodlights (urban ecology and human circadian rhythm be damned) were becoming popular in response to metropolitan deterioration, but the way it reproduced the city's political texture, its zones of social divide. Fifteen years ahead of the physical world, The Garden was projecting a steady expansion of these floodlight zones as rubbled blocks and darkened quadrants multiplied, further splitting the moderate middle, expanding the left and emboldening the right, and generally increasing urban police presence and rural militias to keep up the order. Next week, they were incorporating an epidemic model; next month, space models tracking high-threat meteors and solar flares. In a year they'd begin to see patterns of human responses to the conglomeration of threats exposing the inherent porosity of human borders: national, biological, planetary. But The Garden wasn't a crystal ball. And prophecies were used as much to cement outcomes as to avert them. The Garden merely showed a probable future, and it was here, in the open seam of the present—while it was still open—that Erin hoped to meet Anja again. He scanned the length of street below the office. No unusual movement.

He logged out to take his physical self for a run.

HIS NEIGHBORHOOD was busy for a weekday night, the warm LED glow from the converted gas lamps pleasantly slowing time, softening its blow. Affluent but mixed, and proud of its historicality, the neighborhood had preserved its original facades, the bricks and the moldings, the lush private courtyards, the pattering wedding-cake fountains still delighting plaster cherubs and city birds, enticing the occasional family to spread towels in the plush grass. Erin lived just outside this lambent orb, but his run took him through its center, past the original magazine building, and back to his street where ultramodern condos abutted the Section 8 complex, the defunct bus depot rusting against the state-of-the-art biotech facility that had recently replaced the flower exchange that once supplied the city's florists. From his apartment, Erin could see the lit facility, crowned by rainbows of gray overpasses sheltering the city's climate refugees rerouted from facilities like Angel Island 2, which, along with its historical original, had become submerged by rising sea levels. Jogging up eight floors, Erin unlocked his door, legs burning.

A message was waiting for him, the second in a day. Another Word file.

Time is a relative construct that starts and ends with the body. Your time is running out. But you have

**extra lives in The Garden. Make
your move.**

Erin stared. Was this a threat? Was Anja
working for someone? Titan? It seemed unlikely; the cybertech behemoth was exactly
the kind of company Anja would've made it
her mission to subvert. But high school was
a long time ago. On the other hand, what
if this wasn't Anja? The possibility, kept to a
sibilation until now, hit him, volume turned
up. If this wasn't her, who was it?

He typed, **Who are you?** He typed, **What
do you want?** He typed, **What did you do
to Anja?** Behind him, the apartment expanded like a lung. The last time he'd been
afraid in his own space was in childhood.
He deleted the last question, saved the document, and closed it, heart thumping at the
possibility of a reply.

HE'D GLIMPSED her, or thought he had,
only once post-high-school, when The Garden first went live. Back then, the team was
still dropping in daily to work together in
their virtual office. He happened to look
out the window and see the avatar: an iconic

Robert Smith with a crown of ivy trellising its head. When the avatar saw him, it froze, eyes convincingly wide. Then it was gone, and Erin checked the log. No record of any avatar within a tenth of a mile around the building. He told no one. He'd been sure it was Anja.

Erin had wasted a lot of time in high school searching for things to introduce to her; his only contribution was the band his mother still listened to then, earbuds buzzing, towel over her eyes. He and Anja had caught her at it one day their sophomore year when Luna canceled her seminar and was home early. Anja, transfixed, asked if he knew what his mom was listening to. Erin did know, and Anja had thrust her phone at him. By then Erin knew the beetle headphones welded to her ears were always playing music, but like all things related to her deafness, he'd been afraid to ask about it. Anja, huffing, snatched back her phone. Music = Vibration, she swiped. The revelation detonated his heart. He played her **Pornography.** She side-eyed him but absorbed the album, saved all eight tracks to her playlist, plus the band's every iteration of "The Hanging Garden." It became their soundtrack for the rest of high school, Robert Smith's cackling voice—**fall fall fall jump jump out of time**—caroming through their skulls, sparking manic fireworks of adrenaline and endorphins that baked a kind of sonic palimpsest into The Garden.

You mean like a garden beneath The Garden? she'd written when he shared this observation.

"Something like that," he'd replied. "Do you think Smith's Hanging Garden is like Babylon's gone bad? Like a dream that got lost and turned into its nightmare?"

She tapped her pen. E, everything mutates. But **we** can control G.

"But what if we can't? We don't **have** to be responsible."

If we don't try, we'll be responsible too.

What Erin didn't tell her was that he'd also started looping the song outside the basement, listening to the strangled words tunneling out of Robert Smith's throat like a voice squeezed from far away as the drums hammered down, machine-like, driving nails into the acoustic coffin, closing up

the human echo. It left an ache inside him
that followed him back into The Garden,
bruising the hours he spent there trying to
reconcile his nightmare with Anja's dream.
"Sometimes I don't know what we're trying
to save. I mean, what does an ideal human
future even look like?" he said.

For the first time, Anja too had had no
answer.

TWO PINGS startled him out of a nap.
One a text message from Mortimer (**gale
on standby**). The other a hideous dialog
box flashing on his laptop screen.

The Garden has been breached.
The Garden has been breached.

Panic moved through him, his old nightmare mutating, annexing his brain: a wea-
ponized Garden. He snapped on the VR
headset and clicked the green orb.

But nothing had changed. No one had
introduced a pandemic. No one was breach-
ing their office building. Above, clouds
were hurrying through the sky, stray gusts
tousling the treetops. The dog park was

empty, a few avatars bent like broken umbrellas against the wind. He rode the elevator to the seventh floor.

Everybody was there; Gale was on track to test its prototype, and the team was running preliminary checks. He'd forgotten this synergy, his team in full flow, though the warmth was gone, everyone wary of the hidden spigot, the traitorous leaker. Mortimer strode over.

"New activity?" Erin asked.

Mortimer held up the map. Around the globe, flags had amassed in the largest cities. He pinched the map's surface. The flags dispersed, and the continents gave way to an arterial network of rivers and highways splotched with the green alveoli of the few state parks and refuges still under legal protection. Then the borders of their state appeared, and Mortimer focused on the tiny blue patch just outside their city perimeter. When the map entered streetview, Erin saw the familiar park reservoir less than two miles from them, surrounded by a ring of white avatars standing at attention, their red insignias in perfect alignment.

"It's the same everywhere," Mortimer

said. "Every major park and garden." He zoomed out until the avatars compacted into a circle of white dots that multiplied like white blood cells around other green and blue patches.

Erin's physical phone pinged. **def not titan. too weird,** Mortimer's text message read. Erin returned to The Garden. The spotted globe looked diseased. "Bakteria?" he asked, evoking the catchall spectral hacker group blamed for almost all major cyberattacks in the decade of its activity, including the recent raid on a renowned pharmacological research center. For all its notoriety, the group had remained elusive, leaving no traces in any cyberwreckage. Its signature was a total lack. "Zoom back in," Erin said.

The avatars were still ringed around the reservoir, but they'd pivoted to face out like sentinels. They looked unarmed, but that meant little in The Garden, where new gadgets flourished without their knowledge and often didn't announce themselves.

"Do we need rules for synchronized behavior?" Mortimer asked.

"We're not a totalitarian state," Erin said,

slipping his gaze around the office. No one was looking at him. No one seemed tense or excited. But avatars were as expressive as Noh masks; they could reveal or hide anything.

Across the room, on the weather panel, the storm had engulfed the Northeast; soon Gale would enjoy optimal conditions for its tests, but more of the East Coast would go dark. His physical laptop pinged: a desktop notification. He lifted his headset. Another flashing pop-up:

E is for Erin
E is for Erin

Did you let her in, Erin?

At the bottom, a static image of a beat-up roll-top backpack.

ANJA DISAPPEARED three weeks before graduation. As usual, they'd been working together in his basement after school. His mom had made dinner, and Anja, as she often did, had eaten with them, filling her bowl twice. Then she'd grabbed her backpack, and he'd walked her to her house. It was a chilly night, a damp mist tarrying in the air, smearing the halos of porch lights. As usual, the sidewalk ended too quickly, and as she stepped into her driveway a flash of anguish propelled him to tug her backpack. Anja, stumbling, laughed, a rare husky, joyful hoot, and Erin, ridiculously happy, had turned, leaving her to traverse the few steps to her door.

But Anja never walked through that door. Her dad called just before midnight, and after that it was an unspooling nightmare of police lights and questions. They found nothing: no witnesses; no other missing persons; no trace of Anja's backpack, thought to contain all her electronics; and no body.

Most believed Anja had been taken, but by whom was anyone's guess. Others believed she'd been recruited, maybe by Bakteria, which was all over the news then for attempting to replace governmental archives with fake historical documents. This time, though, it also leaked a trove of undeclassified material related to a Japanese bacteriological warfare unit from the Second

World War, whose crimes the U.S. government had notoriously helped cover up in exchange for their data harvested from human
experimentation—a revelation that gave
fresh ammo to those historians who'd been
trying for decades to substantiate the rumor
that the U.S. military had used the data to
conduct its own bacteriological experiments
during the war in Korea. The timing led
some to believe Anja **was** Bakteria, especially after the local news screened in popular pundits to parse in rapid sound bites
the impact of the leak (it'll be months before we'll know), as well as the manner in
which it happened (an accident of a juvenile
prank), and the broader meaning of it all
in an era of bots and fake news (folks, this
is cyberwarfare, and it's waged by people
as young as high schoolers). Behind Erin's
back, classmates debated whether Anja had
planned the whole thing and ultimately
used Erin to this end.

Erin heard the whispers, which rustled
around him like a paper dome every time
he moved, but his brain registered nothing,
just snips of conversation that flicked and
looped like old film reels that had reached

their end. Would he hear from her? This was the question that kept him going, the pulse of hope prodding his days, one revolution, two revolutions, around the pivot of those final hours, that final minute in view of her door.

But he didn't hear from her, and the semester ended as if on mute. He raked The Garden for hidden messages, jumped at every ping, delivered his mother's food to Anja's dad. Gradually the world drifted away, and in the new vacuum he began picturing her against a white backdrop that he fought to keep blank, swiping away his skulking fears before they rendered a sound, a scene, another human figure. Did he **believe** she was gone? His mother, a low-tech human, was the only one who asked him this question. No answers came, only an echo from the static of his heart—**was** she gone?—and a single image: a girl with beetle-shaped headphones in a permanently interfaced world, the termini of her body fused with the electronic circuitry that connected her brain to the larger network, her neural tendrils curled around every system, penetrating every brain, to switch them on, wake them up, evolve the species for survival. In that world, there were no gods to curse the girl who deigned to intervene; they were all asleep, some dreaming of a girl named Anja and a boy named Erin who'd plant a garden that would save many, while others tossed and turned, trapped in the silence that would ensue when all the squabbling was over and the earth, scorched and fallow, lay waiting for a spring that would come devoid of humanity but full of new life.

Erin slid his headset back on. In The Garden, the office was quiet. Gale was online; the team had momentarily shelved their distrust. On the map, the space suits had not moved. Outside, wind was sweeping the virtual streets, clearing the city for the rain that would soon close the curtains on the sun, triggering all the sensor-operated lights before setting off a network of weather sirens, their blares faithfully carrying the sound of war that had rent the physical world in the previous century. According to The Garden, it would still be several decades before Earth truly began to unburden itself of humankind, but even in the physical realm the signs were proliferating as the somnambulant world—reassured by the stable of businesses that still opened their doors in the morning, the gleaming high-rises that still glittered at night—blundered on, banking on the miracle of science to prolong the dream that something so concrete as a cup of coffee couldn't one day vanish like a hologram. So, what, in the grand scheme, was human survival worth?

Erin lifted the headset. On his laptop screen, the message was still flashing, the backpack still punctuating it like a signature. Was this or was this not Anja? The backpack definitely felt intimate, like a message with a return address. He clicked it. Sure enough, a command prompt appeared, the cursor blinking like a beacon in the empty box. If this wasn't Anja, what did it matter? He unlocked his phone, searched for an old app buried in the app drawer. He spread his hands across his laptop. He typed, deleted, typed again. He sat for a long moment, the distant wail of the city outside like a voice from long ago. Then he pressed Enter.

ECHOLOCATION

Vision and hearing are close cousins in that they both process reflected waves of energy. Vision processes light waves as they travel from their source, bounce off surfaces and enter the eyes. Similarly, the auditory system processes sound waves as they travel from their source, bounce off surfaces and enter the ears. Both systems extract a great deal of information about the environment by interpreting the complex patterns of reflected energy they receive. In the case of sound, these waves of reflected energy are called "echoes."
—Wikipedia

We—Erin, Mother, and I—are visiting (Aunt) Katy, Aunt in parentheses because she won't stand for it, the stupid title, she told us (though she doesn't mind Doctor, we observed), her pointy glare shriveling our tongues so they learned to disobey us before disobeying her again. We're here in Boston because it's summer, and Mother is giving a lecture at a university (**2024: [Re-]visioning the Refugee Crisis**), and Dad's going to a pharmaceutical rep conference despite the global travel alert. Dad's plane is a 787 Dreamliner. It has a cruising altitude of 43,000 feet. Erin says Dad's at least at 30,000 feet by now, but I'm not supposed to think about that.

Erin is three point two five years older than me, which makes him Responsible, but he's plugged into his laptop, unlikely to notice where I am or what I'm getting into, which at the moment is Katy's bedroom closet. Katy's jumble is magnificent. All soft silver like liquid pearls, but I don't touch anything. Not even her gorgeous clutter of shoes, which are stamping her milky button-downs puddled on the floor. In back, something glitters. When I reach for it, the closet blurs. I rub my eyes; the button-downs float and multiply. I shut my eyes and step back, step all the way back into

Katy's room. Breathe. Centeredness is the only way to clarity. Even here, 2,691 miles from Studio Oneness, I hear Kirsten's voice guiding Mother and me and the neighborhood ladies through her breathing meditation. What do you see? Kirsten says. I see a blue smudge and a beige rectangle that morphs into a plastic fold-down table, a packet of peanuts rattling on a napkin. Intention is the gateway to manifestation, Kirsten says. I intend Dad's 787 to fly steady.

*

OKAY, I lined up the shoes. Katy will notice, but Katy's a busy person; she might appreciate the organization. Erin's busy too. He's busy going through Puberty. Puberty makes him irritable in a way he can't explain. I'm supposed to stay three point eight feet minimum away from him. But that can't stop my eyes from traveling.

Erin Before vs. Erin After. There are pros and cons to both.

• Cons: Voice Change. When he laughs, an alien heehaws out of his face. Freaky. Also, he accuses people of thinking things about him they never thought to think about. Very freaky.

• Pros: Greater Intelligence. Which he shows off, but I don't care. Knowledge is a form of Power, and knowledges must be gathered from many different sources. Mother says it's one of the most important things to remember.

"Erin?" My eyes touch his face. "Can unco-surgeons fix things besides cancer?" My voice joins my eyes, and I rub them all over his face; three point eight feet means nothing to sound and light waves.

"**Unco**-surgeon?" Heehaw heehaw. "Did you just say **unco**-surgeon?" Heehaw heehaw.

Sarcasm is a Con. I click my pen and write on my hand to Ask Katy Later.

*

Dinosaurs first appeared 230 million years ago. 65 million years ago, a catastrophic

extinction event ended their dominance. One group is known to have survived to the present. According to taxonomists, modern birds are direct descendants of theropod dinosaurs.
                    —Wikipedia

Why were dinosaurs dominant?

Did theropods survive because they turned into birds?

When did humans appear?

Are we dominant now?

Like what's a catastrophic extinction event?

Erin returns to his Code and refuses to google more.

*

"STOP IT. What's wrong with them?"

My eyes, Erin means. I turn my back and rub them some more.

"I'm warning you, Mai," he says.

I retreat from the living room and rub my eyes In Private.

*

ONCE UPON a time, people thought
robots would take over the earth or take
people's jobs. So far there are still poor people to manufacture things, but Jacki our
neighbor back home says we should prepare
for when the earth turns barren and everyone will have to live like people who still
can't afford things like air conditioners, even
though they themselves assemble them in
boiling factories that squeeze every drop of
their sweat before tossing them out like bug
husks. **Think** of the inhumanity, she always
says. And they don't even get Minimum
Wage, which is required by Law, I always
say. And Jacki's eyes shine. Oh, honey, forget minimum wage; they get nothing, nada
is what they get paid, and who can live on
that, or buy air conditioners, with or without an employee discount? Jacki abhors air
conditioners. They make the rich richer and
the earth hotter and give her a special chill:
the Chill of Monstrous Irony. She makes it
a point to boycott them.

Dad doesn't approve of Jacki. He says he
and Jacki don't see eye to eye, which Jacki says
is because they exist on different eye levels.
Dad and Mother also exist on different eye

levels, but they make it a point to look at each other. Dad says, Nobody should ruin anybody's life, but people need jobs, and companies offer them. What does Jacki do for people besides boycott air conditioners?

Mother doesn't disapprove of Jacki, **per se.** She tells Dad it's the exploitation Jacki objects to. Besides, she says, we have to start somewhere, and every bit counts. Like Jacki, Mother believes today's real war is with the Climate. And she says "we" to spread the responsibility. We, we, I think, like a French person. But Mother also tells me not to hang on to Jacki's every word; hearts can be in the right place but don't always lead to the best results. What Mother doesn't know is that Jacki's connected to The Universe. People like Jacki are burdened by Knowledge, which they feel so clearly they can no longer live like they don't see it. Such people are often shunned by Society, which is set up to encourage Blind Complacency. One day The Truth will prevail and reorder the world as we know it, but Jacki's skeptical if one day will be soon enough. Even Erin, who avoids Jacki, can't deny it could happen. The End, I mean.

*

2:43 PM. Birds are chirping in the gutters, squirrels are making brown waves in the grass. Sunset is not until 7:47 PM. Which means five hours four minutes of daylight left. I make my way to the center of Katy's living room and breathe.

*

EXPLOSIVE DECOMPRESSION: **A steep drop in cabin pressure, causing distention, blistering, even popping of air-filled materials**—such as maybe the eardrums and lungs, we think. Erin says the statistics are low, only ten passenger planes since 1954, which was seventy years ago. But low doesn't mean never. Does it?

*

"WHAT THE HECK?"

JAPANESE SUICIDE TORPEDO "KAITEN" FOUND. **Thursday, volunteer divers still searching for Malaysian Airlines Flight**

370 nine years after its disappearance found what they believe is an intact Japanese World War Two–era manned torpedo known as the "Kaiten" . . . [To read the full story, subscribe or sign in]

Kaiten (回天), literally "Turn the Heaven," were suicide crafts used by the Imperial Japanese Navy at the end of World War II. Manned by the Special Attack Unit, the first Kaiten was a Type 93 torpedo engine attached to a cylinder that became the pilot's compartment. Early designs allowed the pilot to escape after final acceleration toward the target, but this was later dropped so that, once inside, the pilot could not unlock the hatch. The Kaiten was fitted with a self-destruct control in case the attack or vehicle failed.

—Wikipedia

"So someone's in this thing?" Erin says, peering at the news article's greenish underwater image. "Is he, like, vacuum-sealed—like **preserved**?"

Effectiveness [edit]: Despite the advantages of a manned craft, US sources claim only two sinkings were achieved, while some Japanese sources claim a higher number.

—Wikipedia

"This is insane," Erin says. "When **was** World War Two anyway?"

*

"ERIN, CAN we check on Dad's plane?"

*

KATY HAS six windows: one in the kitchen, one in the bathroom, two in the bedroom, two in the living room. My favorites are the ones in the living room overlooking a courtyard with one fountain and one oak tree that scatters light in the summer and pelts the windowpanes in the fall until the first snow brings out the notice Courtyard Now Closed For Your Safety. Erin wonders why they even bother;

nobody ever goes out there. When I asked why not, he said it's because the courtyard's an idea, something to look at and be reassured by, like a museum. Look at this brownstone, five stories high and shaped like a U, hoarding that patch of grass and those twittering birds splashing in that fountain that's only pretending to be ancient, like something that's been there and will be there forever and ever—

—but won't? I guessed.

Erin rolled his eyes. What we need to ask is who's the beneficiary? Who is it reassuring?

Not Jacki, I guessed again, filing away the word: beh-neh-fishery.

Exactly, he said, prouder of himself than of my Educated Guess.

Is that why Katy bought the apartment?

Erin frowned. Erin has a crush on Katy, even though he's in love with Anja, who is a better programmer than him and draws in a notebook and is complicated. You have zero clue, he said.

I clicked my pen and wrote on my hand to Ask Katy If Fountain Is Fake.

*

4:12 PM. I kneel on the couch and push my face into the living room window screen. Four floors down, the cherubs on the fountain look sketched. "I bet Anja would love that fountain. She'd adore the naked cherubs," I say.

Erin, who is also on the couch, pulls me from the screen. "You're going to rip it," he says.

I stop for a minute, then push in again, more carefully. "Was Anja born deaf? Is it weird that she doesn't know your voice?"

Erin turns a page in his book.

"What does Anja draw, anyway? Does she draw you?"

He turns another page.

"Anja said she saw you signing. She knows you practice. Do you sign to her, Erin?"

Erin plunks down his book and plods to the bathroom. If Katy were here, he'd close the door, but Katy's at work, so I listen to him pee. He pees a long time, then flushes and blasts the tap. When he returns he has two spots on his jeans where he dried his hands.

"Mindfulness is the way to save water," I say.

Erin picks up his book. He's in hardcore Do Not Disturb mode. But this means he can't tell me to scooch three point eight feet away, so I scooch closer.

"Does Anja draw because she misses sound?"

Erin doesn't even twitch. Puberty is powerful. In the window, a fly materializes. It taps and taps the glass, then drops and buzzes along the sill. "I bet Anja would let you make out with her in that courtyard," I say.

Erin slaps his book. He's glowering, but at the fly, which just hopped from the window to the coffee table. Erin's a fly killer. Mother hates it when he uses a book, but books are his weapon of choice, and he's about to bring it down. In my mind, I picture a giant hand plucking the book and frisbee-ing it across the floor. But if I'm good, Erin might speak to me, so I say, "Nice! People will pay you big money when flies take over the earth."

Erin's eyes flick toward me, then he slams down the book and inspects The Damage.

*

"MAI, YOU cow! What'd you do that for?"
Erin snatches his book sprawled on the
floor and glares at me. He's a master glarer.
Which makes me think I'll miss it if I never
saw it again.

*

**Whales are descendants of land-living
mammals. They are the closest living
relatives of hippos. The two evolved
from a common ancestor around 54 million years ago. Whales entered the water
roughly 50 million years ago.**
                              —Wikipedia

Why did whales enter water and not
hippos?
Will one outsurvive the other?
What happened 54 million years ago?

*

THE 787 is two point two five times as
long as the biggest known whale. It holds

the Guinness World Record for the longest passenger jet. Seven is a lucky number in many cultures, and so is eight. At
over 40,000 feet, even the 787 is like a fly
squeezed inside a giant fist of air.

Also, Malaysian Airlines Flight 370 was
bigger than the biggest known whale, and it
vanished like it never existed.

*

"ERIN, DO you think they'll open the
torpedo?"

*

KATY'S COURTYARD ends at a wall, on the
other side of which is a lawn, overgrown
with thickets preparing to ambush the stone
house with the faded patio, two lawn chairs
sunning on it. Erin says he's seen people
lounging there, but I think what he saw
were ghosts.

Can you see ghosts during the day? I
asked Katy when she got home last night.

You mean me, personally? Or do you
mean can you see them because they exist
during the day? she asked back.

Both, I said, impressed by her fine distinction, up there with Spock and Sherlock Holmes, the Greatest Descendants of the Age of Reason and Enlightenment.

Well, I've never seen ghosts, day or night. But that doesn't mean they don't exist, she said.

Can you always see things that exist?

You'd at least see the evidence, I'd think.

Can you **only** see things that exist?

Katy thought about this. I hope so. But sometimes people see what nobody else does.

Like Sherlock Holmes, I said.

Heehaw heehaw. Mai's in love with Sherlock Holmes.

I'm **not** in love with Sherlock Holmes.

Katy snatched my hand. Don't, she said.

She's been rubbing them like crazy, Erin told her.

Do they hurt? She peeled back my eyelids. It doesn't look like conjunctivitis, but it doesn't mean it won't be. I'll see if I can get some drops.

Katy's Enlightened; she looks and also sees. But that doesn't mean she always knows. Seeing is not always knowing, and seeing cannot always solve all problems. Humans often see only what they want to see or believe they're seeing. Dad said that, believe it or not. Does that mean if nobody wants to see you, you don't exist? What about if you want to see but you can't? Or if you can hear but not see? I decided not to ask in front of Erin.

*

"GREAT. KATY's going to kill you."

Erin's in the kitchen, jabbing me with his toe. I'm evacuating Katy's below-the-sink cabinet: cleaner (chemical); dishwashing pods (chemical); recycling bag with twenty-three take-out containers plastic #6. "Did you have a good chat with Anja?"

Erin stops jabbing. He plods to the fridge and clatters out an ice cube. He leans on the counter, crunching it. The sound makes me shiver. "You're a weirdo, did you know that?"

"You're Prejudiced, did you know that?"

Erin walks away, and I lean into the cabinet. Then I close my eyes and open my pores and feel the cold peeling off the U-shaped pipe. The cabinet itself is warm and scratchy and smells like mold. I run my fingers over the braille of the wood, the nicks and chips like secret dimples, the damp patches like half-peeled scabs, then I touch something: a spongy nest. My fingers shriek, but I don't let them shrink. Darkness is not the enemy; Fear's the enemy—it's the number one enemy of the human species. Jacki does not support Fear. Think what'd happen if you always reacted or made decisions only out of Fear. Jacki chooses to prepare by (a) doing what she can to prevent The Worst, and failing that (b) doing what she can to survive with Integrity.

*

DAD POOH-POOHS The Worst. Next thing you know, I'm doomed because I was born on a Friday the thirteenth, he says.

Dad believes in Reason; he believes it will prevail. Mother wishes he were right, but it's humans she doesn't trust. Look where Reason and technology and science got us, she says.

*

"I WANT to see the plane. I want to **see** it."

*

KATY'S A doctor; she believes in all possibilities, fundamentally. Still, she lives like she doesn't believe in The Worst. Yesterday, she had one tube of tomato paste, three apples, and one tub of organic hummus in her fridge. Katy doesn't plan for Eventualities. When she sees a Lack, like in her fridge, she seeks Abundance, like in the supermarket. Katy fixes things. Which is how we ended up at the supermarket after she got home from work last night. And because it's summer, it was still light out, the gray streetlights holding their breath, and Katy said, Look. I looked up and saw a shadow blip across the sky. When I blinked, the shadow lurched and swallowed the clouds. When I rubbed my eyes, the shadow smudged and strobed like distant lightning before breaking into pinpricks of light that fused into one pair of eyes belonging to one crow perched on the telephone wire, watching the passage of our groceries.

*

"MAI?"
"What?"
"You know what."
And I do. Erin's my brother; he doesn't need to be in the same room to know what I'm doing. Jacki calls it the Mind's Eye, which is a knowing that's independent of seeing and that beats seeing because seeing doesn't always add up to knowing. Feel that tingling on the forehead? That's how you know you **know.**

I sit firmly on my hands and draw my awareness away from my eyes to my forehead and concentrate.

*

The term "human" refers to the genus Homo (H.). **Scientists estimate that humans branched off from their common**

ancestor, the chimpanzee, about 5–7 million years ago and evolved into several species and subspecies now extinct. Debate continues as to whether a "revolution" led to modern humans ("the big bang of human consciousness"), or a more gradual evolution. According to the Out-of-Africa model, modern H. sapiens evolved in Africa 200,000 years ago and began migrating 70,000 to 50,000 years ago, replacing H. erectus, inhabitant of Asia, and H. sapiens neanderthalensis, inhabitant of Europe. Out-of-Africa has gained support from mitochondrial DNA research which concluded that all modern humans descended from a woman from Africa, dubbed Mitochondrial Eve. Both human and chimpanzee DNA, to which human DNA is approximately 96% identical, are undergoing unusually rapid changes compared with other mammals. These changes involve classes of genes related to perception of sound, transmission of nerve signals, and sperm production.

—Wikipedia

Why did humans split off from chimpanzees?

How come some humans survived and not others?

Why are we changing like no other mammals?

Are we all changing, or only some?

How rapid is rapid?

Who was Mitochondrial Eve?

Where was Adam?

*

"DO YOU think we'll ever know who's in the torpedo?"

*

5:45 PM. Two hours two minutes left. Out there in the world, there are gorillas who have learned to sign, and humans who have learned to see like bats and whales. Daniel Kish is such a human. And so is Ben Underwood. Ms. Alvarez-Johnson called it human echolocation.

*

Human Echolocation: A learned skill whereby humans use sound, such as palate clicks, to navigate the environment.

Clicks (mouth): Clicking sounds made by placing the tongue on the palate and snapping it back. Mouth clicks are used most often by the blind to determine the distance, size, and shape of objects and locate them, but they may also be valuable to rescue workers, such as firefighters.
—Wikipedia

But **how** do you stop the earth and sky and sea and people from erupting like a sudden sun blinding the bluest sky, leaving an endless archipelago of beached fountains leaking algae, a verdant hieroglyph of a lost civilization, fluorescing in the permanent dark.

*

"ERIN? JUST at first, will you read to me if I go blind?"

Erin looks up. At first his eyes are blank. Then they widen, tadpoles of fear darting across them. He wakes his phone: Mother won't be home for another hour, and Katy even later. He drums the table. Drums and drums. Then he looks at me, pulls a chair next to his own, lifts the three point eight feet rule, and I know he **knows,** and he's going to tell Mother.

*

The Sun is approximately halfway through its main-sequence evolution. In 5–6 billion years, it will enter the red giant phase, during which its outer layers will heat up and expand to eventually reach Earth's current position. Recent research suggests that the Sun's decreased gravity will have moved the Earth out, away from the danger of engulfment, but it will not prevent Earth's water from boiling and its atmosphere from escaping into space. Long before that, however, as early as 900 million years from now, Earth's surface will already be too hot for the survival of life as we know it.

In another billion years, the surface water will have disappeared.
                    —Wikipedia

Will whales shrink to the size of moles and enter the earth?

Will they have learned to see underearth by then?

Where will humans be?

Will they have learned to see under-earth too?

Why do we exist, Erin?

Is anyone else out there?

How will they find us?

Will they tell our story?

What's going to happen to us, Erin? Are we going to bring about The End?

Are we, Erin?

Are we?

Are we?

AUTHOR'S NOTE

So many things—books, art, film, music, experiences—have catalyzed this collection into being, and it is impossible to list them all here. But I do want to mention a few. "I Stand Accused, I, Jesus of the Ruins" is in part a rewriting of Ishikawa Jun's "Jesus of the Ruins" (1946), and the Rōjin and The Heavenly Curtain Hotel's House of Hope are from Hotta Yoshie's "The Old Man" (1952). Both short stories have been translated into English. "Pavilion" is in direct conversation with Jorge Luis Borges's "The Garden of Forking Paths" (trans. 1958).

I would also like to note that the snatch of lyrics reproduced in "The Garden, aka Theorem for the Survival of the Species" is from "The Hanging Garden" by The Cure, and the lines that appear in the Rōjin section of "I Stand Accused, I, Jesus of the Ruins" are my translation of lyrics from the song "Utsukushiki Tennen," which was popular in Japan at the turn of the last century. The Wikipedia extracts in "Echolocation" are based on the following Wikipedia entries found at the time of writing: "Human Echolocation," "Dinosaur," Uncontrolled Decompression," "Kaiten," "Whales," "Human," "Sun." I should also note that "Urashima Tarō," the fairy tale that begins "Passing," is a cultural staple in Japan. There are many variations; I've summarized the one I heard most often. Finally, the passage quoted toward the end of "Passing" is from Kimiko Hahn's provocative zuihitsu-style poem "Blindsided," found in her book **Volatile** (1999).

Over the course of writing this book, I've often been asked about its historical content—how much was drawn from real people and events—and whether I consider it historical fiction. These are deceptively complex questions. What I can say is that my concern was less to capture a time, place, or event than to responsibly represent that time, place, or event. For this reason, this book is foremost engaged with the texts and media, scholarly, popular, and fictional, that have represented and discussed this history, and the concept of history, from myriad perspectives.

As for historical fiction, I feel that, as a genre, it often takes for granted the fundamental accessibility of history—as though history is an objective occurrence bound to a time and place, and it's largely a matter of pinning down the details: what people wore, how the streets looked, the "facts" of what happened. I hope this collection will complicate this idea and spark questions about how history is made, how it is lived, remembered, reproduced, and used, and how ultimately unbound it is by the time and place in which it is grounded. The Second World War didn't start and end with specific people and events; its roots reach back to values seeded long ago, and its sundering effects have hardly lost their spark and propulsion. The consequences are still unfurling, and these days I find myself wondering how my philosophical grandfather, who worked for a Japanese company that built warplanes during the Second World War, would have evaluated our world's trajectory. He died naturally four years ago, a full century after his birth in 1916.

ACKNOWLEDGMENTS

This first book has taken so long to write that I have many people to thank.

Early writing teachers and advisers: Chris Tilghman, Steve Almond, Sheila Emerson, and Jonathan Strong for encouraging this direction long ago.

Friends and family who lent their energy at various crossroads: Alan Cohen, Allison Paige, Anna Ritter, Hsuan Wu, Janet Generalli, Janet Thielke, Jen & Keith Leonard, Patricia Grace King, Stan Tam, Shane Clifford, Shetal Shah, Steph Belmer & Aaron Richmond, Sophia Lin & Jake Hooker, Tal Zamir, Timothy & Tana Welch, and my community at FAWC that pivotal year. A special thank you to Maria Koundoura for the vital sanctuary of her home, table, and conversation; Joanna Luloff, my delightful friend, who engaged with many of these stories; Matthew Neill Null, one of the most discerning and supportive writers I know: I cannot thank you enough.

Thank you to my singular parents and lovely brother. To Barb Modica, Larry Mateja, and their geodesic dome where part of this book was completed. To Mary Bernardi and Rema Bernardi for keeping an eye on our journey. To Marty Luloff for opening his home (and pie stash) at a critical juncture. Thank you also to Mario Modica: I wish you were here to read the rest of the book.

I'm grateful to the Rona Jaffe Foundation, Beth McCabe, and the RJFWA jurors (I wish I knew who you were). I'm grateful to the invaluable Fine Arts Work Center in Provincetown and Jaimy Gordon, whose words have bolstered me in enduring ways. Many, many thanks to Laura Furman and the **O. Henry Prize Stories** jurors, including Molly Antopol and Edith Pearlman. Thank you to Bill Henderson and **The Pushcart Prize.** Thank you: **Copper Nickel, Witness, The Antioch Review, Prairie Schooner, The Southern Review,** and especially Paula Deitz and Ron Koury at **The Hudson**